THE CHRONICLES OF KIBBLESTAN

REVOLUTION

ANDREA RAND

COLIMAR PRESS

Book Layout ©2013 BookDesignTemplates.com

Cover Design: Tim Jessell
www.timjessell.com

The Chronicles of Kibblestan: Revolution/ Andrea Rand. -- 1st ed.
ISBN 978-0-9967491-0-7

For Maren and Colin, who first explored Kibblestan. And for Russ, who believes in me more than I believe in myself.

CHAPTER ONE

"We are the Voyagers, campers of goodwill.
The vulture is our symbol, but we never eat roadkill.
We always stick together, our loyalty is high.
As long as we're united, like vultures we will fly!"

— *Vulture Voyager Theme Song*

The group of boys laughed as they hollered the words around the afternoon campfire, but Ellis' lips barely moved. He should have been happy. His troop had taken first place at the Vulture Voyager Survival Games. He'd passed all his wilderness exams. And he'd proudly received the Regurgitating Raptor Patch to sew on his Vulture Vest that proved he was no longer a fifth-grade Fledgling—he'd flown up to full Vulture rank. But instead of enjoying the campout's closing ceremony, he stomped off toward his tent, kicking up gravel along the way.

This campout was even more important than when he had graduated from the humiliating Egg rank. He was now a Vulture. It was a big deal. A *way* big deal. And

Dad should have been here to see it, like all the other dads.

But he wasn't. He had to work. Again.

Ellis trudged up the sloping ground toward the blue tent he shared with his best friend, Colin. It was zipped tightly shut, but that didn't muffle his dachshund's lonely whimpers coming from inside.

Oh Philecia. He wouldn't have to lock her up like this if she'd just act like a normal dog, instead of like some freakazoid.

"Hey! Wait up!" Ellis turned to see Colin trekking up the path. "Dad says it's time to pack up."

"Okay," Ellis said. "But don't let Philecia out. After she went crazy running from the fireflies last night and peeing all over the marshmallows, I don't think anyone wants her getting loose."

"Oh, I don't know," Colin said. "She wasn't *that* bad."

Colin was being polite. He was *always* polite.

"Come on, Colin. She was horrible. Not only did she keep us from making s'mores, she peed on Duane Ratsman's cell phone. It's a wonder either one of us is still alive."

Frantic yapping erupted from inside the tent. Ellis unzipped the door and stuck his head inside. His small brown dachshund cowered in the corner, her pupils constricted and drool flying as she barked furiously. "Philecia, it's me, girl."

"What's wrong with her?" Colin asked.

"I don't know." Ellis crawled into the tent. "Come on, girl. It's okay."

Philecia pressed deeper into the corner. Her eyes darted to the ceiling, to the walls—everywhere but the ground.

Something small and dark scurried across the nylon floor and disappeared underneath Colin's sleeping bag. Philecia's barks escalated into a dog scream.

"Did you see that?" Ellis asked. He crawled to Colin's bedding and lifted the sleeping bag. A lizard scampered out from underneath and through the open door.

"A lizard?" Colin said as he entered the tent. "Your dog freaked out that much because of a tiny lizard?"

Ellis felt his face grow hot. Philecia's brown eyes bugged out and her body hunched as a yellow puddle formed on the floor. Ellis smacked his forehead. "Really? Again? It was just a lizard! A teeny tiny lizard. Did you really have to pee?"

Colin wrinkled his nose. "Gross!"

Colin quickly gathered up his bedding and crawled out of the tent. "I'm going to the car," he called as he hastily made his exit.

Ellis glared at the brown dachshund. "You're no fun to bring on campouts, you know that?"

Ellis looked around for something to soak up the urine and settled on using the t-shirt he'd worn the day before. He scrunched up his face as he mopped up the warm liquid. Philecia sat in the corner watching him, head hung low.

"Yeah, you should feel sorry," Ellis continued. "Why can't you be like a normal dog and chase stuff instead of peeing at every little thing that moves? It's so embarrassing."

Ellis wadded up the soiled t-shirt and backed out of the tent to find a plastic garbage bag. Instead, he found Duane Ratsman.

Duane stood as solid as one of the trees in the forest and seemed almost as tall. Ellis was by no means small for an eleven-year-old, but Duane Ratsman? He was a beast. Duane crossed his pink freckled arms and curled his lip in a sneer, displaying sharp jumbled teeth that would make any dentist see dollar signs.

"Where's that weiner dog of yours? I'm gonna stomp its head for peeing on my phone."

This was not good. Dropping the t-shirt, Ellis reached behind him and pulled the flaps of the tent shut.

"Philecia's not here," he said, meeting Duane's pale eyes. "I already put her in Mr. Rooper's car."

Duane shot a thick wad of spit through his jagged teeth. His doughy face brightened. "Then I'll get my revenge on *you!*"

Ellis tried to dodge Duane's gorilla hands but wasn't fast enough. In a flash he was trapped in a headlock, listening to Duane's familiar cackle and gagging at the sour stench of his sweaty armpit. Ellis dug his feet into the ground, pushing hard against Duane's body, but it was like pushing against a concrete wall.

"Come on, Ratsman! Let me go!" Ellis' arms flailed, landing punches to Duane's lower back, but he couldn't get any power behind them from his awkward position. Duane grabbed a chunk of hair at the base of Ellis' neck and yanked.

"Ow! Cut it out!" Ellis hollered, but then another sound cut through Duane's wicked laughter. Philecia's barks pierced the air.

"The weiner dog!" Duane shouted. "So it *was* here!"

Duane grabbed the band of Ellis' underwear and yanked so hard his feet left the ground.

"Wedgie ala Ratsman," Duane grunted.

"Stop it!" Ellis shouted.

"Can't lie to me and get away with it."

Duane shoved Ellis to the ground. He landed on his chest, panting, his face inches from the dirt. Duane planted his boot on Ellis' back.

"Keep your weiner dog out of my face," he growled. Then he lumbered off down the trail.

Ellis groaned and rolled onto his back. Philecia jumped out of the tent and lathered Ellis' face with slobbery kisses.

"Philecia, stop!" Ellis pushed her away. He stood up and wiped the drool from his cheeks.

Colin ran up the path, out of breath.

"You okay? I saw Duane come down the trail with that stupid grin on his face. He didn't mess with you, did he?"

Ellis shrugged and looked away. "Doesn't matter. I'm fine."

The two friends finished packing up the tent then loaded everything into Colin's dad's SUV.

Two hours later they reached the outskirts of town. They turned into Ellis' neighborhood and drove down his street—a dead end road lined with houses backing up to an open field. Beyond the field lay an ugly gray forest.

The SUV came to a stop in front of Ellis' house.

"Thanks again, Mr. Rooper," Ellis said. "Sorry my dad had to cancel last minute."

"It's no problem." Mr. Rooper smiled, but Ellis couldn't help but wonder if he was secretly tired of dragging him along to everything. Ellis did so much with the Roopers these days, someone might mistake him as one of them—if not for his dark hair and tan complexion. All the Rooper kids were blonde and pale.

Ellis walked to the back to unload his gear.

"Wait! I've got something for you." Mr. Rooper rummaged in the glovebox then walked over to Ellis and handed him a brochure. On the cover a boy in a Vulture

Voyager uniform smiled back at him. "*Are you a boy who loves adventure?*" the brochure read. "*Are you ready to make lifelong friends? Come and join the Vulture Voyagers!*"

"It's our new recruitment brochure," Mr. Rooper explained. "We're going to have a contest to see who can bring in the most new members, with a party at the end of the summer. You and your dad can be on a team ..." His voice trailed off as Ellis looked at his feet. Mr. Rooper swallowed. "Or, you know, you can always be on our team."

Ellis forced a smile. "Sure, Mr. Rooper."

Ellis stuffed the brochure in his back pocket as he watched the SUV drive off. Then he whistled to Philecia and dragged his camping gear to the garage. He punched in the passcode to the garage door opener and the door creaked and squealed as it lifted off the ground. Before the door made it halfway through its journey Ellis' shoulders slumped.

The garage was empty.

He dropped his gear on the concrete, silently cursing himself for getting his hopes up. Of course no one was home. What did he expect?

Ellis let himself into the house and saw a note on the kitchen table from his mother.

"*Ellis – Grandma's cats are throwing up again and she's really upset. I'm going over there after I'm done helping Dad at the shop. There's ice cream in the freezer if you're hungry. Love, Mom."*

Ellis crumpled the note and threw it on the floor. He ignored the ice cream in the freezer and went back out to the garage.

Click-click-click. Philecia's nails tapped the concrete as she followed him to the shelf full of power tools and Christmas decorations and boxes of clothes he'd outgrown. He found his basketball and dribbled out to the driveway to shoot some hoops. As the sun dipped lower in the sky he heard his dad's beat-up Honda chugging down the street. Philecia scampered out of the way as the small car rolled into the garage.

Javier Garcia got out. He wore a navy polo with "Garcia's Glacial Goodies" embroidered on the chest. A matching cap compressed his curly black hair.

"Hi Ellis." He waved absently as he looked at his cell phone. "Sorry I'm late. Bruce called in sick so I had to teach Marcia how to close. Sure hope she doesn't forget anything."

Ellis scowled. Who cares?

Javier stuffed his phone into his pocket then reached into the car and withdrew an unlabeled ice cream carton. His smile was like a kid on the last day of school as he walked toward Ellis. "Guess what. I think I finally have it. Ninja Nosejuice—the ice cream flavor you've been begging me to create. I colored the caramel swirl green and I think it just might work."

Ellis crossed his arms and grimaced.

Javier's brow crinkled. "What's wrong? I thought you'd be excited." Javier paused and scratched his chin. Then his eyes brightened. "Oh yeah. How was the campout?"

Ellis shrugged.

"Come on, tell me about it."

"Why should I?" Ellis snapped. "Don't pretend like you're all interested. You couldn't care less about me being a Vulture, or getting beat up, or being humiliated in front of my whole troop because my stupid dog freaks out and pees all over the place. I did just fine. Didn't need you anyway."

Ellis dribbled the basketball down the driveway.

"Ellis, I ..." Javier sighed and rubbed the back of his neck. "I wanted to be there. I did. It just didn't work out. You know how it is. I've got to run the shop."

Yes, the stupid shop. Garcia's Glacial Goodies, home to forty-three flavors of ice cream and Dad's American Dream. If Ellis ever complained about time spent at the shop Dad was quick to remind him of just how lucky they were to live in America and own their own business. Grandma and Grandpa had risked everything fleeing Cuba, all so their kids would have a chance at a better life. Javier did not take that lightly, and neither should Ellis.

"Look, I'm sorry," Javier said. "Marcia's not ready to run the shop alone during the weekend rush. I can't risk customers coming and not having a good experience. This isn't Cuba, it's America. You work hard to beat your competition and if customers don't like my shop, they'll find ice cream somewhere else. And we can't afford that. You want to be able to pay for stuff like your Buzzard Club, don't you?"

Ellis shot a basket, throwing way too hard. The basketball ricocheted off the backboard and bounced toward the street. Ellis looked into Dad's hazel eyes. They flashed golden green in the sunlight, so much like his own.

"It's Vultures!" Ellis hollered. "Vulture Voyagers, not buzzards. All you care about is the stupid shop. You don't care about me. You never do anything with me anymore. Well, I got news for you. I hate the shop. I hate ice cream. And I hate you!"

There, he'd said it. Screamed it. And it felt so good.

Yet the stunned look he saw on Dad's face, the worried crease in his forehead ... speechless, hurt ...

Ellis turned and ran. Down the gravel path that led from his driveway, past his backyard, and into the field beyond. He ran and ran, not thinking of where he was going or how far he'd come. He ran until the lump filling his chest exploded and he had to stop as sobs erupted from his aching lungs.

Ellis bent over and choked out sob after sob. He coughed and sputtered, until finally he was able to take a deep breath. He took a few more before straightening up.

Something scratched the back of his leg. He looked down. Philecia's brown eyes stared up, soft and loving. He hadn't even realized she was following him.

At least she cared.

He scooped her into his arms, and when she lapped his cheeks with kisses, he didn't push her away. Okay. Maybe he had been a little hard on her. Right now she was the coolest dog in the world.

Ellis looked toward home. He didn't want to go back. Not yet. Let Dad wonder where he'd gone. A solid line of trees caught his eye from several yards away. Wow. The edge of the forest. He'd never come this close to it before.

Ellis wandered closer, examining the layers of peeling bark and crusty knotholes that scarred the massive gray trunks. He'd never seen trees so big. This forest was ancient. Quiet, too. Like everything inside was holding its breath.

"You can play in the field, but stay out of the forest," Dad always said. "It's not our property and besides, you never know what might be back there."

What was Dad doing right now anyway? Sitting in the driveway, waiting for him to cool off and return? Or had he gone in the house? Was he relaxing and not even thinking about Ellis anymore?

Probably.

Ellis swallowed hard.

"I'll show him," he thought. "I'll go in the woods, and he can't stop me. And if I don't come back, he'll know it's his fault. His fault for being such a mean dad. He'll know he made me run away and he'll wish he'd spent more time with me instead of the stupid shop. He'll be sorry for the rest of his life."

Ellis hugged Philecia to his chest and stepped into the trees.

A draft of frigid air seized him and held on tight. Weird. He put Philecia on the ground and rubbed his arms, shivering. The cold air stung his nostrils and made his boogers freeze.

You never know what might be back there ... The tiny voice whispered in his mind but Ellis ignored it. He pressed deeper into the shadows.

The gargantuan trees rose up like bark-covered sky-scrapers. The farther he hiked, the thicker they became, their web of gnarled branches blocking out the sunlight. Ellis stopped and rubbed his tingling hands together. This adventure was turning out to be cold and dark and not much fun. Maybe he should just go home. He turned to go back and that's when he noticed.

Philecia was gone.

.

CHAPTER TWO

Ellis looked all around. No sign of her. His heart flipped like it was on a trampoline. This was silly. She couldn't be far. He cupped his hands around his mouth and called. "Philecia! Come here, girl!"

Ellis stopped. His voice sounded weird. Not like the voice of someone yelling out in the open. His call sounded muffled, like someone locked in a small closet. Or buried in a coffin.

Ellis took a few steps, listening, watching.

Nothing.

He glanced toward the clearing and his heart slammed into his throat.

The trees had moved.

Ellis could still see the light of the clearing far away, but he could swear that the trees had scooted closer together. Their trunks had grown wider, too, narrowing the spaces between them.

Ellis shook his head. It's your imagination. Trees don't move. They *can't* move.

Ellis felt something on his foot. A brown mouse scampered across his shoe. It circled in front of him, then zigzagged back and forth.

A rustling sound. The mouse jumped and scurried behind a tree. Ellis turned as Philecia charged out of the shadows.

"Philecia!" Ellis reached down and caught his dog mid-stride. Relief flooded into him, making is arms feel weak. He cuddled the dachshund against his thumping chest and let out a deep breath. "Whoa, girl. You can't go running off like that. You scared me."

Philecia squirmed in his arms. What did she want? He looked where the mouse was hiding. Had Philecia been chasing it? Actually chasing it? Philecia whined but Ellis clutched her tight. No way he'd let her back down. They were going home. Time to ditch this creepy forest. He turned toward the clearing and stopped short.

The clearing was no longer there.

Ellis turned in a circle, clenching his teeth to keep them from chattering. This was crazy. The clearing couldn't have disappeared, could it? Philecia and the mouse had distracted his sense of direction. That was all.

Something darted across the ground. The mouse. It now ran in circles, pausing every few moments to look up at the trees, shake its head, then resume its circles again, faster than before.

Great. Even the mouse looked lost.

Ellis took his best guess of which way was home and started walking. To his surprise, the mouse followed. Each time he stole a glance over his shoulder the mouse would stop and sit back on its haunches, avoiding all eye contact as it absently played with its tail. As soon as he turned back around the pitter-patter behind him resumed.

Ellis had not walked far when he heard a distant rumbling.

Philecia let out a low whine.

"It's okay, girl. It's only thunder." He paused, then added. "Nothing else."

Up ahead a light flickered between two trees. Was it the clearing? He quickened his step and the scampering behind him did the same.

The rumbling grew louder.

Ellis slowed down as he approached two of the thickest trees he'd seen yet. This was weird. The light only shined between these two trees and no other. It flashed and dimmed, beckoning him to come closer. Ellis peered through the lit space and his heart plunged to his stomach. It wasn't the clearing. Everything looked dark and fuzzy, and in the distance there was an ominous greenish-yellow glow. A sweet metallic smell hung in the air that was strangely familiar.

Ellis looked behind him. The trees had changed again. He wasn't imagining things. They hardly looked like trees anymore. They looked like one big, shadowy mass eager to swallow him forever. He had to get to the light. Any light.

Ellis clutched Philecia tighter and squeezed between the two trees. A piercing shriek drilled his ears, rising above the rumbling thunder. At the same time, a frantic, squeaky voice spoke so quickly he could barely understand what was being said.

"I don't want to die. No I don't! No I don't! No I don't! I just want to go home. Yes I do. I do!"

Ellis blinked at his surroundings, trying to make sense of the confusing sounds. The sky was black with swirling clouds and the air was hot and still. In the distance a volcano erupted. Its greenish-yellow lava spewed upward in angry, fiery bursts, lighting up the sky before settling on the horizon.

Philecia vibrated in his arms, shaking uncontrollably. Ellis tightened his grip. "It's okay," he whispered, his voice as shaky as his dog.

The squeaking started again, coming from the direction of the ground. "Please take me with you. I don't want to be alone. No I don't! No I don't! Let's be friends. Please, please, please!"

Philecia whimpered, and Ellis stumbled back, nearly dropping her. He was hearing more words—but this time in his dog's whining voice. "I don't want to be friends with you. You have those beady eyes and teeth that could gnaw my tail in two. Besides, I have Ellis. He's the only friend I need."

Ellis placed Philecia on the ground before she slipped from his hands. He felt numb.

Philecia pointed her nose toward something brown and furry. The mouse. It hopped up and down, clenching its paws into tiny fists. "You think you're so high and mighty, being canine. Mice need friends, too, yes they do. Besides, I wouldn't be here if you hadn't chased me around the forest. You got me all lost, yes you did. Why'd you do that, hmmm? Hmmm?"

Philecia kept up the whimpering sound. "I'm supposed to chase things like you. I'm a dachshund."

The mouse stuck out its chin and crossed its arms. "But you don't have to be such a meanie."

Philecia's floppy ears went limp. "Look ... I'm not a meanie. It's just ... I'm sick of disappointing Ellis, okay? He's my human, and he got a wedgie because of me and ... Oh forget it. You're just a mouse. You don't understand dogs and their humans."

Ellis plopped down on the grass. It felt soggy beneath his jeans but he didn't care. He was listening to his dog have an argument with a mouse, in a land that didn't look anything like home. Soggy jeans were the least of his worries.

"I know, I know, dogs care so much about their humans." The mouse's chatter was earsplitting. "But some humans aren't that great, you know. Some poison mice, yes they do. Or set traps." The mouse sat back on its haunches, paws on hips, and scowled up at Ellis. "What about you?" it demanded. "Do you do things like that? Do you? Do you?"

Ellis' vocal chords were slow to cooperate. "Like— like what?"

"Poison me! Trap me? Would you? Would you?"

"N-no," Ellis managed. He squeezed his eyes shut and massaged his temples. Maybe he was dreaming. Could this be the weirdest, most lifelike dream he'd ever experienced? He pressed his fingertips to his forearm, grabbed a bit of skin and pinched.

"Ow!" he yelped.

It wasn't a dream.

The mouse squeaked on, barely pausing for a breath. "I have a bad feeling about this place, yes I do. We need to stick together, yes we should. Let's be friends. Please, please, please!"

The mouse grabbed its tail and stroked it, looking first at Ellis, then to Philecia, then back to Ellis.

Philecia looked wary. "I don't know. I guess I'll do whatever Ellis wants." She looked at Ellis and cocked her head. "Can you understand me, too?"

Ellis nodded, speechless. He pulled Philecia to him and hugged her close, as his mind tried to grasp what was happening. This was real. It wasn't a dream. He took a deep breath and cleared his throat. "I think the mouse is right. We need to stick together."

The mouse broke into a huge grin. Its square teeth twinkled like two sugar cubes as it nodded and pranced about.

"We're friends now. We're friends! We'll get out of here together, yes we will. Yes we will."

The mouse tugged at Ellis's pant leg. He knelt down, putting Philecia on the ground. The mouse grinned and did a flying leap, landing squarely on Philecia's head. Philecia winced.

"Introductions, introductions. My name is Matilda, yes it is. Pleased to meet you. So very, very pleased!"

The mouse stuck out a tiny paw and before he knew what he was doing Ellis shook hands with the rodent.

Philecia stared up, cross-eyed. She shook her head and the mouse went flying.

"Philecia!" Ellis scolded. "Don't do that."

"But it was on my head," Philecia protested. "What if it pooped?"

Matilda lay on her back, her hind legs sprawled above her head. "I'd never poop on anybody, no I wouldn't." She popped up and dusted herself off, fixing Philecia with an indignant scowl.

"Let's just get back home," Philecia said.

Home. Yes, they needed to get back home. But it was easier said than done. The tree trunks had widened so much there were no longer spaces between them. Ellis ran his hand along the trunks. They were smooth and solid, like a giant wall of petrified bark. Ellis fought the panic rising in his throat.

Philecia and Matilda stared up, wide-eyed. Why'd they look at him like that? He didn't have answers. He was just a kid.

They walked to a field of tall grass a few feet away. In the dim light he could see patches where the grass had been trampled or smashed into a sort of path.

"I guess we can follow this trail," Ellis said. Maybe it'll lead to another way out."

He entered the field, Philecia on his heels. Matilda ran in circles around both of them.

"Will you cut that out?" Philecia snapped. "We're going to trip over you."

Matilda stopped, looking hurt. "You don't have to be so bossy."

"I wasn't being bossy. I was just ... Ick! What's on my paws?" Philecia stopped and lifted her feet, one by one. When Ellis knelt to examine, his jeans got wet.

"Hold still, girl," Ellis whispered. He took Philecia's front paw and tried to see it in the volcano's greenish-yellow light. Her paw glistened, covered with some kind of substance that looked like jelly. "Does it hurt?"

"No. It just feels weird. It's sticking to the pads of my feet."

Ellis felt the ground with his fingers. Between the clumps of trampled grass were layers of cool wet slime.

He stood up and rubbed his fingers together. As the slime dried it became thicker, turning into a rubbery ball that clung to his skin. The strange metallic smell wafted through the air.

"I don't know, Philecia," Ellis said. "The ground seems to be covered with the muck, whatever it is."

"Wait a minute." Philecia's eyes bulged. "You don't think it's poison, do you?"

"Hmph. Now you know how mice feel." Matilda said.

Philecia ignored her. "What if I get sick? Or what if it never washes off? I can't have sticky paws. I won't be able to run fast. I might get stuck somewhere and something could eat me. I—"

Ellis lifted Philecia into his arms and she settled down. They continued walking. His shoes made a sloshing sound with every step. The slime got deeper. The metallic smell grew stronger.

Ellis stopped. He recognized the smell.

Once, he was flying down the sidewalk on his skateboard at school. He didn't see the concrete stairs leading to the parking lot until it was too late. The skateboard hit the first step and kept going. He pitched forward and tumbled down the concrete stairs. He landed on his chin, his bottom teeth slicing clean through his lower lip.

The blood streamed from his face, filling his mouth while painting the sidewalk red. Ellis remembered the taste. He remembered the smell.

The blood tasted metallic.

It smelled metallic.

It smelled like this slime on the ground.

CHAPTER THREE

Ellis felt something tugging his pant leg. He looked down. Matilda clung to his jeans, hitching a ride to avoid the rising slime. They continued down the trail and when it came to an end Ellis paused, looking left and right. To his left was nothing but blackness. If only he had a flashlight, he could see what was there. Maybe somewhere in that blackness was a way home.

But then again, what if it didn't lead back home? What if it led to something else? Like something that was super hairy, or scaly, with sharp claws and Tyrannosaurus teeth?

A tremendous screech ripped through the air. The sound was loud, *so* loud, and guttural. It resembled the caw of a prehistoric bird—a huge bird, whose throat was shredded and raw.

"What was that? What was that?" Matilda shinnied higher up Ellis' leg.

Philecia pawed at her ears. "Ouch! That hurt. Why do dog ears have to be so sensitive?"

The screech faded, replaced by the steady rumble of thunder.

"I know! I know what it was," Matilda cried. "It was an owl. A big, monstrous owl that wants mouse casserole for supper, yes it does. Hide me! Hide me!"

Ellis searched the sky and saw nothing but churning clouds. He plucked Matilda from his pant leg. "It's okay," he told her, hoping she didn't notice the tremble in his voice. "I think whatever it was is gone." He raised his hand to his shirt and Matilda gladly dove inside his front pocket.

Whatever it was is gone. Whatever it was is gone. The words repeated in his brain. If only he could believe them. He looked toward the volcano. At least this direction had some light. In fact ...

Ellis squinted. Could he be seeing things? Something moved in the distance—a white oval shape that vaguely shined in the dim light. He plodded toward it and as he drew closer he noticed other white shapes as well. They stayed in one place, but shook back and forth. What were they?

Ellis trudged ahead. The ground slanted downward and the slime grew deep, turning into the most disgusting lake of all time. The mushy stuff crept up his thighs, then reached his waist. The deeper it got, the harder it was to move. The gunk was so thick, like walking through rubber cement. And the metallic, blood-smell had changed. It was even more pungent, and becoming overwhelming.

"Ugh! That smell makes me want to puke," Ellis muttered.

Philecia stiffened in his arms. Her ears perked up and she scratched Ellis' forearm.

"Ow! Philecia—"

"Go back," she cried. "We've got to go back." Philecia's claws dug into Ellis' skin as she frantically tried to scramble over his shoulder. "We've got to get out of here. Ellis, get me out of here!"

"Philecia, stop it! I'm going to drop you."

From Ellis' pocket Matilda's voice floated up. "I'm all for going back. Too stinky out there, yes it is. Too stinky."

"Guys, I know it smells bad but there's something moving out there. We got to go see—"

"NO!" Philecia barked. "Get away, Ellis! As fast as we can. I know that smell."

Philecia's nails dug even deeper into his shoulder. That was enough. Ellis held the dachshund out in front of him, face to face. "That hurt, girl. Stop climbing on me. We're going to go see what's moving over there."

"But the smell," Philecia moaned.

"Yeah, I know it's bad. It smells like blood, but—" Ellis stopped himself mid-sentence. Oh no. Why'd he let that slip? To the dog who freaked out at the buzz of a June bug and slunk away if a toad hopped across her path? Now she'd really go nuts.

But she didn't.

Philecia didn't pee or anything. She gazed at Ellis and looked so strange ... almost wise, as if something was taking place in that mind of hers that was far beyond mere animal instinct.

"Ellis," Philecia said slowly, deliberately. "It isn't blood. I'm a dog and I know smells. It's the smell that we fear most. It can make a hungry wolf come running, but tells a dog to get away as fast as possible."

Philecia paused, eyes round. "Ellis, what I smell is death."

Death? Like rotting bodies or something? Ellis quickly looked on either side of him, half-expecting to see a bloody corpse float by. He tried to steady his breathing, but it wasn't easy. Death. Philecia smelled death.

Screeeeeech! The awful sound tore through the air and Ellis jumped, nearly dropping Philecia. He looked toward the sky. What in the world made that sound? Another shriek echoed through the landscape and the air fell silent. All was still for a moment, then the thunder resumed its steady beat.

Ellis hugged Philecia to his chest, like he used to hug his teddy bear when he'd lie awake at night and worry about creepy things living under his bed. If only someone else were here to hug, like Mom or Dad.

Philecia's ears pricked up. "Ellis, did you hear that?"

"The thunder?"

"No, it wasn't thunder. Between the thunder."

Ellis closed his eyes and listened. The thunder rolled through the sky like an approaching locomotive. But then it passed and in that brief silence before the next thunderclap Ellis heard a soft mewling.

He opened his eyes only to find Philecia's brown ones boring into him.

"You heard it?" she asked.

"Yes." Ellis hesitated. Continuing forward meant walking toward death. The further they walked, the stronger the smell. Yet where there is death, there once was life. And the white shapes in the distance continued to move.

Ellis took a deep breath. "Let's go."

Ellis focused on the white shape closest to him. It looked like a huge egg, about the size of a football, but narrower. It kept wriggling back and forth before pausing, as if to rest.

The thunder clapped louder than usual, delivering a crushing smack to the sky. A new burst of lava shot high into the air, lighting up the world. For a second, Ellis could see clearly. He could see that the slime he walked through was bronze. He could see that palm trees stood in the distance. And he could see that the white shapes had faces.

Panicked, desperate faces.

"Look! Look!" Matilda hung out of Ellis' pocket, pointing. "Look at the faces! Alien monsters!"

The crying grew louder as Ellis pushed through the slime, which now reached his chest. He drew up beside the first white face.

The creature was unlike any he'd seen before. Its face was thinner than a human's, the nose long and pointed. The skin was white—not white like paper—but white like the moon on a foggy night. The hair was a slimy mass of blonde curls and its eyes were large and almond-shaped, and filled with terror.

The thing struggled to keep its head above the slime, but was quickly losing its battle. It raised its arms above its head, exposing hands with three very long, pointed fingers and one thumb. It gasped one last breath then disappeared beneath the muck.

Ellis reached down with his free hand and grabbed an arm. He yanked, pulling the creature back to the surface.

"Quick! Grab onto me," Ellis said.

The long, narrow fingers curled around Ellis' free arm as he hefted whatever it was from the slime. The creature was the size of a toddler. It wrapped its arms and legs around Ellis' torso and clung to him like a koala to a tree.

Ellis wobbled on his feet.

"Don't drop me!" Philecia cried. "The slime's too deep."

"I know," Ellis said, breathing heavy. "We've got to find higher ground."

Ellis' arm ached from holding Philecia for so long, and now with this new alien-looking thing wrapped around him, he could hardly move. He took two more steps and sank deeper.

"We've got to go back," Ellis panted, knees threatening to give way. But just then he heard more cries. Louder cries. Cries that were directed at him, he was sure of it.

Ahead three more white shapes jerked back and forth. But this time Ellis knew what they were—the desperate faces of drowning creatures. The face closest to him sank below the slime.

No! Ellis moved forward, ignoring his wobbly knees and the pain in his shoulder. He tried to find the spot where the creature disappeared. The slime pursued his armpits. He lifted Philecia higher as he searched underneath with his free hand. The creature clinging to him gasped and tightened its grip.

Ellis turned in a circle, searching the sea of goo.

Nothing.

Cramps seized his arm, threatening to make him drop Philecia. He had to go back. He worked his way backward, trying to block from his mind the fading cries of the other drowning creatures. The cries were for him and he was failing. Failing!

In the distance two faces remained. "I'll come back for you! Hang on!" he yelled.

Ellis retraced his steps until the slime was only ankle deep. His elbow creaked as he straightened his arm and released Philecia to the ground. He tried to unclasp the creature's hands from around his neck.

"Let go of me! I've got to go get your friends." Ellis peered into its face, but its eyes remained squeezed shut. Ellis reached around his waist and unlocked the creature's legs. It tumbled to the ground then curled into a ball, chin on its knees, silently rocking back and forth.

"Watch him," Ellis told Philecia. He sloshed back through the slime. There had been two faces left. Ellis strained his eyes as he waded deeper, looking ... searching ...

Where were they? He hadn't been gone that long. He'd hurried as fast as he could. He had!

But it hadn't been fast enough. The creatures were no longer there.

Ellis waded back, his chest heavy.

"Did you find them?" Philecia asked.

Ellis shook his head, unable to meet her eyes. Unable to meet anyone's eyes.

"I-is any-anybody else a-alive?" The creature's voice was soft and high, the sound of a very young child. It looked at Ellis with hopeful eyes, its face mottled with tears and slime. Ellis cleared his throat. "No ... just you."

The light went out of the creature's eyes and its whole body shook. "I want my mom," it whispered. "I want Dreya. I never got to say good-bye. She took them. I never—never got to—to—" It broke into sobs.

Matilda poked her head out of Ellis' pocket. Her nose twitched as her beady eyes took in the sight. She scampered down the front of Ellis' shirt.

"Oh no, no, no. Don't cry. Please don't cry." She stroked the creature's leg with her paw. "It'll be okay, yes it will. You will find them. You will. You will!" The creature looked down at the little brown mouse and Matilda offered up her best bucktoothed smile. The creature's tears slowed.

"Who are you?" Ellis asked.

"I'm Jenkins. I want my mom. I want to go home!"

I know the feeling, Ellis thought ruefully.

"I'm Ellis. And this is Philecia and Matilda. Where do you think your mom is?" Ellis braced himself, praying it wasn't one of those he couldn't get to in time.

"I don't know. She took them. She took my mom and my sister, Dreya, and left me all alone. She took them and left me. She left me."

Jenkins burst into new sobs, his shoulders hunched and trembling.

A horrible scream ripped through the air, puncturing the endless rumble in the clouds. Matilda stuck her paws in her ears and scowled up at the sky. "There's that screech again. I hate it! I hate it! It sounds like an angry owl. An owl looking for mouse casserole."

Jenkins lifted his face, eyes wide. "It's her!" He rose to his feet and searched the sky, his eyes taking on a new gleam in the volcano's yellow-green light. "There! There she is!" Jenkins pointed to the horizon. A dark shadow broke from the clouds and swooped toward the ground. It hovered momentarily, then shot up into the swirling darkness.

"Who is that?" Ellis asked.

"Fandrella," said Jenkins. "She's our ruler. She's saving us Petikins from the slewedge." Jenkins sniffed and wiped his nose with his sleeve. "Hey! Did she send you to save Petikins, too?"

Ellis shook his head.

"We just got here. In fact, we're lost. Do you know the way out of here?"

"Here? You mean my village? It got attacked by Snotlins. We had to leave in a hurry and that's when— when everyone got washed away by the slewedge." Jenkins lip quivered. "They all washed away. My home. My friends. Everything." Jenkins sank to his knees and wept a fresh flood of tears.

Ellis looked down at the slimy muck covering his shoes. Slewedge. The stuff was called slewedge and these Petikins had washed away in its depths. No wonder it smelled like death.

Ellis sat down beside the little Petikin, his eyes avoiding Jenkins' sad face. What could he do? How could he get him to quit crying? He awkwardly placed his arm around Jenkins' shoulder, mimicking what his parents had done whenever he'd had a crisis. But the worst crisis he could remember was when he'd gotten the stomach flu on Christmas and spent all morning throwing up instead of opening presents. That was nothing compared to what this kid had experienced. A skinny arm placed around his shoulders couldn't be much comfort.

But Jenkins didn't pull away, and eventually he stopped crying.

"What about your dad?" Ellis asked. "Did he go with that flying thing—what'd you say it was called—Fansomething?"

Jenkins shook his head. "He's not with Fandrella. My dad disappeared a long time ago. It's just my mom and Dreya and me."

Ellis sighed. "I wish I could help you. I don't even know where I am. We came through that forest over there, but now we can't get back."

Jenkins looked up, curiosity on his grimy face. "That forest? The Grand Forest?"

"I don't know what forest it is. It's those trees on the other side of the field. That's where I live, beyond that forest."

"But no one can get through that forest. The trees are all closed up."

"We somehow did. But you're right. The trees closed up after we got through. Now they're like a big wall of rock."

"There's just got to be another way out, yes there does," Matilda said, crawling on Jenkins' arm. "Can you think of a way? Can you? Can you?"

Jenkins slowly shook his head. "If there was a way out of Kibblestan, I'd be long gone by now. My whole family would." He paused, sniffling. "The Snotlins keep attacking all over the place. Everyone's drowning in slewedge. No one has a home anymore. Or family." Jenkins' voice caught at this last sentence.

"Kibblestan," Matilda said. "What's that? What's that?"

"What do you mean, what's that?" Jenkins said. "It's here. This land. From the Grand Forest all the way to Latinab, where the volcano is."

Kibblestan. Latinab. Ellis wracked his brain, trying to remember any geography lessons at school that mentioned either of these places. Maybe they were places that kids didn't learn about until high school. *Or maybe kids don't learn about them at all, because they're magical, and once you set foot in them you never return—*

Ellis squashed the thought and rose to his feet.

"So the end of Kibblestan is that volcano over there?" he asked.

Jenkins nodded.

"Then maybe there's a way out between Kibblestan and Latinab. Maybe we should go that direction and—"

The ground trembled, making Ellis wobble on his feet. He glanced at Jenkins, who looked terrified.

"You get earthquakes much?" Ellis asked uneasily.

Before Jenkins could answer, the ground shook again. This time it was even more intense. Philecia's fur stood on end as her body quaked. Matilda scampered to the top of Jenkins' shoulder and grabbed onto his golden curls to steady herself. But Jenkins took no notice. He remained frozen in horror, watching the shadows.

"Ellis," Philecia's voice was strangely high. "It's coming closer. I can smell it all around us."

"What?"

"Death."

The ground vibrated so hard that Ellis was knocked off his feet. Something tall and black and leathery stepped out of the darkness.

CHAPTER FOUR

The horrifying creature towered twice as high as a basketball hoop. Its head was shaped like an iron—horizontal across the bottom and pointed at the top. Its large dark eyes looked like two shiny globes and its tough skin was black and smooth as a bat's wings. Its skinny neck sprouted up from heavy shoulders and it had two arms and two legs, just like a person. But instead of hands it held out two clicking pincers covered in stiff, black hair.

Ellis couldn't move. His mind screamed, Get up! Get up and run! Yet he remained planted on the soggy ground.

The thing lumbered forward, the ground shaking with each clunky step. When it was only a few feet away it paused, cocked its head and made a slurping sound. Its mouth became a fountain of drool as frothy liquid dripped from its face. It stuck out a long, skinny tongue that wriggled up and down, like a dark purple snake searching for something to strike. Above the tongue were two nostrils that glowed orange-red.

"Mouse casserole! Not mouse casserole. No! Please no!" Matilda's shrieks broke Ellis from his trance and he tore his eyes from the horrendous sight.

Jenkins stood, his mouth frozen in a silent scream. Philecia lay sprawled on her back, paws in the air, lips pulled back in a crazy, terrified grin. She'd done this same thing twice before, once to a turtle and once to a lizard. It was her way of saying, "I submit. I give up. Do with me what you want, just make it quick and painless."

The horrible monster leaned toward them, tongue swirling. A stream of bronze-colored mucous slowly crawled out of each glowing nostril and trickled down its face. Ellis gagged as the metallic stench filled the thick, balmy air. *Slewedge.*

Ellis clambered to his feet and grabbed Jenkins' shoulder.

"Come on!" he cried.

"It's a Snotlin!" Jenkins gasped. "Stay clear of its tongue. And its pincers. Stay clear—"

Jenkins' warning was too late.

"Aaaaa!" Ellis bellowed as the Snotlin's pincers snapped shut around the waist of his jeans and he was lifted into the air. His lower back exploded in pain as the razor sharp hair covering the Snotlin's pincer poked through his jeans.

Ellis swung his arms and kicked his legs as he rose above the ground. Jenkins reached up to him, his long, pointed fingers splayed. Matilda ran in circles as she clutched the sides of her face. And Philecia—Ellis could not believe his eyes. Philecia was no longer laying on her back with that goofy grin on her face. Philecia looked like a dog gone insane. Her fur stood on end as she hopped back and forth and barked her dog scream.

Ellis' cheek felt funny. Something was touching it but he couldn't see what. The strange sensation bore into his flesh, with just enough pressure to be slightly painful. Ellis reached up with his hand just as Jenkins shouted, "No!"

His hand wrapped around a narrow fleshy tube that was rough and sticky.

"It's the tongue, Ellis." Jenkins shouted. "It's the tongue!"

The tongue? That long purple thing? Ellis thought he might puke. He clawed at the squishy muscle, scratching, then yanking. At last the pressure let up on his cheek. He ripped the tongue from his flesh and vigorously shook his hand until it was free.

Ellis gasped for breath. What could be next? His chest felt so heavy, his ribcage tight. Breathing was difficult, painful. His flailing arms and legs slowed. His head grew fuzzy and the world faded away.

Tchooooooooooo!

Ellis was pulled back to consciousness. Worse than the rumbling thunder and the squawk from the thing called Fandrella, this noise shook everything in its presence.

Warm liquid showered down, and Ellis slipped from the Snotlin's grasp. He landed in a flood of slewedge that raced along in waves. Ellis gasped for breath and splashed about as he struggled to swim in the thick, slippery goop.

Tchoooooooooooo!

The sound slapped the air again, and Ellis held his breath as a new flood of slewedge poured his way. A towering wave caught him, somersaulting him over and over without mercy. Blood pounded in his ears as he sucked in a mouthful of slewedge. He clawed to the surface, hacking.

Disgusting! The goop tasted like a dirty penny covered in salt. He gulped the humid air and paddled his arms as he rode the current. Matilda floated by, stretched out on her back with paws in the air.

That's it! Put your feet downstream. How many times had the Vulture Voyagers taught him to do that if caught in a raging river? And Dad thought the Voyagers never taught anything useful. Ellis struggled to put his feet out in front of him.

A violent burst from the volcano lit up the sky, illuminating a dark wall of palm trees ahead. The ground sloped up on either side. Where was he? Had he washed into a stream of some kind?

The slewedge seemed a little cooler now, and less thick. But the current was still too strong to fight.

"Ellis! *Heh heh heh* Ellis!"

Philecia's panting voice. Ellis tried to look behind him but the rushing swells smacked his face. "Phelicia! I'm here! Keep swimming. Don't give up."

Philecia swept past, her eyes bulging and short legs moving in the fastest dog paddle he'd ever seen. Next Jenkins passed by, frantically waving his arms and kicking his legs. Ellis watched them disappear into the jumble of palm trees. Seconds later Ellis followed.

The stream curved to the left, then to the right. At last the current slowed. Ellis planted his feet on the velvety streambed and stood up. The wild ride was over.

He trudged up the embankment and collapsed. He looked around. Where was everyone? They had to be close. He gazed across the stream. Had they climbed out the other side?

Excited squeaking interrupted his thoughts. Ellis turned to see Matilda scampering down the embankment.

"Oh Ellis! Ellis! Ellis! You're, you're here!" Matilda bounced up and down. "Those Snotlins sneezed, yes they did. But we got away. We got away. Now we just have to find the others, yes we do—"

Ellis interrupted. "Snotlins? There was more than one?"

Matilda nodded her head so fast Ellis thought it might pop off her shoulders. "Yes, there were. Lots of them. A whole army, yes they were. They creeped up behind your Snotlin and *Choooo!* They sneezed all at once and that's what made the flood of slewedge, yes it was. It was!"

Ellis rubbed his forehead. All he could remember was dangling above the ground as everything went black. Maybe it was a good thing he hadn't seen the army of Snotlins. Seeing one was enough. "What about Philecia? And Jenkins? Have you seen them?"

Matilda shook her head.

Thrrrrrrr. A strange purring sound came from downstream. What was it? Not thunder. In fact, the thunder had disappeared.

It sounded like a cat's purr, but louder. Ellis looked around. Dense vegetation rose up on either side, overgrown with twisting vines and giant, weepy leaves big enough to cradle a newborn baby. Massive tree roots burst from the mossy ground and a dark green canopy blocked the sky.

They were in the middle of a jungle.

And jungles had jaguars.

Ellis' heart pounded.

Thrrrrrrrrrrrr! A small shape moved through the diluted slewedge. It was way too small to be a swimming jaguar, but Ellis still sat motionless, hoping to stay unnoticed as whatever it was drew near.

"Look! Look!" Matilda jumped up and down, squealing. "Something's ·coming, yes it is. Something's coming!"

So much for remaining unnoticed. The small form took a turn and headed straight for them. As it got closer Ellis realized it was a huge rat floating on a raft. It balanced on its hind legs and held a long stick in its paws that it used to steer. Attached to the raft was a motor of some sort—the source of the purring sound.

The rat guided the raft to the embankment and leaped onto shore, its movements light and graceful. "Okay, Fred, you can stop now." The purring ceased.

Ellis scooted backward as the curious rodent headed his way. It walked on its hind legs and was a little taller than Ellis' knee. It wore a pair of tattered burgundy pants that reached its knees and a flimsy gray hat with a feather sticking out on one side. Its eyes sparkled.

"Here you are!" Its voice was rich, with no trace of squeakiness. "You must be Ellis, I presume?"

Ellis stopped scooting backward, speechless.

"They sent me to find you," the rat continued. "We are lucky it wasn't too far. Now if you'll follow me this way ..."

Ellis didn't move.

The rat's whiskers twitched. "Forgive me my lack of manners." It removed the hat from its head and long, wavy hair tumbled to its shoulders. The hair was light, unlike the rat's charcoal fur, and the texture silky.

Matilda gasped.

"Allow me to introduce myself." The rat placed its hat over its heart. "I am Rabio, Keeper of Kibblestan. I am honored to meet you."

Matilda clapped a paw over her mouth, muffling a squeak.

Rabio turned to her and grinned. "And you, m'lady." He made a sweeping bow, locking eyes with the blushing mouse. Matilda's chest bobbed up and down, her face fixed in a frozen smile.

"How do you know me?" Ellis asked.

Rabio straightened up. "Your friends downstream. I pulled them from the slewedge, with Fred's help, of course. They sent me to search for you. Someone from beyond Kibblestan." His eyes gleamed. "Come quickly! We mustn't dally. You never know when a band of Snotlins may attack with their virulent sneezes."

Rabio walked down the bank and Matilda scampered after him.

"Rabio! Rabio! I didn't tell you my name. I'm Matilda, yes I am. Matilda."

Ellis climbed down the embankment. The raft was made out of palm branches and looked quite soggy. At one end rested a very strange insect. It was bigger than any hissing cockroach or tarantula or creepy crawler Ellis had ever seen. Its body was the size of a rabbit and its cream-colored wings stood as tall as Rabio. It stared up with two round, burgundy eyes.

"This is Fred," Rabio gestured to the insect and its wings vibrated in greeting. "He is my partner in salvaging what is left of Kibblestan. Come! Sit on my raft and we shall go back to your friends."

Ellis hesitated. What if that bug had a giant stinger? Or what if it bit like a mosquito, and made your entire skin turn into a huge itchy bump? That thing was way too big to squish if it tried to attack.

But Matilda did not hesitate. She practically flew as she leaped up front. "Sit by me, Rabio! Okay? Okay? Sit up here by me?"

Rabio nodded and stepped on beside her. He motioned to Ellis. "Master Ellis? Your friends await us."

Ellis gave Fred one last look. The insect hadn't done anything when Matilda jumped on board. And Rabio seemed trustworthy enough. Ellis climbed onto the raft, but his eyes never left Fred.

Rabio grabbed his stick and pushed off from the bank. "Okay, Fred. Power up!"

The strange insect lowered its bottom half toward the water while its furry legs gripped the raft. Its long wings moved in a circular motion, acting as a propeller as they slapped the slewedge mixture over and over. They drifted down the stream and Fred's wings shifted to high gear. The purring sound returned.

They forged ahead and soon Philecia and the small Petikin named Jenkins came into view. Philecia jumped up and down on her hind legs. Rabio steered the raft to shore and Philecia leapt aboard, covering Ellis' face with slobbery dog kisses.

Ellis hugged her wriggly body. "Good girl, Philecia. You're a good girl." He held the dachshund out in front of him. "And I saw you. You were barking. You barked at that Snotlin."

Philecia's tail wagged faster than Fred's wings. "I did, Ellis. And I didn't even pee!"

Ellis scratched Philecia behind the ears. "But that Snotlin was scary. How'd you do it?"

Philecia's tail slowed. "I don't know. I-I guess I've never seen you in danger before. I mean, real life-and-death danger. All I could think was protect! Protect! I love you so much, Ellis. If anything happened to you, I ..." Philecia nuzzled into his arms.

Jenkins stepped onto the raft, looking unsure. Ellis patted the space next to him. "It's okay. You can sit here, dude." The little Petikin looked relieved and smiled as he took his seat. Ellis smiled back.

"Everyone settled?" Rabio pushed off the shore and Fred fired up his wings. The raft slowly snaked its way down the stream, cutting through the tunnel of tangled trees and vines. The air was humid and still, and the rumbling thunder remained eerily absent.

"Rabio," Ellis leaned forward. "Where are you taking us? Can you get us out of Kibblestan?"

Rabio's eyes did not leave the surrounding shadows.

"I am taking you where I take all of the refugees I rescue. It is a place that is secret, and is untouched by slewedge."

The ground vibrated and their raft surged ever so slightly.

Rabio stopped paddling and stared into the dark, twisting trees. His eyes grew bright and his whiskers twitched.

"I felt something, Rabio," Matilda chattered. "Our raft kind of tossed, yes it did. What—"

The ground shook again, harder this time. The vines swung back and forth and the raft lurched forward. Ellis held his breath, watching the trees.

Something moved.

CHAPTER FIVE

"Rabio," Ellis whispered, his eyes still glued to the trees. "Something's over there."

Rabio didn't reply. He paddled faster and faster. Fred's wings beat so quickly they were barely visible. Ellis gripped the side of the raft with white knuckles.

Tchoooooooo! A row of Snotlins burst through the trees as a storm of slewedge rained down.

"Hang on everybody!" Rabio shouted. He flung down the paddle and dropped to his belly. Slewedge flooded the stream, overflowing the banks and tossing the raft like it was a sock in a washing machine. Ellis wrapped one arm around Philecia, while barely hanging on with his other hand. Jenkins clung to his shirt and wouldn't let go. Matilda threw herself down beside Rabio and scooted so close she was practically underneath him. Waves of slewedge-laden water crashed on top of them, covering their bodies with a warm layer of stinky slime.

Ellis squeezed his eyes shut and mashed his lips together, trying to imagine he was riding a boogie board in the ocean instead of a fragile raft in a whirlpool of snot. A few terrifying moments passed, then the waves calmed and the raft steadied.

Ellis opened his eyes. The Snotlins were gone.

The jungle's canopy kept them shaded as the current whisked them along. Downstream, shafts of sunlight cut through the trees. A moment later they were propelled into a warm blanket of sunshine as the jungle came to an abrupt end and the stream emptied into a stagnant pond. The raft crashed onto a boulder and Ellis blinked, squinting in the first sunlight he'd experienced since entering Kibblestan.

The murky pond smelled of slewedge and moss and rotting wood. The front part of the raft had ripped apart, and Rabio and Matilda scampered up the large rock.

Ellis slid into the pond, his shoes sinking into the soft, mud-covered bottom. The slewedge-water only came to his waist, so he carried Philecia and let Jenkins ride piggy-back as he traipsed toward shore. He dropped Philecia onto the ground and looked around.

Mounds and mounds of sand stretched out as far as the eye could see. Gone were the black, churning clouds. Now the sun shined with painful intensity. The slewedge crusted over as it dried on Ellis' skin, and a prickly thirst scratched his throat.

"Come with me." Rabio offered his paw to Matilda and she giggled nervously as she clasped his paw with her own. The two rodents slid down the face of the boulder and swam to shore.

"I fear this is Kibblestan's last place of refuge," Rabio said, gesturing to the miles of sand. "The slewedge hasn't reached here and I have yet to hear of a Snotlin in this desert. It is not an environment that can easily sustain life. Only the boarusks dwell here, being such hardy animals."

Fred whirred over to Rabio and hovered above his head.

"We must repair the raft," Rabio told him. "Go and fetch additional boarusk hair and branches." Fred nodded, then buzzed away over the closest sand hill.

Rabio smiled at Ellis. "Come! You can join the others in my refugee habitat."

Ellis frowned. He didn't want to go to any habitat. He just wanted to find the way home.

But close by Jenkins sat on the ground, his sad eyes distant. What about that poor little guy? Where was he to go?

"Are there any Petikins in this refugee habitat?" Ellis asked.

Rabio nodded. "Absolutely, Master Ellis. There are many different creatures who have survived the Snotlin sneezes, Petikins included."

Ellis chewed his lip. If they went to the habitat, maybe Jenkins would find someone he knew. Who knows, maybe he even had family—some cousins or grandparents or something—who were there waiting for him.

They followed Rabio to a clump of palm leaves a few yards away. Rabio grabbed each leaf and dragged it aside, revealing a gaping hole in the soft desert floor.

"Squeeze in there, if you will. The suction will do the rest."

Suction? Ellis peered inside. Nothing but blackness. Was there even a bottom?

"I'll go! I'll go, yes I will. I will!" Matilda clapped her paws. The little mouse ran right past Ellis and jumped as high as she could. For an instant she lingered, suspended in mid-air as she looked at Rabio and said, "You coming?"

She plunged down the hole and disappeared from sight.

"Who is next?" Rabio smiled, but nobody made a move.

"How deep is that hole?" Ellis asked.

"I can sense your hesitation, dear boy, but I can assure you, it is the safest place we can lead the refugees at this moment."

Something grabbed Ellis' hand and he looked down. Jenkins stared up at him, lip quivering. Ellis gave the Petikin's hand a reassuring squeeze.

"Rabio-o-o-o-o! Rabio! Are you coming?" Matilda's squeak echoed from far away.

Ellis looked at Philecia. Her brown eyes watched him expectantly as she slowly twitched her tail. Ellis tightened his lips and nodded. "Let's go," he said.

He stepped forward but Jenkins clung to his hand. Ellis gently pried his fingers away. "It's okay, dude. You'll come down the hole, too. Come right after me." Ellis stepped to the edge. "Philecia, you follow me, too. Here I go."

Ellis closed his eyes and held his breath. He stepped into the void and was swallowed by darkness. He slid through a rocky tube, skinning his elbows and ripping his jeans. He tried to slow his descent by pressing his feet to the sides but it didn't do much good. When the tunnel's steepness leveled out a strong suction pulled at his clothes, his skin, his entire body. Ellis caught his breath as he was dragged through the remainder of the tunnel. He fell several feet and landed on a mound of palm leaves.

Ellis blinked and looked around. He sat in a room illuminated by silvery-white light. The walls were slimy and lumpy and glowing, and were covered with eyeballs that stared back at him—dozens of them.

"You made it, yes you did. Yes you did!" Matilda sang as she skipped about.

Ellis raised one eyebrow. "Matilda? Er—do you see something weird about the walls?"

"Hmmm? Walls? They're lovely, aren't they? Silver-white and bright—just like the stars, yes they are. Just like."

But stars were a million miles away and did not have eyeballs that watch your every move. Ellis inched closer. The walls were covered with star-shaped slimy creatures, some the size of a deck of cards, others as big as Ellis' head. He reached out a finger and touched a pointed leg. The creature jiggled and its eyes glared. His finger came away coated with clear, wet residue.

"Don't touch the starjelos!"

Ellis whirled around to see a rat wearing an orange bonnet, lavender blouse, and a long brown skirt with white lace leggings underneath. Her fur was a rich cream color and her large sapphire eyes twinkled in the silver light. Like Rabio, she stood on her hind legs and was nearly as tall as Ellis' knee.

"You see, anything that comes in contact with the starjelos' sensitive outer lining has the potential to decrease its liquid content, and they tend to get grumpy— or maybe you already knew that?"

"Um, no," Ellis replied. "I've never heard of starjelos before."

"But of course." The rat looked sympathetic. "Not every refugee is familiar with the wonderful creatures who reside below the earth." She smiled with understanding. "I am Raquel."

Before Ellis could introduce himself there was a ringing sound, and the ceiling moved.

Ellis jumped.

"It's doing it again. It's doing it again." Matilda
hopped up and down, pointing.

Something flat, speckled and scaly covered the ceiling. It had no eyes and was so featureless it looked like a
giant amoeba. Its dark cavity of a mouth sucked in air.
As it inhaled, its lungs expanded like two inflating gray
balloons beneath a layer of shiny, translucent skin.
Philecia tumbled out of an opening in the ceiling and
landed on the palm leaves. The thing's lungs quickly de-
flated, followed by a deafening burp that smelled like
rotten fish and vomit. Ellis' stomach lurched.

"Thank you, Leon!" Raquel smiled up at the ceiling.

Philecia shook herself and looked around. "Ellis!" she
cried. The loyal dachshund scampered to Ellis, wagging
her tail.

Raquel's eyes bounced from Philecia to Ellis. "If you
don't mind, can I ask what ... I mean, who you are?"

Ellis understood. They had to look really weird to
everyone around here, just like they looked strange to
him. "I'm Ellis and this is Philecia," Ellis did his best to
smile, but the sickening stench from Leon's burp was
making him queasy. Sweat dotted his forehead and he
tried not to breathe through his nose.

"That's Matilda," Ellis pointed to the brown mouse who was busily preening her fur. When she heard her name she looked up and smiled.

Raquel's eyes shined. "And what village do you hail from?"

"Village? We're not from Kibblestan. We came from that dark forest over —I don't know— it was way back before you get to the jungle."

"The forest? Surely not the Grand Forest? Nothing gets through there."

Ellis wiped his brow. Finally the air was starting to clear. "We did. But now we can't get back. It turned solid again. Do you know a way out?"

Da-ding! The bell rang out, and the amoeba thing sucked Jenkins into the room. The little Petikin ran and hid behind Ellis, wrapping his arms around Ellis' leg as his eyes darted around the room.

A moment later Rabio dropped through the opening.

"Rabio!" Matilda rushed to his side. "I love your habitat, yes I do, yes I do. Where do we go now? I'll go wherever you go, yes I will. I will!"

Rabio gazed at Raquel. Her long lashes fluttered. Matilda's whiskers twitched. Suddenly the little brown mouse didn't look so excited.

"I see you've met Raquel," Rabio said, bowing in the cream-colored rat's direction.

Raquel's eyes traveled to Ellis, studying him from head to toe. "Pardon me for asking, but you aren't—you aren't some kind of Kootie, are you?"

Ellis wrinkled his nose. The only kind of cootie he'd ever heard of was the case of cooties Sarah Jackman had after trying to kiss two boys in second grade. "Cootie? I don't have the cooties!"

Rabio stroked his whiskers. "What she is asking, Master Ellis, is if you are a part of that long lineage of Kooties who have served as Kibblestan's rulers for generations. Like Fandrella. You and she could pass for the same species, except ..." He walked toward Raquel. "My darling, he is not a Kootie. Look at his feet. They are not talons. He does not fly. He's ..." Rabio raised an eyebrow. "Forgive me, but what are you exactly?"

Ellis looked from one rat to the other. "I'm a boy. A human. I'm—I'm from America. Have you heard of it? America?"

Raquel and Rabio shook their heads.

"Well, that's where I'm from. I can leave Jenkins here, but Philecia and I need to keep going. We've got to find our way back home."

But what if there wasn't a way back home? What if he never saw Mom and Dad again? What if the last words Dad ever heard him say was *I hate you?*

Ellis swallowed and shoved the thoughts from his brain before his heart exploded.

Raquel eyed Philecia. "And what is the long creature who travels with you? Is that what rats look like in your world?"

"Huh?" Ellis looked at Philecia, who'd turned pink beneath her fur. "Philecia's not a rat. She's my dog."

Rabio's eyebrows raised. "Dog? I never would have guessed."

Raquel walked toward a wall with a circular entrance to another tunnel.

"Please follow Raquel," Rabio instructed. "I must return to my duties and repair my raft before resuming my search and rescue missions."

Matilda looked heartbroken. "You're not staying? But I thought you would, yes I did."

"My dear mouse, there are countless others who are struggling against the slewedge. I must go and rescue them. I leave you in the competent paws of Raquel. She will show you the habitat."

"But ... but ..." Matilda's buckteeth glistened as she gnawed her lower lip. "I'll come with you, yes I will. I can help."

Rabio shook his head. "I appreciate the offer, little mouse, but you need not risk your life with me." Rabio turned to go.

"H-h-have-have y-you ..." The childish voice was barely audible.

Rabio turned back around. "Yes?"

Jenkins came out from behind Ellis' leg. He shuffled his feet. "H-have you seen my mom?"

"Your mother?"

"Y-yes. My mom and my sister. They're-they're gone. I need to find them."

Rabio scratched his chin. "I just might have, son. I've rescued many and brought them here. If you will follow Raquel—"

"No!" Jenkins shook his head. "No, they're with Fandrella. Fandrella called out to us and she took my mom and sister just in time. We almost drowned."

Rabio frowned.

Jenkins continued. "Where'd they go? Did she bring them here?"

Rabio's jaw tightened and he closed his eyes. When he opened them they were filled with sorrow. "I am sorry, son. Fandrella has not brought anyone here. I—" Rabio opened his mouth as if to say more, then closed it again. "I'm sorry." He bowed his head and turned away.

Jenkins' eyes welled up. "I want my mom ... I want my mom!" His body trembled as tears streamed down his splotchy face.

Ellis found himself once again feeling helpless as he awkwardly wrapped his arm around Jenkins' shoulders. "It's okay, dude," he whispered. "We'll find your family. Everything'll be okay."

Ellis caught Raquel watching them, a strange look on her face. She scampered to Rabio and whispered something into his ear. Rabio looked their direction, shrugged and whispered back.

What were they whispering about? It was rude, and confusing.

Rabio walked toward the exit and Matilda chased after him. "Rabio! Rabio! Are you really leaving now? Really? Really?"

"Yes, I am Matilda. I must go."

The dejected look on Matilda's face was not lost on Rabio. He dropped to one knee and clasped her paw. "Farewell, dear mouse. Until our paths cross again." He raised her paw to his lips and kissed it. Matilda wobbled on her feet.

Rabio waved to the room then scaled a ladder made of vines to the exit in the ceiling. He climbed into the opening, his long, rubbery tail hanging down. "Okay, Leon. I'm ready."

The gray speckled amoeba thing exhaled with a whoosh. Rabio's tail disappeared. Leon closed his mouth, but not before expelling a loud belch that polluted the air. Several clear droplets of who-knows-what rained down.

That was enough to get Ellis moving. "Come on, guys. Let's go."

They followed Raquel through the opening in the opposite wall. A circle of yellow light winked in the distance. Drops of sweat clung to Ellis' floppy bangs. It was so warm and stuffy. Were the walls closing in? He took a deep breath and focused on the light up ahead. Now it flickered blue.

At last Ellis reached the end of the tunnel. He stepped out and looked around, taking in the sight.

The room was huge, and very crowded. Swarms of insects flew by—large insects, some the size of a giant bumblebee, others the size of a flying cat. They buzzed noisily while their abdomens lit up, some bright yellow and others royal blue. The walls were covered with them, but oddly enough, the insects with blue lights clung to the wall on the left and the insects shining yellow plastered the wall on the right.

Philecia jumped up against Ellis, her eyes bulging. Ellis reached down and petted her. "It's okay, girl," he whispered. "They're only fireflies. You've faced a Snotlin. This is nothing."

The shining insects were not the only ones crowding the space. Small, milky-white people clustered about. Petikins! Surely one of them would be willing to take care of Jenkins.

A pack of dogs—all of them large and scruffy—padded around the room, sniffing. Their coats were varied—some long, some short, in different shades of brown, black and gray. They weaved through the crowds on stealthy paws, and though they didn't look like each other, they all had one thing in common—a wild, untamed look in their eyes.

"Right this way," Raquel motioned. They followed the rat further into the room. Jenkins stuck to Ellis' side, and Matilda pranced along, nearly bumping into a very strange animal. It looked like a small terrier with a pink vulture head and long, silver fur, with four purple talons for feet. Its bloodshot eyes jiggled in their sockets and its mouth was lipless and leathery.

"Watch where you're going!" it snapped.

Matilda backed away. "You don't like mouse casserole, do you? It's disgusting, yes it is!"

The strange animal scowled and scampered off.

Matilda let out a sigh of relief. She was soon overtaken by the excitement of so many new creatures. "My name's Matilda, yes it is. Yes it is!" She disappeared into the crowds, extending a paw to anyone willing to shake it.

Ellis wished he could blend in so easily. He towered over everyone, and while he received all kinds of curious stares, no one made an effort to welcome him. One Petikin sporting a thick black beard with eyebrows to match glared at Ellis. He shoved his way through the crowd until he reached Raquel, his considerable belly straining the buttons on his shirt.

"More?" The Petikin's dark eyes never left Ellis. "Just how many more refugees is your Rabio going to bring down here? It's crowded enough!"

Raquel placed a dainty paw on the Petikin's hairy arm. His sleeves were rolled up and above his elbow was a burgundy arm band with two R's embroidered in gold. "Now don't you worry, Blotu. There's plenty room for newcomers. It might feel a little tight but the important thing is that Rabio's saving lives. We'll worry about space later."

Raquel's answer did little to satisfy the Petikin called Blotu. His bushy brows drew together and his puffy lips curled up in a sneer. He turned and stomped off, shoving aside any Petikin who got in his way.

Raquel smiled, but it was a poor attempt to mask the concern on her face. "You must excuse him. Some of these refugees have lived here since the first Snotlin attack. They're anxious to leave. I understand it's upsetting. They've lost their homes. Many have lost family ... " Raquel's voice trailed off and her eyes went distant.

Ellis couldn't blame anyone who wanted to leave. The air in this crowded room smelled worse than a gym bag. But at least it was a safe place for refugees to go.

"You're doing the best you can." Ellis said.

The rat smiled underneath her orange bonnet. "Yes. Yes, we are. Now please, make yourself comfortable. I will be back later." She scampered through the crowds and disappeared through the exit.

Comfortable? This place could never be comfortable. But maybe they could at least find a place to sit down. As they made their way toward the back, a dog studied them from several feet away. It reminded Ellis of a black wolf, with a thick, matted coat and hungry yellow eyes. It stood very still, ears erect, tail twitching.

Its gaze traveled to Philecia.

It slowly licked its chops.

CHAPTER SIX

Ellis stared at the hungry-looking dog. It was so huge. It could gobble Philecia up in one bite. He glanced at his dachshund. She'd obviously noticed the dog. Philecia's ears were plastered flat against her head, her tail tucked between her legs. Ellis knew what would happen next. Pee.

He grabbed Philecia and slowly backed away. Thankfully, the wolfish dog chose not to follow.

They picked their way through the crowds, and found a space to sit down. Philecia curled up in Ellis' lap and Jenkins rested his head on his shoulder. Something skipped along Ellis' back and he jumped.

"Sorry!" A brown mouse leapt from his shoulder and disappeared into the shadows.

"I want my mom. I miss my mom," Jenkins whispered over and over.

"Jenkins," Ellis said, "there are a lot of Petikins here. Do you recognize any of them? Do you have any relatives? Maybe an aunt or cousin or something?"

"No. Just me. All by myself." His voice cracked.

Matilda popped out of the crowds and headed their way. "I've been looking all over for you, yes I have." She waved her arms dramatically. "We need to get out of here, yes we do. Before the big fight. I don't want to get drowned in bug guts, no I don't. No I don't!"

"Drowned in bug guts? What are you talking about?" Ellis asked.

"The fireflies. They hate each other. Always have. The Yellows think their light is best because it's cheerful. The Blues think theirs is best because it's pretty. They always lived on opposite sides of Kibblestan, yes they did. And now they're sharing the same space and they hate it. They want to kill each other, yes they do. They're going to splat each other against the walls. I don't want to get smothered in flying bug guts, no I don't."

Ellis scratched his head. "Matilda, who told you this?"

"Everyone!" The mouse threw up her paws. "Everyone's talking about it, yes they are. And some Petikins are talking about fighting, too. They're bored. There's nothing to do here so they might as well fight. It's what they say, yes it is."

Ellis looked around. Did Raquel know about this?

The strange animal with the long, silver fur and vulture head scampered up to them. "Odds are, Blues three to one. What's your bet?"

"Um, we're not betting." Ellis said.

The animal's eyes looked like two throbbing golf balls wrapped in a web of veins. It stared at Jenkins. "Haven't I seen you before? Tell me your name."

Jenkins raised his head from Ellis' shoulder. "It's Jenkins. Jenkins Jabbermeyer."

The animal looked like it just swallowed a mouthful of puke. "Jabbermeyer! No wonder you're by yourself and stuck with these weirdos. You're a Jabbermeyer. Serves you right."

"Now wait a minute—" Ellis started to say, but the animal scurried off through the crowds.

"What was that all about?" Philecia asked.

"It's a lizamum," Jenkins said. "They're mean. That one lived in my village. He was always gossiping and saying rude stuff."

"But what did he mean about being a Jabbermeyer?" Ellis asked.

Jenkins looked away and mumbled. "I don't know. Some Petikins just didn't like us. Me or my family. Mom and Dad used to tell me and Dreya to ignore anyone who's hateful, and that it wasn't our fault." Jenkins' voice caught and he swallowed. "Then Dad disappeared."

The crowd roared and pushed toward the front of the room. Ellis stood up to see what was happening. Voices shouted.

"Gimme some! I need that!"

"Here! Raquel! I'm starving!"

"Please! My children! They didn't get to eat last time. Don't make us be last. Please."

The refugees descended on the cream-colored rat that stood atop a makeshift cart just inside the tunnel entrance. The cart rolled into the room, pushed by a large animal that looked like a wild boar. It stood upright on tall, lanky legs and was covered with course dark fur. A pair of tiny wire-framed glasses with round purple lenses perched on its snout. Long, stringy hair that belonged on a hippie grew on its head.

It carelessly snorted while Raquel tried to settle the crowd. "One at a time!" she hollered. "There's enough for everybody. Please, keep calm and wait your turn."

But no one stayed calm. Blotu led a group of Petikins, all wearing burgundy armbands with RR embroidered into them. They trampled over the smaller animals—chipmunks, mice, insects—to get to the cart first. When they reached it they shoved Raquel aside and grabbed at what was inside. They dragged out a hairy carcass that resembled the animal pushing the cart. They struggled under its weight before dropping it to the ground with a thud.

"It's a dead boarusk," Raquel called. She glanced at the animal standing next to her.

It casually nodded as it picked at its teeth with a hoof. "Yeah. You can chow down on the dude. Cool?"

Raquel shouted louder. "The boarusks have agreed to give us their dead. Rabio will be bringing more. So please! Share with each other. Remember there are many mouths to feed."

When Ellis realized Raquel had brought food, he felt a sharp pang in his stomach. But he couldn't bring himself to join in the fray. Mice and chipmunks were being squashed beneath the Petikins' wooden shoes. Dogs ran forward, barking. Several ripped the boarusk carcass away from Blotu and his friends. They growled and violently shook their heads, pulling at opposite ends of the meat. More dogs joined in until it finally tore apart in a fresh splatter of blood.

In seconds the meat was consumed and the dogs padded away, licking blood from their whiskers. Raquel shook her head sorrowfully before following the boarusk with the cart back into the tunnel.

This was crazy. A few Petikins had managed to tear off some morsels before the dogs took over, but most of the refugees got nothing. If every feeding time went like this, half the refugees would starve.

A mother chipmunk emerged from the mob, her brood of five babies following close at her heels.

"But Mama, I'm hungry."

"Me too," another tiny voice whined. "When is it our turn to eat? When?"

The mother chipmunk gathered her babies in an embrace and put on a false smile. "Next time, sweeties. Next time food is delivered it will be our turn. We just need to be patient a little longer."

Her tear-filled eyes revealed the lie but her babies were too young to notice. They nuzzled into their mother's belly and drifted off to sleep.

Ellis couldn't stay any longer. This place was nuts, and wasn't helping him find his way home. Besides, the dogs looked at Philecia the same way he might look at a gooey cheese pizza. Not good.

"We're not staying here," Ellis said. "Let's find someone to take care of Jenkins and go."

Philecia nodded and Matilda bounced up and down, clapping her paws. "I agree, I agree, yes I do. Let's get out before the bug gut fight. Let's go! Let's go!"

Jenkins hung his head, and Ellis took his hand. "Come on, dude. I've done what I can. There are people of your own kind here. You don't want to come with me. I'm going back to my own world."

Jenkins nodded, but didn't look up.

They made their way to a small group of Petikins. There were two women, three men and a boy about Jenkins' age. The boy had glossy black hair and lay on his stomach, looking extremely bored as he traced lines on the ground with his pointed finger.

"Excuse me," Ellis said. The group of Petikins looked up and couldn't hide their astonishment.

"It's a Kootie!" one man breathed.

"Does Fandrella have a brother?" a woman asked.

"They can't be related. His feet aren't talons. He's something else."

A man whose mouth was lost beneath a charcoal bristly beard stepped forward. "You're not a Petikin. Go find someone of your own kind."

Ellis pushed Jenkins forward. "This is Jenkins. He is your kind. We're looking for someone who may know him." Ellis shifted his gaze from Bristlebeard to the two Petikin women. "Can you help him find his family?"

"He won't be findin' his Dad, that's for sure." The voice belonged to the black-haired boy. He still lay on his stomach, smirking.

Ellis frowned. He tightened his grip on Jenkins' shoulders. "Can any of you help—"

The boy interrupted, a wicked grin on his face. "His old man disappeared in a puff of smoke! Poof!" He rolled over and laughed.

Ellis fought the urge to stomp on the boy's face. How could anyone make fun of someone's dad being missing?

"Smartyn, be nice!" One of the women scolded, then smiled apologetically at Ellis.

"But it served him right." Smartyn sat up and pointed. "You're Jenkins, right? Jenkins Jabbermeyer?"

Jenkins nodded slowly.

Bristlebeard raised his eyebrows. "Jabbermeyer? As in Thornton Jabbermeyer?"

Now everyone in the group stared at Jenkins.

Bristlebeard growled. "Speak up, boy."

Jenkins raised his head. "Yes. Jenkins Jabbermeyer. Thornton is my dad."

Bristlebeard moved toward Jenkins, a staircase of horizontal lines crossing his forehead.

"I'll not be helping any Jabbermeyer, ever!" Bristlebeard looked at Ellis. "I don't care how big you are. You can't make us take him in. And you won't find any Petikin who will. He's *your* problem."

Bristlebeard turned away and the Petikin men followed. The women exchanged uneasy glances.

But the boy named Smartyn continued to grin. "Yah, I remember when you left school. Best day ever in class. Your dad was such a weasel."

Without warning Jenkins pounced. Ellis was just as startled as Smartyn, who couldn't react quickly enough to get up off the ground. Jenkins straddled the boy and pinned him down, fists flying.

"Don't you say that about my dad! Take it back! Take it back!" Jenkins hollered. He landed punches to Smartyn's nose and left cheek before Smartyn could get his arms in a position to fend off the blows. The two young Petikins rolled on the ground, but Jenkins ended up on top.

"Break it up! Break it up!" One of the other Petikin men rushed over and grabbed Jenkins' shoulder, but Jenkins twisted away.

"Jenkins!" Ellis yelled. As much as Jenkins was giving the punk what he deserved, this wasn't helping him find someone who'd take care of him. In fact, just the opposite. Ellis lifted Jenkins off the struggling boy. Smartyn scooted back, shouting, "See! He's a Jabbermeyer! They're all mean. Get him away. Away!"

"You were the one being mean!" Ellis hollered. By now a crowd of more Petikins had gathered. And at the name Jabbermeyer they all shook their heads and grumbled.

"What's going on here?" A gruff voice demanded. Ellis turned and saw Blotu. Oh great.

Bristlebeard shook his fists in the air. "This Jabbermeyer boy attacked Smartyn! He's nothing but trouble. Get him out of here. We don't need anymore Jabbermeyers."

Ellis felt like clawing all the bristles off the Petikin's face. "Fine!" he said. "We're going. Who wants to be with Petikins like you anyway."

Ellis grabbed Jenkins' arm and steered him away. Philecia and Matilda followed.

"Boy, you really showed him, yes you did." Matilda skipped along, punching the air. "One – two – *pow!* One – two – *pow!*"

When they reached the tunnel leading out of the room Ellis crouched down beside Jenkins. The Petikin's white face was scraped and dirty, but his smoky eyes were different. They were no longer filled with scared tears. Something within Jenkins had awakened.

"Sorry," Jenkins spoke the word, but Ellis knew it wasn't true. Nor should it be. "Are you mad at me?"

"No." Ellis said. "That kid deserved it."

Jenkins dropped his gaze and was silent.

Ellis continued. "It's okay. It's just ... Look, I don't know what the big deal is about being a Jabbermeyer, but I had hoped to find someone of your own kind, you know, to help you."

Jenkins gazed around the room, a faint smile on his lips. "Guess that didn't work too good, did it?"

Matilda crept in between them and jumped up and down. "Stick with us, Jenkins. Stick with us!"

Jenkins looked up at Ellis. "I don't want to stay here. It's just like my village all over again. No one likes a Jabbermeyer."

"And you really don't have any idea why?"

Jenkins shrugged. "Not really. My parents said it was too complicated for me to understand. Whenever someone would say something mean to me or Dreya,

Dad would just say to be nice and forgive, and that he was working on making things right."

Ellis scanned the room. The Petikins stayed huddled on one side, the blue fireflies hugged one wall, the yellow fireflies hugged the other. The dogs lay in a big pile on top of each other, with a few strays pacing back and forth. The lizamum flitted from group to group, trying to eavesdrop while its leathery mouth pecked at any crawling insects. The mice had retreated to the shadows and the family of chipmunks cuddled together into one furry ball.

Everyone was with their own kind. The groups had been formed, and Jenkins was not going to be welcomed into any of them.

CHAPTER SEVEN

Ellis smiled at Jenkins, hoping to mask the doubt that was flooding into him, choking him. What was he going to do with the little Petikin? He had no clue. But he couldn't leave Jenkins here by himself. No way.

"I guess you're coming with us," he said. He put an arm around Jenkins' shoulder.

Ellis led the way through the narrow tunnel, ignoring the feeling that the walls were closing in on him. At the end of the tunnel, he peeked into the room. Raquel paced back and forth as she twisted the folds of her skirt. The bell rang and Leon filled his lungs. Rabio fell into the room.

Burp! Leon's belch smelled even worse than before. The pungent stench of rotten fish and vomit made Ellis' eyes water. He slapped his hand over his nose and mouth, gagging, and stayed put until the air could clear.

Raquel rushed to Rabio and grabbed his paws, her voice panicked. "Rabio! When will the next food be here? We need food! It's getting really bad down there."

"My darling, the boarusks are making every effort to collect their dead. Is it really that dreadful?"

"The worst I've seen. They practically trampled me to get the food. Some of the Petikins got to eat this time, but the dogs ... the dogs are vicious. I can see it in their eyes. They're fighting their instincts, but I don't know how much longer they will resist. I'm afraid they'll be driven to do what it takes to survive, even if it means eating their fellow refugees."

Rabio's brows drew together. "They need to hold on. I risk my life every time I go on a rescue mission. The least they can do is share what little food we have to keep everyone alive."

"I try to tell them that, but they don't seem to care. There's a poor little chipmunk family who hasn't eaten in I don't know how long. Each time I come with food I try to get it to them, and each time something bigger—a Petikin or a dog—wins out. I'm afraid those poor little chipmunk babies aren't going to survive."

"Me too." Ellis and his friends stepped out of the tunnel and both rats jumped, startled.

"M-master Ellis!" Rabio said. "What brings you and your party back here? I—er—did you not find our habitat to your liking?"

"No, it's not to our liking," Ellis said flatly. "What Raquel says is true. Everyone down there is like—going crazy! And the dogs seem wild. They look at Philecia like she's a sausage or something. And Jenkins, well, none of the Petikins seem to like him too much."

Jenkins hung his head. "It's because I'm a Jabbermeyer." He mumbled the statement, but the words were not lost on Rabio and Raquel. Both rats straightened up, eyes shining.

"I knew it!" Raquel said. "I knew you looked familiar." The lovely rat scampered over to Jenkins. "Thornton's son? Are you one of Thornton's children?"

Jenkins nodded, confusion on his face. "Yeah. How does everybody know my dad?"

Rabio approached Jenkins and tenderly placed a paw on his shoulder. "Your father was a good friend of ours. He was a good Petikin. Don't let anyone tell you something different."

"I *know* he's a good Petikin. He's the best dad in the world," Jenkins' voice caught, but his eyes had the same fiery look in them as they did after his scuffle with Smartyn.

"There's got to be someplace else to go," Ellis said. "Raquel's right. It's only a matter of time before your habitat explodes."

Matilda nodded her head, eyes wide. "Explodes into bug guts, yes it will! Yes it will!"

Rabio raised his eyebrows.

"The fireflies," Ellis explained. "They're planning on smashing each other."

Matilda squeaked so fast she was hard to understand. "Yessir! They hate each other, yes they do."

Rabio clawed at his long silky hair and looked at Raquel. Raquel held his gaze. The tension in her face lingered a moment, then seemed to melt. She closed her eyes and nodded. Rabio turned back to Ellis. "There is another place," he said slowly. "We just wanted to delay moving the refugees until it was absolutely necessary."

"Where is it?" Ellis said.

Rabio hesitated. He looked at Raquel again, and she nodded her reassurance. Rabio motioned for Ellis and his friends to come closer. They huddled together like a group of football players discussing a secret play.

"The entrance is right beside us." Rabio's voice was a whisper. "The starjelos are camouflaging it. We've kept it a secret because we're protecting the poor chap who lives there."

"Someone's there already?" Ellis asked, surprised.

Rabio nodded. "A Petikin lives there all by himself. He is a friend to Raquel and I." Rabio paused, and looked at Jenkins. "And was a good friend of your father's."

Jenkins' eyes widened.

"But we cannot let anyone else know that he is down there," Rabio continued. "You see, his life is in danger."

"Why is his life in danger?" Ellis asked.

"He discovered something. It is something about the starjelos. If Fandrella ever finds out, she might try to destroy them all, and our friend in the process."

"Why?" Ellis asked. "Can the starjelos hurt Fandrella? Can they blow things up or something?"

Rabio shook his head. "No, nothing like that. Come. I will show you."

Their huddle broke apart and Rabio walked to the opposite wall that was covered with starjelos. He picked up a long stick lying on the ground and gently prodded one. It's eyes shot open then drew together in a frown.

"Forgive me for disturbing you," Rabio said. "We need to get through." Rabio tilted his head and flashed a winning smile at the star-shaped, gelatinous creature. "I do so appreciate your understanding."

Rabio's charm did not completely erase the annoyance in the starjelo's eyes. But it was enough to make it cooperate, as it curled its legs toward its body until it looked like one iridescent ball. It moved up the wall, smashing over the other starjelos. The starjelos stuck to each other, and the shiny sphere grew like a rolling snowball, creating a path toward the ceiling. A narrow door made of spindly sticks was revealed.

Rabio raised a paw. "That's enough. Thank you!"

The starjelo ball stopped and Rabio gently pushed on the door. It swung open into darkness.

"Quickly, quickly, now," Rabio instructed. "Climb inside so we can cover this up again."

No one moved. It was pitch black inside. How could they see where they were going?

Rabio twirled his whiskers. "But of course, allow me to go first. I shall show you the way." The handsome rat turned to the glowing walls. "Is anybody at maximum capacity?"

An unusually swollen starjelo unstuck its pointed leg from a wall as if it was raising its hand. Rabio walked over and stuck his rear end toward the starjelo. It wrapped one leg, then two, then three legs tightly around Rabio's long, rubbery tail. Rabio pulled the starjelo from the wall with a pop. It wrapped itself snugly around the rest of the tail, looking like a giant wad of starlit chewing gum.

Rabio leaped through the doorway. "Now follow me. We must make haste!"

Matilda clapped her paws. "We're coming, Rabio! We're right behind you, yes we are. We are!"

Matilda scampered after her beloved rat, but Jenkins and Philecia waited for Ellis to lead them. He stepped into the tunnel and waved to Raquel as she closed the door behind them.

Wow. It was dark. Ellis stuck his hands out in front of him and stepped carefully, following the bright, lumpy orb on Rabio's tail. This passageway was much longer and curvier than the tunnel to the refugee habitat. There were so many turns. Which direction were they going? Were they headed deeper into the desert? Or traveling underneath the jungle?

The ground sloped down the further they went, and the air grew damp and cool. The passageway widened and finally opened up into a new room. It looked nothing like the habitat.

Starjelos were sprinkled all over the place. A bed was pushed up against the far wall, its mattress thin and worn. Clumps of straw poked out from tears in the fabric. On top of the mattress was a dark red blanket and a lumpy pillow, its fluffiness long gone. Above the bed there was a dark hole in the wall, another entrance to yet another tunnel.

Rabio turned in a circle, frowning. "Hmmm. He's not here. He must be exploring again." He walked to the middle of the room where a black cauldron hung above a circle of smooth, round stones. Rabio climbed up the side of the cauldron and stuck his tail inside. "Here you go, my squishy friend." When he brought his tail back out, the starjelo was gone.

"Oh my, oh my!" Matilda's paws flew to her cheeks. "Are you going to cook that poor starjelo? Are you?"

Rabio smiled and shook his head.

"No, I'm not going to cook it, little mouse. The starjelo will be de-liquified."

"De-liquified? What do you mean, Rabio? What do you mean?"

"Tis the discovery Fandrella would surely hate. The starjelos collect water. You see, there are underground streams running all throughout this place, and the star-jelos stick to the walls and use their filaments to constantly collect it. Their cells are so dense and pliable; they are able to store incredible amounts of water in relation to their size."

"Oooooh!" Matilda breathed.

Rabio grinned. "It was a remarkable discovery, considering everything that happened in your village." Rabio looked at Jenkins. "Your father wanted to dig a system of underground channels around your village, then bring a colony of starjelos to live there and extract the groundwater. Your village would have its own source of fresh, clean water. In fact, he'd drawn up the plans and recruited some Petikins to help him make it a reality when he disappeared."

Jenkins' eyes became misty. "I remember. I remember Dad working at his desk. He was always real excited. He said he was working on something that could make our village the best one in Kibblestan. But he wouldn't tell me what it was because it had to stay secret."

Ellis scratched his head. "I don't get it. You said that—what's her name? Fandrella? That thing that flies around would want to destroy the starjelos? Because they provide water? Why?"

Rabio sighed. "Well, it's just, Fandrella has a strange way of seeing things. Trust me, she wouldn't have liked Thornton Jabbermeyer's idea. Especially in your village."

Rabio paused. "In fact, I think she would have done anything in her power to stop it."

Jenkins looked up. "What do you mean?"

Rabio dropped his gaze. "I hate to say it aloud. I really do. It's just ..." Rabio looked up, his eyes soft. "I think Fandrella might have had something to do with your dad's disappearance. Either her, or her supporters."

Jenkins jaw dropped. "Fandrella! But she's our ruler! She takes care of us. She's saving Petikins from the slewedge. Why—why would she do something to my dad? He never did anything wrong."

Rabio walked over to the bed, reached up and patted the tattered, worn mattress.

"Come sit down, and I shall tell you the story."

CHAPTER EIGHT

Ellis sat on the bed, Philecia on his lap and Jenkins by his side. Matilda eagerly perched next to Rabio, who stood before them and began his story.

"Before the Snotlins arrived and flooded Kibblestan with their deadly slewedge, the Petikins in your village lived in peace. They had an abundance of food sources—nut vineyards, oingo fruit trees, beety leaves, and the like."

Ellis wasn't sure what all these things were, but he got the picture.

"However, the closest water source was that stream we went down, that's now contaminated with slewedge."

Jenkins nodded. "I remember. It was far away."

"Yes it was, young Jenkins. And not everyone wanted to make the walk to the stream each day. The walk was long, and carrying heavy buckets of water back and forth was quite strenuous. A few Petikins weren't even strong enough to make the journey, and they had to depend upon the kindness of others to bring them the water they needed."

Rabio paused.

"Enter William Wantonburger." A sly smile played on his lips as he said the name. "William was new to the village. He did not have his own garden or fruit tree or nut vineyard, however he did possess two things—a keen intelligence and a willingness to work hard. He told the Petikins that he would haul water to whoever wanted it, in exchange for first pick from whatever food they gathered that day. This would allow him to have the most juiciest, mouthwatering food to trade for whatever he wanted on Village Trading Days. He called himself WCE—Water Carrier Extraordinaire—and the Petikins jumped at the opportunity to not have to make the grueling walk each day.

"William's service became very popular—so popular that in time there were more Petikins wanting water from him than he could provide. He tried walking faster. He tried carrying bigger buckets. He'd get up before dawn and journey to the stream, back and forth, back and forth. Some nights he wouldn't quit until the three moons of Kibblestan shone in the sky. And though his pay was in oingo fruit and vine nuts and beety leaves, there were days when he collapsed on his bed without eating any of them, for he was too exhausted."

"Poor William." Matilda shook her head.

"Yes, little mouse. William needed help. So he decided to raise his price. Whoever wanted the services of Water Carrier Extraordinaire would have to pay him two pieces of food. If the Petikins were willing to pay it, then he could afford to hire a WCA—Water Carrier Apprentice—to help with his workload."

"So what happened?" Philecia asked.

"A few Petikins grumbled and decided the price wasn't worth it, but most of the Petikins were willing to pay the higher price. And soon William Wantonburger not only had the largest, most admirable collection of food to swap at the Village Trading Days, but he also hired his Water Carrier Apprentice, an ambitious Petikin who decided the walk to the stream wasn't so bad if he could get paid from the juicy collection of food William had."

"Oh goody!" Matilda clapped her paws.

"Yes, it was good," Rabio said. "And now that getting water to the village was no longer a problem, the Petikins were able to devote more time to planting, and the gardens and fruit trees and vineyards flourished. Even the Petikins who were never strong enough to carry water before could now grow their own gardens and pay for William's service. They found a certain happiness and dignity in being able to pay their own way, and many became some of the most generous Petikins of all.

"Soon the village became known in surrounding parts for its richness, and the local animals made it a point to stop by and get a free meal. That's what brought Raquel and I there. And the Petikins were glad to share—especially with those from other parts of Kibblestan where things were not so plentiful."

"Wait a minute," Jenkins interrupted. "You can't be talking about my village. My village never had enough food. And no one shared."

Rabio's eyes clouded. "No, Jenkins. It was your village all right. But you were too young to remember."

"Well then, what changed it?" Jenkins asked.

"What changed it is what happened next," Rabio continued. "Fandrella paid a visit."

"Wasn't she impressed?" Ellis asked.

"No. She hated what she saw. She got angry." Rabio's eyes became distant, haunting. "Really, really angry."

"Angry? Why? Why?" Matilda hopped to her feet, paws on her hips.

Rabio's jaw tightened. "She said it wasn't fair."

"What wasn't fair?" Ellis asked.

"William Wantonburger. It wasn't fair that William Wantonburger always had the best supply of food for Village Trading Days."

"Not fair?" Matilda jumped up and down. "But no one else wanted to gather the water, no they didn't. No they didn't!"

"Yeah," Ellis said. "And everyone was happy. I mean, William might have had the best food but he'd worked for it. It's not like he'd stolen it or something."

Rabio sighed. "In her eyes, it wasn't fair."

A slow fire started to burn as Ellis thought of working really hard to start a business, and then someone barging in and declaring that it wasn't fair. He'd had a front seat witnessing the hard work it took to run an ice cream shop. Late nights, working weekends, missed campouts. Dad was no different than William Wantonburger, but no one in America told him it wasn't fair that he owned his ice cream store.

"But what William did *was* fair," Ellis protested.

"Not to Fandrella," said Rabio. "And her idea of fairness was the only thing she cared about. She didn't care that the village was flourishing beyond belief, and even those who had very little before were now being fed. She said that as long as she ruled Kibblestan, everything was going to be fair, fair, fair. No one should have more than anyone else, and William Wantonburger was selfish for charging such a high price for his water service. As ruler of Kibblestan, she declared he must stop being Water Carrier Extraordinaire."

"But how would the village get its water, huh? Huh?" Matilda squeaked.

Rabio's mouth turned down. "The Petikins asked that very same question, little mouse. Fandrella replied that she would provide them the water herself, for free."

"Wow," Philecia said.

Rabio offered a wry smile. "Yes, and that is all that it took for the Petikins to turn on William. Poor William became the most unpopular fellow. Fandrella's incessant talk of fairness had birthed a bitter resentment in many Petikin hearts. Now they were angry at William for charging such a high price for something Fandrella was willing to give to them for free. How selfish he must be—he and his apprentice. William could see he was no longer wanted, and he promptly left the village. His apprentice went back to his home, but life for him and his family would never be the same. Meanwhile, the Petikins anxiously awaited their free water service."

"And? Did they get it?" Ellis asked.

Rabio nodded. "Yes. The first time Fandrella flew to the village to deliver the free water she was greeted by cheers of adulation. But as she smiled down at the crowd I noticed there was something different about her. Her entire forehead pulsated, like her brain was swelling up and stretching her skull. Her skin was different, too. It was no longer fair, but waxy and yellowed. You could see her veins throbbing, twitching like underground worms trying to break free from her skin."

Ellis shuddered, glancing at the round opening above the bed. Fandrella sounded creepy. Surely she wasn't anywhere near this underground, was she?

Rabio continued. "Fandrella delivered the water alright. Do you know how?"

"How?" Ellis asked.

"By flying to the stream and filling her mouth with water, then flying back and spitting it out."

"Gross!" Ellis made a face.

"The water the Petikins received was warm and slimy, and even though Fandrella, being a Kootie, can hold enough water in her mouth and throat to fill an entire bucket, there was never enough. When the Petikins complained and asked Fandrella to carry buckets instead of using her mouth, she said carrying heavy buckets would make her arms hurt. And when they pleaded for her to make more trips back and forth, like William Wantonburger had done, she said she didn't have the time. She reminded them that the whole reason she was providing the water in the first place was to create fairness in the village, because she cared so much about them." Rabio twirled his whiskers. "But you know what? If she truly cared about them, she would not have done what happened next."

"What happened?" Philecia asked.

"Well, soon the Petikins' fruit trees and nut vineyards and gardens started to wither. If something didn't change soon, the Petikins would be facing a food shortage. They came to the conclusion that they were going to have to carry the water themselves again. Many Petikins reluctantly made the daily walk to the stream and hauled the water back to the village, while a few settled for Fandrella's warm, slimy water. But do you know what Fandrella did when she found out?"

"What?" Ellis asked.

"She screamed that it wasn't fair."

"You're kidding!"

"No, Master Ellis, I tell you the truth. Fandrella threw a fit, saying that it wasn't fair for certain Petikins to get bucket loads of fresh water while others used the little bit of spit-filled water she provided."

"But that doesn't make sense. Why should she care if the Petikins got their own water?"

"Because that would mean that some Petikins would have more than others. If the Petikins were free to get their own water, the ones who were stronger or faster, or more determined, would end up with more. She wants everyone to have the same thing, even if it means that everyone has less. To her, that is what's fair."

Ellis' head spun. This Fandrella was whacked.

Rabio continued. "And the worst was yet to come. Fandrella said since the Petikins could not be trusted to be fair on their own, she would force them to be fair. She recruited dogs to guard the stream day and night, and attack any Petikin that came near. Then she assigned a small group of Petikins to be Resource Redistributors—the R & R. Their job was to keep tabs on everyone in the village, and inform her of who was in deepest need of water."

The R & R. Ellis remembered the gold R's embroidered on the burgundy armbands worn by some of the Petikins in the habitat. "Did they wear armbands? Was Blotu one of them?" he asked.

Rabio nodded. "Ah, yes. Blotu was their leader, and he relished his power. Now obtaining water to grow your gardens was no longer dependent upon your own hard work, but by who you knew in the R & R. If you were friends with an R & R, or you had something to bribe them with, they would tell Fandrella to bring her water your way. And to make matters worse, Fandrella decreed that since the dogs were too busy guarding the stream and didn't have time to hunt, and the R & R didn't have time to tend their own gardens, everyone in the village must give them a portion of their food to use at Village Trading Days. If anyone did not do so, they would be punished severely for being selfish.

"Eventually, the R & R's had more food than anyone else in the village. But nobody dared to call an R & R selfish, for they could keep you from ever seeing water again. The Petikins found themselves in a cruel sort of bondage, all in the name of fairness."

Ellis shook his head, disgusted.

Rabio continued. "That's when Raquel and I considered leaving the village. Not only was the food scarce, but the Petikins had changed. Before, they were happy to share. Now they clung to what little they had and waited for Fandrella and the Resource Redistributors to provide for everyone else. And if anyone ever mentioned trying to find water on their own, the R & R immediately accused them of being selfish just like the 'evil' William Wantonburger. And do you know who suffered the most under this new regime?"

"Who?" Ellis asked.

Rabio looked at Jenkins. "Thornton Jabbermeyer, the Water Carrier Apprentice."

Jenkins straightened up. "My dad? My dad was the Apprentice?"

Rabio nodded. "Yes, young Jenkins. Your father was William Wantonburger's Water Carrier Apprentice."

"So that's why! That's why no one liked us."

"I am afraid that is correct. Your father became the symbol of selfishness and greed, despite the fact that he was one of the most generous Petikins Raquel and I ever met. Raquel and I stuck beside him, even when many of his friends deserted him, for fear of being called selfish too."

Jenkins' eyes brimmed with tears. Rabio hopped onto the bed and looked deep into the little Petikin's eyes. "Your father was a very good Petikin, Jenkins. Never doubt it for a moment. He was not despised because he did evil. He was despised because Fandrella convinced the Petikins to change their definition of what is evil."

A scuffling sound came from the round hole above the bed. Everyone jumped off as a Petikin popped out and somersaulted onto the thin mattress. He had shaggy black hair and snappy brown eyes. His arms were muscular and his white skin bore scrapes and scars. He was short—even for a Petikin—but what he didn't have in height he made up for in thickness, his heavy shoulders set upon a barrel chest. His black hair flopped into his eyes and he lifted it from his face and stared in surprise.

"Whoa! What be goin' on?" His voice was rough, like he had a cold in his chest.

Rabio stepped forward. "It's okay. They can be trusted." Rabio turned and made a sweeping bow. "May I present to you, Mr. William Wantonburger."

CHAPTER NINE

The scruffy Petikin looked confused. "Refugees are they? But why ye be bringin' them here?"

Before Rabio could answer Matilda smiled and made a curtsy. "I'm Matilda, yes I am." She twirled about. "William Wantonburger, what a lovely name, yes it is. Kind of like cheeseburger. Or hamburger."

"Or mouseburger," Philecia grinned as Matilda turned to her in horror.

But William wasn't paying attention. He stared at Ellis the way someone might stare at a big hairy gorilla—something cool to see, but only at a safe distance. Ellis stepped forward. "My name's Ellis. I'm a human from America."

William's expression didn't change.

"America," Ellis continued. "It's–it's another land. It's not Kibblestan."

"Master Ellis travels from beyond the Grand Forest," Rabio explained. "He's from the Other World."

Ellis nodded. "Yeah. And this is my dog, Philecia."

Philecia wagged her tail and William's eyebrows shot up. "Dog? Ye sure?"

Philecia's tail stopped wagging.

95

Rabio walked over to Jenkins. "And do you know who this is?"

William shook his head.

"This is Jenkins Jabbermeyer. Thornton's son."

William's eyes widened. He hopped off the bed and grabbed Jenkins shoulders, looking him up and down. "Jenkins? Well, I be a boarusk's behind! By golly, ye were only a wee baby. Now be lookin' at ye, growed so big!"

Jenkins blushed. William's eyes danced as he grinned down at the little Petikin, revealing square gray teeth in bad need of a brushing. "Ye made it. Survived those Snotlin attacks." But then his smile faded as his eyes traveled to Rabio in silent question. Rabio looked down and shook his head. "It's only Jenkins. Dreya and Ravina are, uh, missing."

Any remaining joy slipped from William's face. His hands fell from Jenkins' shoulders and he bowed his head, clearing his throat. "Tis sorry me is, about your family."

"They're with Fandrella," Jenkins said. "Fandrella took them away but left me in the slewedge."

William looked up, the corner of his mouth twisting down. "Did she now?" William shook his head and sighed. "Course, she still be tryin' to be the big hero," he muttered under his breath. He turned to Rabio. "So, what be bringin' ye here?"

Rabio hesitated, averting his gaze. "We brought a starjelo. It's in the cauldron."

"Ah, did ye now?" William rubbed his jowls. He walked to the cauldron and looked inside. "Wow! And a puffed up one at that. Don't worry, slimy chap. We be deliquifyin' ye in a quickin'."

William grabbed a tool that sat to the side of the cauldron. It had a long wooden handle and attached on the end was a flat star-shaped piece of metal. William stuck it inside the cauldron.

"What are you doing?" Matilda scampered to the cauldron. "Can I see? Can I see? I want to see, yes I do. I do!"

William shrugged. "Why not?"

Everyone gathered around the cauldron as William carefully placed the star shaped metal over the starjelo, lining up the points in the metal with the starjelo's legs.

"Now ye be shuttin' your eyes, little guy," William told the shiny blob. A thin membrane full of mucous crept over each staring eyeball. William gently pressed down.

"Gots to do it just right," William said. "Slow and gentle, or ye hurt the starjelo." As the metal slowly squashed the starjelo, clear liquid squirted out from every side. In less than five seconds the cauldron was over halfway filled with water.

William smiled. "Tis good and pure to the last drop. Taste it. See for yourself."

Ellis stuck his face inside the cauldron and sniffed. It smelled fresh, like rain. Before he could cup his hand and take a drink, something plopped inside the cauldron. Matilda's head bobbed to the surface, her face one big smile.

"Oooo! So fresh, yes it is. And so tasty. So tasty."

Rabio looked at Jenkins. "Long after William left your village and your father stopped being his apprentice, Raquel and I ventured into the jungle one day to hunt for food. We were shocked to run into William. He told us of the fascinating discovery he had made beneath the desert."

William nodded, removing the metal star from the cauldron. "Yep," he said. "T'were by accident that I stepped on a starjelo one day when me be explorin' these underground parts. Unfortunate chap, he was. He be squished beneath my boots but that's when me realized all the water they be sucking up. They be regular water carriers."

"Yes," Rabio said. "When I went back to the village and told your dad about what William discovered, he got more excited than I'd ever seen him. He could not wait to use this discovery to give your village its own source of water, once and for all."

William's dark eyes flickered. "Yep. Me and Thornton, we be makin' our plans, all right."

Rabio continued. "Thornton was in charge of designing a system of underground tunnels to house a colony of starjelos, and William was to figure out a way to transport the starjelos to their new home. Raquel and I were the messengers back and forth."

"Oh, but we be workin' in secret. Not everybody be likin' it, if they be knowin' what we was up to," William said.

Rabio nodded. "The Resource Redistributers were enjoying their power and the bribes that were making them rich. It was only after the plans were complete, and Thornton was ready to dig, that he dared to confide in a few Petikins he thought he could trust." Rabio paused, his eyes clouded. "But someone sold him out, I guess. He left to meet William one night—"

"And never showed." William shook his head.

"He played with me that day." Jenkins' watery eyes were distant. "It was the first time in I don't know how long. He was always working on his plans, but that day he decided to take a break and play with me."

Ellis put an arm around Jenkins' shoulder. So his dad had been a hard worker too. And someone too busy to play with his kid.

"Twas a real shame too," William said. "We be so close to startin' the diggin'. So close."

"After Thornton's disappearance the plan fell apart," Rabio said. "Thorton's secret allies were too afraid that they, too, might mysteriously disappear."

William looked at Jenkins. "Your daddy didn't leave on his own, no sir. Me knows, he loved ye way too much. Ye and your mama and your sister, he be lovin' you lots. He was taken, that he was. He was taken."

Rabio nodded in agreement and Jenkins hung his head. Ellis tightened his grip on Jenkins' shoulder, a lump rising in his throat. He couldn't imagine what it'd be like to have your dad disappear without a word. As much as Dad worked, he still came home at night. He did spend time with Ellis, even if it was only once in awhile. But Jenkins didn't have anyone.

William turned back to Rabio. "So, me friend, ye be takin' me back that memory lane. Thank ye for droppin' by to show me the lad."

Rabio looked at the ground, shuffling his feet. "There's something else," he said. He locked eyes with William. "I fear the refugees are getting restless."

William's brows drew together and he folded his arms across his chest. "Are ye be meanin' what I think ye be meanin'?"

Rabio opened his mouth to speak but the shrill voice of Matilda floated up out of the cauldron. "They're going crazy, yes they are. The fireflies! The fireflies! The Blues want to squash the Yellows, and the Yellows want to squish the Blues. That habitat will be one big bug splatter, yes it will, yes it will."

Ellis walked to the cauldron and looked inside. Matilda was perched atop the deliquified starjelo, which now resembled a star-shaped piece of cellophane wrap floating on water. She smiled at Ellis. "Lift me out, please?"

Ellis lifted Matilda out of the cauldron.

Rabio wrung his paws. "The mouse is right, William. The refugees are becoming violent. They are not sharing the resources we bring them."

"And I don't trust those dogs," Ellis added. "They seem, I don't know, almost evil."

Philecia nodded. "I didn't feel safe. They looked at me like I'm a hot dog or something. I could see it in their eyes, picturing me covered in ketchup and mustard. It was terrifying."

"It's a ticking time bomb down there," Rabio said. "The stresses of living in such close quarters with limited resources is getting to be too much for them to bear. Raquel said when she brought food, some of them nearly killed each other trying to get to it. William, you know I would not ask you if it weren't necessary, but—"

William held up a calloused hand. "Me got it. Ye be needin' more space, and ye be wantin' mine."

Rabio bowed his head. "It is what we have always feared. I am afraid the time has come."

William's jaw moved as if he were chomping invisible gum. His eyes searched the room. "So tis, so tis. It be time to move on. I will go. Let the refugees come. If it bide them time before they kill each other, it be worth it."

Rabio removed his hat from his head. "I am so sorry, William. We can see if the Petikins will accept you. With all that they've been through, maybe they've changed. Perhaps the days of blaming you for their water woes are long behind them."

But William shook his head. "Me gots no desire to live near that lot, no me don't. They be wantin' me blood, some of them, and for no good reason at all. There be hate in their hearts, pure hate. Me can find another place to make me home. Tis just ..." William paused and rubbed the back of his neck, glancing at the hole in the wall above the bed. "Tis a many tunnel to explore. And lately me been feelin' spooky. Somethin' in those tunnels. Somethin' not right."

"What do you mean?" Rabio asked.

"Can't be puttin' me finger on it, no sir. Me just feel like—like me bein' watched." William shrugged. "Probably just me imagination. Livin' by meself all this time, me lonely mind may be trickin'."

"Can we come with you?" Jenkins asked.

Ellis turned, surprised. "You want to go with William?"

Jenkins nodded. "I want to be with William. He knows my family. He likes them. And you'll come with me, Ellis, won't you?"

Before Ellis could answer William interjected. "Ye know, it might not be a bad idea. Me could be usin' the company." His eyes lingered on Ellis. "And protection." William walked over to the bed and reached underneath, drawing out a dark brown backpack made of leather. "Me be gatherin' me things then we be off."

Ellis turned to Rabio. "Are you and Raquel going to be okay? If – if you need me to help…"

"My gracious thanks, Master Ellis, but that will not be necessary. You may be more useful accompanying William into further exploration of the underground. Perhaps you will find more hospitable space for the refugees to make their home."

Perhaps. Or perhaps they would run into whatever was making William feel spooked. But right now Ellis didn't care. For the only perhaps he could think about was perhaps—perhaps one of those tunnels would lead him back home.

CHAPTER TEN

William hoisted his pack and nodded at Ellis. "Ye and your buddies, be grabbin' a starjelo. T'will give us light and water." He peeled a starjelo from the wall and placed it on his shoulder, then shook Rabio's paw. "We be sendin' word on what we discover."

William climbed into the dark hole above the bed.

"I guess we need to follow him." Ellis told Rabio. He reached down and tenderly scratched the rodent on the scruff of the neck. "Thanks for everything. You're a good rat. If I find a place where you and the others can live, I'll send word. I promise."

"I have the utmost faith in all of you." Rabio said. He strode across the room and stopped in front of the exit leading back toward the habitat. He removed his hat and waved it in the air. "From the bottom of my heart, I wish you the grandest luck." He smiled with one last wave then crawled through the exit.

Ellis looked at Philecia. "Guess we better get moving." He stripped a starjelo from the wall. "Come here, girl. Let me stick this on your tail."

Philecia's ears flattened behind her head and she crouched toward the ground. "Will it hurt?" she said.

"Of course not. Rabio did it. Now give me your tail." Philecia raised her tail then squeezed her eyes shut as Ellis lowered the starjelo toward her.

"Tell me when it's over, Ellis. Pleeeease. Tell me when it's—oooo! Tickles!"

When Ellis was satisfied that the starjelo he'd wrapped around his dachshund's tail would stay put, he lifted Philecia into the round hole. She peeked out at him.

"You sure you're coming?"

"You're my dog. You know I'll never leave you. I'll be right there."

Ellis grabbed another starjelo and placed it on his forehead. Its belly felt like a million fine strands of velvet caressing his skin. Philecia was right. It did kind of tickle.

Jenkins grabbed a starjelo and climbed into the hole. Ellis started to climb in after him but paused. Where was Matilda?

"Matilda?" he called. "You coming?"

A strained squeak came from under the bed. "I suppose." It was followed by the unmistaken sound of sniffling. Ellis climbed down and looked under the bed. Matilda sat on her haunches, paws swiping tears from her eyes.

"What's wrong?" Ellis asked.

"Nothing, it's nothing. I'm just–just really going to miss Rabio. He and I, you know, have such a history. I'm afraid he might be heartbroken forever."

The only thing that came to Ellis' mind was Raquel, and the obvious way she and Rabio lit up whenever they saw each other.

"I'm sure he'll be okay," Ellis said. "He has Raq—" The scowl on Matilda's face stopped Ellis mid-sentence.

"Raquel's just a rat friend, yes she is. I'm his soulmate. I am! I am! You think we'll get married someday? Do you? Do you?"

Matilda was asking his opinion? Really? He was an eleven-year-old boy. What did he know about romance? Especially romance between rodents?

"Um, I don't know. Uh—sure."

Matilda scampered out from under the bed. "You are so right, yes you are. Yes you are." She scurried up into the hole in the wall, pausing to call out to the room. "Don't you worry, Rabio, wherever you are! I'll be back, yes I will. I'll come back and find you, and we'll live happily ever after. We will! We will!" She grinned before disappearing into the tunnel.

Ellis took one last look around the empty room, then climbed in after her.

The tunnel was narrow and tube-like at the beginning, but after it curved to the left the floor sloped downward and the walls widened. They followed William's lead, the starjelo on Ellis' forehead acting as a headlamp, the one on Philecia's tail a swinging lantern. Eventually the passageway ended and they entered a huge room with a dome ceiling.

In the middle of the room the floor dropped off into what looked like a giant crater. Ellis walked to the edge and looked down. Many feet below black water rippled in the crater's belly.

"Right this way," William called. They followed him along the edge of the crater, toward the far wall that was dotted with openings. "I be explorin' two of these holes so far. Both of them be havin' other holes inside leadin' to other tunnels. It be a regular maze in there."

Ellis counted. One, two, three, four, five. Five entrances to who knows how many tunnels. What were the chances of one of them leading back home?

William continued. "The middle hole there, me started to explore ... then me stopped. Didn't like it. Gave me a bad feelin'. Spooky."

"So which one should we try?" Ellis asked.

"Me thinks this one." William climbed into the opening to the right of the middle tunnel. "It be good as any. C'mon." William disappeared into the blackness.

"We're coming, yes we are!" Matilda scurried after him into the hole, but Jenkins stayed planted by Ellis' side.

"I guess we're next," Ellis said. "Come on Philecia." Ellis looked beside him. Where was Philecia? He turned around.

Several feet away Philecia cowered, staring at something off to the side. Ellis followed her gaze and his heart leaped into his throat.

They were not alone.

Inside the last tunnel, way over on the end, two eyes stared out from the darkness. Brilliant green eyes, the color of emeralds.

Jenkins gasped and gripped Ellis's sleeve. Ellis felt like a stampede of wildebeests was trampling through his chest. What was it? And what did it want?

Ellis swallowed, though his mouth felt sticky. *Don't panic.* He locked eyes with the green-eyed thing as he slowly picked up his trembling dog and backed away. If the thing was looking for a dachshund-sized meal, it wasn't going to get one without a fight.

Sweat broke out on Ellis' brow and the starjelo on his forehead slid down, blocking his view. He pulled it from his face and got an idea. He flung the starjelo toward the last tunnel. It landed in a glowing heap, its light illuminating the dark opening, revealing the owner of the green eyes.

His skin tingled.

It was the biggest dog he'd ever seen—like a pony that gives rides at a fair. Its long, white fur shimmered and its pointed ears stood erect as it sniffed the air with its long snout. It leaped out of the tunnel, landing on chunky paws attached to gangly legs that were out of proportion to the rest of its body. It lowered its head, watching them as its tail twitched back and forth.

Ellis clutched Philecia tightly and backed away, tugging on Jenkins' shirt so that he would do the same. The dog watched them like a tiger about to go in for the kill. But as Ellis took one backward step after another, the dog's burning gaze did not focus on him. Nor Philecia.

The dog's eyes trained on Jenkins.

What did it want with Jenkins? Jenkins had been through enough. He didn't need some weird over-sized dog stalking him.

Ellis stepped protectively in front of Jenkins and drew a quivering breath. "Go on!" he called. "Go away. Scram!"

The dog didn't move. It studied Jenkins as if in a trance.

"Why is it staring at me?" Jenkins' voice was a squeak. "Make it go away."

"I'm trying." Ellis said.

"Oooooh! What a pretty dog!" Ellis looked around. Matilda beamed down at them from the tunnel. "William, there's a dog out here, yes there is, yes there is. Come and see!"

A soft chime rang out. It sounded like the jingle of a tiny bell, the kind that's found on a kitten's collar or an elf's shoe.

Ellis looked every which way. "Did you hear that?"

Philecia's floppy ears perked up. "I did."

Ellis looked back to the white dog. It crept forward then jumped from side to side, landing awkwardly on clumsy legs as its beautiful green eyes danced. It opened its mouth.

Ching. The tiny bell sound rang again. The dog stood up on its hind legs, tipped its head back and formed an *O* with its mouth.

Chiiiiiiiiiiiing. The delicate chime floated through the air. The dog took a breath, tipped its head back and howled again.

Chiiiiiiiing.

The dog lurched forward and that's when Ellis realized—the legs and feet so out of proportion, the clumsy moves—even though this dog was huge, it was still just a puppy. It pounced toward Jenkins, tail wagging. Jenkins hopped back a step, but started to smile.

Ellis stepped aside and the dog bowed down in front of Jenkins, its green eyes hopeful. Its tail rose in the air, wagging even faster.

"Ching. Ching." Its bark was like a song.

"He wants to play," Philecia said. "That's a play bow he's doing. That's how we dogs say we want to play."

Sure enough, Ellis knew this well. How many times had Philecia challenged him to a game of fetch by striking this same pose after dropping a tennis ball at his feet?

Jenkins held out a hand for the dog to sniff. But it had no interest in sniffing it. It had no interest in sniffing any of them. It paced toward the last tunnel, then circled around and returned to Jenkins.

"This is weird," Philecia said, her voice trembling. She cleared her throat. "L-let me down, Ellis. I-I need to try something."

"You sure, girl?"

Philecia swallowed. "Yes, yes. Put me down."

Ellis did as Philecia told him.

Philecia inched toward the white dog. "Hey, you," she said. The dog glanced at her and Philecia cringed. But when it didn't try to bite her head off she straightened back up.

Philecia crept forward, then moved her rear toward the dog's face and lifted her tail. "Hello," she said.

She wanted him to sniff. Gross! But then again, that was what dogs do.

Except this one.

The white dog looked at Philecia like she was a major weirdo. Then it pounced in front of Jenkins, paced to the tunnel, and circled back again.

Philecia shook her head. "I don't know, Ellis. That dog isn't like any I've met before. He didn't even want to sniff under my tail. And no dog ever gives up that chance. I mean, never."

"I think he wants me to follow him." Jenkins' eyes shone.

The white dog stood on its hind legs and jumped. "Cha-chiiiiiiiing!" came its ringing response. It bounded into the last tunnel, then stuck its head back out.

"Come on, Ellis." Jenkins' face was bright. He ran to the tunnel and scrambled inside.

Ellis followed Jenkins. But was this last tunnel the right one to explore? Should they trust the white dog? Or was it some kind of a trap? He picked up the starjelo he had thrown and put it back on his head. "What do you think?" he called to Matilda and William.

William poked his head out above Matilda's. "We be following, to be sure. To be sure, young lad. Me never seen such a creature in these underground parts. Never ever. He be quite fascinating, he is."

William and Matilda ran over and climbed into the last tunnel. Ellis lifted up Philecia, then crawled in himself. They made their way through the passageway, the white dog loping ahead and Jenkins doing his best to keep up with it.

Suddenly Philecia stopped and snorted, the fur across her shoulders one big bristle.

"Wait," she said.

Ellis stopped walking. "What's wrong?"

Philecia's nose twitched.

"Something ... I smell something ... different."

Different? Like something bad? "Hey Jenkins!" Ellis called. "Wait up!"

Jenkins paused and the white dog paced back and forth while Philecia put her nose to the walls, to the floor and to the air again. She looked confused.

"Well?" Ellis said anxiously. "What is it?"

"I'm not sure. It's a mixture of smells. Some are familiar, but some ..."

The white dog reared up then landed in a play bow. It wagged its tail and turned in a circle.

"Ching. Ching. Ching." It barked.

"Look how excited he is," Jenkins gushed. "He's got something important to show us. I just know it."

The dog nodded and smiled the only way a dog can smile—mouth pulled wide, tongue flopping out. It turned and galloped ahead. The tunnel curved to the right and the dog's green eyes lit up, like two flashlights shining emerald beams of light into a room at the end of the corridor. They followed the dog into the room, but stopped short when they saw what awaited them inside.

"Well I'll be!" William gasped.

Ellis squinted, not sure if he was seeing correctly.

Then Jenkins started to cry.

CHAPTER ELEVEN

The white dog's green spotlights had settled on a small, withered figure leaning against the far wall. He was curled up in a ball, his long, scruffy beard resting on two knobby knees that poked out through holes in his tattered pants. The light bounced off his bald head and he squinted, shielding his extremely pale face with splayed hands, each containing three very long fingers and a thumb. He was a Petikin.

"Ruthertold! That's so bright. Your light's so bright!" The Petikin's voice sounded scratchy and unaccustomed to being used. The green light disappeared and the white dog trotted up to the Petikin and nuzzled him with his nose. The Petikin remained hunched over, and blinked repeatedly as his eyes recovered and absorbed the sight before him.

"Wha—who?" he stammered.

A few starjelos dotting the walls gave off a dim light but it was not enough to satisfy Jenkins. He grabbed the starjelo from Philecia's tail and ran to the Petikin. He held it in front of his tear-stained face, choking back sob after sob. Yet his mouth drew up in a smile.

"Dad! Dad, it's me. It's Jenkins!"

The grizzled Petikin gaped in shock. His shaking hand reached out and caressed Jenkins' cheek. The moment his bony fingers touched Jenkins' skin, a smile appeared under the bush of wiry hair. His gray eyes misted.

"Jenkins," he croaked. "Jenkins! My son, my boy! You-you're alive. You're here. You're here!"

Thornton Jabbermeyer reached out and pulled his son into a desperate embrace. His head sank into Jenkins' blonde curls and his shoulders heaved as he silently wept.

"Oh Jenkins! Jenkins! I thought I'd never see you again. Never!"

Father and son clung to each other as if their lives depended upon it. Jenkins buried his head into his Dad's shoulder and started bawling.

"Dad! Oh Dad! I – I thought you were gone for good. I missed you so much!"

Ellis smiled through the tears stinging his eyes as he imagined reuniting with his own dad. How good it would feel to collapse into the strong, protective arms of his father.

At long last Thornton's arms went slack. He pulled away and surveyed Jenkins from head to toe. "Your mom. Dreya. Did you bring them with you?"

Jenkins bowed his head as fresh tears flowed.

"She took them, Dad. She took them away from me and flew off somewhere."

Thornton's eyes widened. "Who? Who took them?"

"Fandrella. Dad, we were drowning in slewedge. Everyone was. Fandrella swooped down and picked them up and flew off. I thought she'd be back to get me, but she never came back. She never did."

Thornton's knuckles turned a searing white as he gripped Jenkins' shoulders, panic assaulting his weary face. His whole body trembled, and he clenched his broken teeth.

"Fandrella!" He choked on the name. "Fandrella has them? Your mom and sister are with *Fandrella?*"

Jenkins' tears froze as he looked at his dad with confusion.

"Yeah. But I'm sure they're somewhere safe and when the Snotlins go away and the slewedge goes back down, we'll find them."

Thornton slumped over like someone had driven a sword through his chest. He cupped his face in his hands and jerked his head from side to side.

"No! No! No!" he wailed. When he raised his head his bloodshot eyes were wild. "You don't understand. They're not okay. Nothing is okay. Fandrella's gone mad. She's not who she pretends to be. She's always loved power but now ... something has her in its grip and she's—she's different." Thornton's fearful eyes darted around the room like those of a caged animal on the brink of losing its sanity. He shouted at the top of his raspy voice. "She's evil! Pure evil! She's destroying Kibblestan!"

Thornton buried his face back in his hands and heaved sob after sob. Jenkins stumbled backward, lips quivering as he looked helplessly around.

William quickly stepped forward. "There, there, now, Thornton. You're scarin' yer boy." William leaned down and tried to peer into Thornton's face. "Ye calm down now, okay? Tis me! Yer friend, William. Things gonna be okay."

Thornton raised his head, blinking. "William?"

William smiled. "Tis me, old chap. Tis me. Me buddy, ye be alive. What ye be doin' here? Why ye disappear on us like ye did?"

Thornton stretched out his leg and that's when they realized. Thornton Jabbermeyer was a prisoner.

A metal ring surrounded his ankle. Attached to the ring was a charcoal gray rope that was several feet long and disappeared into a tiny hole in the stone wall. The skin on Thornton's ankle had long ago started to rot away. The metal had dug a purple trench in his skin that looked like raw steak that someone had sneezed on. Ellis was no medic, but even he could tell Thornton's wound was serious.

"We need to get that off of you," Ellis said, stepping from the shadows.

Thornton's eyes bugged. "Wha-what is that? A Kootie? Fandrella sent another Kootie?"

"His name is Ellis, Dad," Jenkins said swiftly. "He saved my life. If it weren't for him I'd have drowned in the slewedge."

Ellis felt his cheeks flush. Jenkins made him sound like some kind of hero or something, but he sure didn't feel like one.

"Me wondered the same thing, me did," William said. "No, Ellis is not a Kootie. He be from beyond the Grand Forest, from the Other World. What it be called?"

"America. I'm a human from America. And this is my dog, Philecia." Philecia nodded her head before Matilda hopped in front of her and curtsied.

"And I am Matilda, yes I am. Pleased to meet you. So very, very pleased."

Thornton's eyes drank in the sight of so many new visitors.

"So Thornton, me buddy," William said. "Who did this to ye?"

Thornton shuddered. He looked over his shoulder at a round opening in the wall behind him—an entrance to yet another tunnel. His eyes searched the room.

"Ruthertold?" Thornton rasped. The white dog bounded over to the opening and stuck his snout inside and sniffed. Then he stepped back and shined his green light inside. He bounced over to Thornton, sat down and shook his head.

"*Ching. Ching.*" Ruthertold barked. He shook his head again.

"Very well then," Thornton said. "Coast is clear." He looked down at Jenkins. "My leaving was none of my own doing. Surely, you've known that. I was betrayed, by whom I am not sure. But our plans to build a starjelo colony to provide water to our village did not remain secret. Somebody told Fandrella, and the knowledge sent her into a rage. She sent a band of chatzkies to attack me. There was nothing I could do."

William stroked his chin. "Chatzkies. What be chatzkies?"

Thornton's breath quickened. "You've not seen the chatzkies? They've not attacked anyone else?"

William shook his head. "Not that me be hearin', and me hears a lots from Rabio."

"They're those engineered dogs," Thornton said. "They're tiny brutes with pointed ears and needle teeth. They may seem harmless at first, but they're not. *She* engineered them. *She* made them."

"Who?" William said.

"Fandrella! I told you, something's wrong with her. She's gained powers no Kootie has ever had. She's living in Latinab, in the belly of the volcano and she somehow makes things. Things that are evil."

William snorted and shook his head. "Oh me poor buddy, me poor friend. Yer mind's a gone a bit soft, this talk of livin' in a volcano and makin' evil dogs. Me don't likes Fandrella, but she not be doin' that stuff. Tis impossible."

Thornton crawled toward the center of the room, wincing as the metal ring rubbed against his rotting flesh. "William, I tell you it's true," he gasped. "All of it. Ruthertold, show them. Show them!"

The great white puppy pounced in a play bow and wagged his tail. His green eyes sparkled with mischief as his mouth pulled back in a smile and he started trotting in circles around the group of friends. His trot turned into a run and finally a sprint as he circled the room, faster and faster.

Suddenly gold and silver sparks shot out of Ruthertold's paws. At first Ellis thought it was caused by the friction of his paws hitting the stony ground, but this was not the case. Ruthertold's paws had left the ground. He was flying, gliding in circles while the sparks filled the room like fireworks falling through the sky. Ellis' jaw dropped. It was beautiful.

The sparks banded together and took on a life of their own. They swirled like a tornado, climbing higher to the ceiling before spreading out and forming the shape of an eyeball that stretched the circumference of the stony room. Ellis no longer stared at dark, granite walls. He stood inside a glittery sphere with gold and silver sparkling on every side. Straight ahead the eyeball's pupil stared out, its black surface rippling like a dark river at night.

"Just wait," Thornton said. "Watch the pupil. You will see."

Ruthertold's eyes cast their emerald beam at the jiggling blackness and the pupil's surface became still. Now it resembled a big circular movie screen with an image of a black hole filled with yellow-green flames. Ellis felt a mysterious pressure tug at his stomach, like an invisible hand snatching his insides and pulling him forward.

Ellis' feet remained planted on the ground as his spirit seemed to leave his body and he was sucked into the pupil. Now he wasn't staring at an image, he was inside the image, hovering above the flaming hole as a clap of thunder exploded and greenish-yellow lava came spewing toward him.

I'm gonna get hit! I'm gonna get hit! Ellis opened his mouth to scream but no sound came out. He raised his hands to protect his face, but his hands were not there. Nothing was there. He was invisible, like a dream, yet everything felt so real. The lava shot up out of the hole and straight through Ellis. Ellis didn't feel a thing.

The invisible hand clamped around his torso, pulling him down inside the pit. Ellis looked above as shooting lava filled the angry, black sky with malicious light of its own. What was this? Where was he? Had he died and didn't even know it? But this couldn't be heaven.

Ellis sank deeper and deeper into the chasm as walls of black lava rock rose up around him. Greenish-yellow flames flicked their fiery tongues in greeting. A girl's giggle floated up from beneath him and Ellis felt like his heart had been replaced by a popsicle. The giggle was sinister. Evil. It was the laughter of someone very angry.

Or insane.

CHAPTER TWELVE

Ellis looked in every direction. Black walls. Green flames. Cruel laughter. He hadn't made it to heaven. This was the place that was opposite of heaven. With a name that could get you in big trouble if you say it at school.

Ellis panicked. He clawed at the air above and kicked his invisible legs. He writhed against the mysterious pressure gripping his insides, willing it to please, please, let him go. Set him free from this dark, horrible place.

His feet touched the ground. He turned and nearly bumped into a very odd-looking girl. She stood a few inches taller than him and had stringy, long blonde hair that looked like it had been washed in a swamp. Her face might have been pretty, if her skin weren't so tight. It was stretched to its limit over high cheekbones and a pointed chin, and a skull that was one size too big. The color of her skin was strange, too—grayish-green, like someone who's ridden one too many roller coasters after downing a plate of greasy nachos.

She wore a long, light-blue dress with a high, white collar and puffy sleeves that reached her wrists. She shot her arms into the air, splaying hands that looked human—four fingers and a thumb—tipped with thick fingernails that were ragged and broken.

The moment she raised her hands a loud thunderclap sounded from above. A new spray of lava exited the pit and burst into the air. She tipped her head back and laughed, displaying tiny, white teeth that were perfectly square.

The girl didn't notice him. In fact, her eyes burned straight through him.

"That will keep them busy!" she cackled. Her voice vibrated, as if the skin inside her throat was loose and flappy. What was she? A dark angel? She kind of looked human and yet ... She lifted a few inches off the ground and that's when Ellis noticed what was sticking out from beneath the folds of her gown, where her feet should be.

Two black talons.

This was a Kootie. It must be the Kootie called Fandrella. And he wasn't dead. He'd been pulled inside the volcano of Latinab. He should feel hot. No, he should be burning up—melting like a marshmallow at a Vulture Voyager campout. But he felt no heat, even as the greenish-yellow flames continued their dance.

"What's going on, boss, huh? Huh? Fandrella, what's going on?"

Ellis turned toward the smooth, urgent voice. A tiny dog the size of a Chihuahua stood in the opening of one of three large holes in the wall. Its head was way too big for its body. It had short white fur with blue-gray splotches and small, pointed ears. Its eyes looked like two fuchsia ping pong balls that bulged out of its skull, and they matched a hot pink bow neatly tied around its head. Its snout was small and dainty, but as it smiled at Fandrella, Ellis couldn't help but notice its teeth. They were skinny and sharp and silver, like two rows of drool-covered needles.

The strange dog jumped out of the hole in the wall and trotted over to Fandrella on paws that were no bigger than marbles.

"Charro, darling." Fandrella scooped it up in her arms. "I'm sending those Snotlins over to one more village. Then Kibblestan's destruction should be complete."

Charro wagged her stump of a tail and grinned as she shinnied up Fandrella's arm to her shoulder.

"Yes! Yes!" she said. "Then I'll be in charge, won't I?"

Fandrella blinked slowly, a sly smile spreading across her face. "Of the other chatzkies, of course."

Charro balanced on Fandrella's shoulder. "But I'm already in charge of them. I want more."

"You'll be in charge soon enough. The few creatures who I save from the slewedge will feel so indebted to me they'll have to obey and do what I say. And that will include listening to you, my pet. Kibblestan is starting anew. It will now be called Fandrellaville, and this time I will force it to be fair. And there'll be no pesky Bob to interject his stupid opinions, either."

Charro leapt to the ground and spun in a circle, chasing the nub that was her tail.

"No Bob, no Bob," she sang. Then she stopped. "Where is Bob, anyway?"

Fandrella's pale green eyes flashed burgundy.

"I don't know and I don't care. Stupid drooling, homely unicorn. He was such an embarrassment. He looks like a donkey with an exploding zit on his forehead. I never would have brought him here if Kootie law didn't require it." Fandrella paced back and forth, her voice an octave higher as she mimicked someone. "Every Kootie leader must have a unicorn adviser to ensure they have perspective. Bleh, bleh, bleh."

Fandrella knelt in front of Charro and scratched the dog under its neck. "No one took him seriously, anyway. But they'll take you seriously, my pet. Once they see those special teeth I made you. You, my dear, are my proudest creation yet."

Charro raised up on her hind legs and pranced. "Better than Snotlins!" she sang. Then doubled over, laughing. "And better than that goofy white pup you made. Oh, what a joke that thing is. Ruthertold can't even bark right. Sounds like a doorbell or something."

Fandrella grimaced, her voice ice. "Do not mock my first attempt. I despise being mocked. Besides, it wasn't my fault. Bob drooled all over the concoction before it was sucked into the flames to be made real. That has to be the cause of his stupidity. Even the Snotlins can read the messages I send up into the sky. Ruthertold can't understand a thing."

Charro giggled. "Yeah, he looks at you like you're an idiot."

Fandrella's eyes narrowed to glowing slits as her hands reached for Charro's neck. Charro jumped back in surprise and panic, but before Fandrella could crush her windpipe they were interrupted by another voice. This one was low and slurred, sounding like a cow with an extremely bad cold.

"I'b dun, Maw!" Ellis sprang back in horror as a Snotlin squeezed out of one of the three holes in the wall and landed on the ground. "Maw, Maw, be not feel so good. Mah nose hurts."

Though the Snotlin towered over her, Fandrella looked up at it like it was an ant she could squash.

"Have you been crawling around in the desert again?" Fandrella demanded.

"Aw, geeeez, Maw." The Snotlin hung its iron-shaped head and its shoulders slumped beneath its black cape. Its nostrils looked like two round holes filled with burgundy clay instead of fiery pits trickling slewedge.

Fandrella closed her eyes and drew a breath, clearly irritated.

"Stop calling me Ma," she said through clenched teeth. "I'm not your mother. I don't know why you Snotlins can't get it through your rubbery brains that just because I created you, I'm not your parent. I'm your master."

The Snotlin nodded. "Sorry, Maw." Its arms swung back and forth as it clicked its black, hairy pincers.

Fandrella sighed. She continued, her voice clipped. "I have told you and told you to never go to the desert. The sun will dry up your nostrils like a slug who is sunbathing. Get over here now, and I'll fix you up."

The Snotlin made a slurping noise and its long purple tongue slid out of its mouth and hung down to one side, nearly touching the ground.

"Charro!" Fandrella commanded. "Bring me the chalice."

Charro grinned and scampered into the dark shadows then quickly returned, carrying a goblet in her mouth. She pranced past the Snotlin, holding her head high, as she presented the cup to Fandrella. Fandrella took the goblet and held it up in the air. It looked like it was made of bone. Fandrella tipped her head back and started to shout words that made no sense. Her voice vibrated even more, sounding like she was gargling.

"Snoo-snotlin yo-ho-joe ... soupy floop ... flayer may."

The sounds meant nothing to Ellis but they apparently meant something to the volcano for the interior walls started cracking, spilling tiny streams of yellow-green lava. The lava oozed down the walls and Fandrella walked over and held the goblet under one of the streams. The lava dripped into the goblet and immediately sizzled. Smoke rose from the cup and formed the shape of a skull. The skull seemed to grin, bearing rows of pointed teeth and for just a tiny moment, so fast Ellis almost missed it, two blood-red slits flashed in the smoky skull's eyes. Then they faded as quickly as they came. The skull shape dissipated as the smoke spread out and traveled up the volcano.

Fandrella lowered the chalice in front of her face. She smiled faintly as she placed one finger to the side of her nose, closing that nostril. She inhaled and then blew through the remaining open nostril. Clear droplets sprayed out and landed inside the cup.

"Ma-a-a-aw?" The Snotlin grunted.

"Shut up!" Fandrella snapped, watching the contents of the goblet. Whatever she saw inside of it must have made her happy, for she smiled and let out a chuckle from deep within her chest. "Arootay! Avinay! Anakinoosteray!"

Fandrella shoved the goblet in the air at the same time yellow-green flames descended from above. The flames spun around each other, forming a spinning hourglass shape inches above Fandrella's hands. Fandrella let go of the goblet and it flew up inside the twirling flames. The flames spread out and gently bounced the bony cup up and down before crawling back to the volcano walls, leaving the goblet suspended in the air.

"It is ready." Fandrella smiled as she reached up and grabbed onto the goblet's stem. She walked to the Snotlin and held it out. "Drink. Now."

"Aw, Maw," the Snotlin slurred. "Do I hafta? Whad if id tastes bad?"

The silent rage in Fandrella's face gave the Snotlin no choice. Its purple tongue slithered toward Fandrella, moving back and forth like a cobra watching a snake charmer. Finally, it sensed where to go and the tip of the tongue disappeared into the chalice.

The sound of the Snotlin drinking was noisier than a St. Bernard drinking water out of a toilet. It slurped and slurped, the mysterious concoction sloshing around the white cup until every drop was consumed.

The Snotlin withdrew its tongue and let out a hiccup that sounded like a car horn. Then it backed up against the wall.

"Whad now, Maw? Ow!" The Snotlin grabbed its nostrils. When it withdrew its pincers its nostrils were no longer clay-colored. They were bright orange-red pits, alive with tendrils of slewedge that looked like wriggling maggots.

Fandrella smiled. "All better. Now, up with you. Join your ranks and finish ridding Kibblestan from all the selfish evil that lurks there. Do your duty. Now!"

The Snotlin nodded and walked away from the wall. "N-kay. Sen' be up. Bud I sure sneeze a lot up dere."

Fandrella closed her eyes and her nostrils flared. "That's the entire point, dimwit!" she shrieked. She raised her arms and a loud clap of thunder boomed. The volcano shook and fresh lava shot into the sky, carrying the Snotlin with it.

Fandrella paced back and forth, gnashing her tiny, square teeth and balling her fists. Charro cowered by the wall, then took one timid step after another toward her seething master.

"B-boss? You okay?" Charro crouched, ready to jump away should Fandrella turn on her.

But Fandrella didn't. The rage left her face as she looked at the tiny dog. "It will all be over soon, my pet. And when it is, I will send those idiot Snotlins into a lake and we'll never have to deal with them again." Fandrella's smile dripped of malice. "They don't know they can't swim."

Charro grinned and the yellow-green flames glared off her metal teeth. But Ellis only saw that for a second, for the invisible hand around his torso was taking him up, up out of the volcano and back through the pupil. The next thing he knew he was back inside the underground room.

And something smelled funny.

CHAPTER THIRTEEN

Ellis watched the gold and silver sparkles fade, but the funny smell lingered. The black pupil disappeared as well, and once again they were surrounded by the dark stone walls that made up Thornton Jabbermeyer's prison. Everyone looked around like they were in shock, except the white pup called Ruthertold. He paced back and forth, sniffing the air.

Jenkins, who was cuddled next to Thornton, lifted his head from his father's chest. "What was that? Was that *real?*"

Thornton tousled Jenkins' hair. "It's Ruthertold's secret. He can show you the past. If it weren't for him, I'd have died a long time ago. Not only did he bring me food and water, but he showed me memories that gave me the strength to keep going." Thornton smiled as he looked into Jenkins' eyes. "He took me back to all the best times of my life, like when I married your mother, and when you and Dreya were born. And that time we played Knights Throwing Up—that game you made up. Remember?"

Jenkins stared at his father with amazement. "I remember. It was the day you disappeared. You played with me that day." Jenkins grinned. "And you made the best throw up sounds."

Thornton chuckled. "Crazy game, but one of my very best memories."

Jenkins smiled and wrapped his arms around Thornton's neck. Ellis' heart flip-flopped as he thought of his own dad. It must be way past bedtime at home. Was Dad missing him? Was he holding onto memories? His throat tightened. Or was Dad thinking about those hateful words he had shouted before running away? Fresh tears stung Ellis' eyes that he couldn't blink away.

"So what we just saw was the past?" Jenkins asked. "Fandrella did all that? The Snotlins are all because of her?"

Thornton nodded.

The funny smell seemed slightly stronger now. Ellis wiped his face as he wrinkled his nose. What was it? It was sickeningly sweet yet vaguely familiar. He glanced down at Philecia, who was sitting beside him. She was sniffing the air just like Ruthertold.

Ellis leaned down and whispered. "Do you smell something funny?"

Philecia's black nose twitched back and forth with a life of its own. "Yes," she answered. "It reminds me of something. Oh, what is it?"

Ellis looked at the others, but no one else seemed to notice, they were so caught up in conversation. And where was Matilda? He didn't see her anywhere.

"Well, Thornton, me friend," William said. "Ye be tellin' the truth. Me's sorry for thinkin' ye be off yer rocker."

Philecia put her snout to the wall and stood on her hind legs, sniffing higher and higher.

"But, what's going to happen to Mom and Dreya?" Jenkins asked. "And all the other Petikins Fandrella saved from drowning? Where'd she take them?"

Philecia stepped back from the wall, balancing on her hind legs. "I know!" she said loudly, smiling and wagging her tail. Everyone stopped talking and looked at her. "Your grandma, Ellis."

Now everyone looked at Ellis. William's brows lowered. "What she be talkin' about?" he growled. "Your grandma be helpin' Fandrella hidin' them?"

"Oh no—no." Ellis said quickly. "Er—the smell. That's what Philecia's talking about, right?"

"Yes," Philecia yapped. She spun in a circle. "It smells like your grandma in here."

Ellis scratched his head. How could it smell like Grandma? And yet ... now that Philecia mentioned it, he *could* remember a similar smell whenever Grandma came to visit. And one time ... Yes, he remembered her spraying a liquid on her skin. Its smell was funny, but not nearly as funny as its name. She called it toilet water and Ellis had totally cracked up. But Grandma insisted on wearing the stuff, even though it smelled like rose petals soaked in cough syrup.

Thornton sat up straight. "The smell?"

Ruthertold let out a low, urgent whine from deep within his throat.

The odor was growing stronger. Thornton sniffed the air. His eyes clouded and he started to tremble. His voice was a hoarse whisper. "Chatzkies. They're coming."

"That smell is chatzkies?" Ellis asked.

Thornton nodded. "They like to wear perfume. That Charro—she wears it the most." Thornton's teeth started chattering and he drew his arms across his chest, hugging himself as he rocked back and forth. "Run. Get out of here. You don't want to be here when they come. Trust me."

William clawed at his chin, his eyes skeptical. "Uh, Thornton, me buddy. Me knows ye been through a lots, but those chatzkies, they uh—well, to tell ye the truth, they don't be lookin' too tough, me friend."

Thornton leaned forward, sputtering for words. "Not tough? *Not tough?* Just look at my neck, William. Look good and hard."

Thornton turned his head to one side. Two lines of angry maroon dots marred the side of Thornton's neck.

It looked like someone had used a marker with a very fine point to draw them except each dot had an indention in its center. And the lines were not made of ink, but of scar tissue.

Thornton straightened his head, his voice grim. "When those chatzkies attack, they're so fast you don't see them coming. Their bites feel like nails being hammered into your flesh. And they don't bite over and over, no. They sink their teeth down to the gums and stay. Get Jenkins out of here. All of you. Go."

"Or maybe we be stayin'. Can fight the critters."

"It's too risky, William. When they attacked me they bit my hands, my back, my neck, even my face. Those needle teeth tore all the way through my cheek and sliced my tongue. Another chatzkie stood on my head and said if I tried to run or scream, it would gauge out my eyes. And she meant it, no question."

Thornton shook his head, horror flooding his eyes as he relived the memory. "Then Fandrella showed up. Told me I was a threat to my village with my plans to make a new water supply using starjelos. She said it would disrupt her ability to keep things fair and equal and that I must be punished. She brought me here with the chatzkies still stuck to me, and when they finally let go I nearly bled to death from all the tears in my skin. I lost so much blood I passed out."

"Oh, Dad!" Jenkins hugged his father tight.

The smell grew stronger, but no one moved.

"They're coming, I tell you," Thornton said. "Get out of here. Now."

Jenkins gripped his dad tighter and buried his face in Thornton's shoulder. "I won't leave you, Dad. I won't go."

"It's okay, Jenkins. It's okay." Thornton stroked his son's curls. "All they do now when they come here is laugh at me. Horrible laughs, too. But I don't know what they'd do if they saw all of you." Thornton pushed Jenkins away, holding him at arm's length as he looked into his eyes. "You must do what I tell you, Jenkins. Get away now. You can't risk what the chatzkies might do."

Jenkins scowled and puffed out his lower lip. He lunged toward his father but Thornton kept his arms out, blocking him. "No, Jenkins. No!" Thornton grabbed Jenkins' arms as he writhed this way and that. Thornton looked to William. "Get him out of here, William. Get him to safety. I'm sorry I can't come with you."

"Oh yes you can. You can!" Matilda's unmistakable squeak pierced the air. Ellis looked toward the sound as the little brown mouse stepped out from behind Thornton, her face beaming as she massaged her jaw. "That was tough, yes it was." She opened and closed her mouth a few times. "What was that rope made of, anyway? Hmmm?"

Rope? Ellis crouched behind Thornton. The charcoal rope connecting the ring around his ankle to the hole in the wall had been gnawed in two. Thornton Jabbermeyer was free.

Ellis grabbed the end of the rope and shoved it in Thornton's face. "Look! Matilda chewed it in half."

Disbelief swirled in Thornton's gray eyes, then he let out a cry as he leapt to his feet. "I'm—I'm—"

"Free!" Jenkins finished his father's sputtering sentence. But there was no time for celebrations, for the sweet smell of chatzkies became so strong Ellis' eyes started to sting.

"Quick!" Thornton said. "Go to the tunnel." William readjusted the starjelo on his shoulder and led the way into the dark passage from which they'd come. Thornton hobbled, his legs not used to walking, and Jenkins gladly wrapped his arm around his father to help steady him. Matilda scampered close behind and Philecia trotted along, ears flat against her head, eyes worried and tail between her legs.

Ellis followed into the tunnel but paused when Ruthertold stayed behind. He leaned into the room. "Come on, Ruthertold," he said. But Ruthertold lowered his head and whined.

Ellis went back into the tunnel. Philecia was waiting for him. "Hey Thornton," Ellis called down the passageway. "Ruthertold's not coming."

"It's okay," Thornton yelled over his shoulder. "He's been around chatkies plenty of times. He probably wants to distract them to give us a head start."

Ellis looked down at Philecia. The others were getting further away, but Ellis found it hard to follow. It just didn't feel right to leave this wonderful puppy all by himself in a room full of chatzkies.

"Oh no," Philecia looked up, shifting from paw to paw.

"What?" Ellis said.

"My starjelo. It's still in there."

Just then insane cackling exploded from inside the room.

The chatzkies had arrived.

Ellis kept his back against the tunnel's wall, and carefully peeked around the corner.

Two chatzkies bounded through the room, laughing hysterically as they dodged in between Ruthertold's giant paws. They looked like Charro—Chihuahua-type dogs with oversized heads, bulging eyeballs, and needle teeth, but they weren't white with blue-gray splotches.

Instead, one chatzkie was glossy black, with eyes that were a deep sapphire blue. It swiped at Ruthertold's snout with its tiny paws, then cackled like a demon when Ruthertold snapped at it and missed.

The other chatzkie was light tan in color, and its purply black eyeballs looked like two swollen clots of blood. It giggled like a maniac as it ran figure-eights through Ruthertold's legs. "Ruthie, Ruthie Ruthie-Roo! Can't catch me!"

Over and over Ruthertold tried to stomp on the chatzkies but was always too slow.

"Ahem." The crisp sound cut through the laughter and both chatzkies stopped their tormenting and looked at the round opening in the wall. Two fuscia eyeballs lit up, glaring beneath a hot pink bow.

Charro.

She pulled back her lips in a grimace, drool glistening against her sharp silver teeth. "Didn't either one of you notice? Thornton. He's gone."

She jumped down from the hole and paced back and forth, eyeing Ruthertold.

"Where is he, pup? Did you see him?"

Ruthertold's green eyes sparkled. He sat down and cocked his head.

Charro glowered. "Oh, of course you don't know anything, you useless bunch of fur. What about you, Jetta?"

The black chatzkie shrugged. "Maybe he got so skinny he slipped out of his ankle brace." Jetta let out a laugh as her blue eyes rolled in opposite directions.

"Yeah," said the tan chatzkie. "Or maybe he died and something crawled in here and ate him."

"Oooo, that's a good one, Tawni," Jetta snickered. "Or maybe his insides blew up and he got sucked up by maggots."

Tawni collapsed into a fit of giggles. "Or maybe he was so hungry he ate himself up." The two chatzkies rolled on the ground, laughing so hard that tears streamed from their eyes.

But Charro wasn't laughing. She trotted to the gnawed off rope hanging from the wall. "It's broken. The rope's ripped apart."

Charro glared at Ruthertold. "You wouldn't dare ... " she said under her breath. Ruthertold cocked his head to the other side. His eyes danced.

"Course he wouldn't, Charro." Tawni said. "His messed up teeth are too soft. You know that."

"Yeah," Jetta added, then sang. "Gummy teeth, gummy teeth, gushy wushy gummy teeth."

Tawni joined in the chant as they circled Ruthertold and took turns spitting at him.

Charro scowled. "Well, something cut the rope. It didn't just break on its own."

"Maybe Thornton got so hungry he chewed it through," Tawni said. "Doesn't matter anyway. It's not like he can go build that starjelo colony now that everything's flooded."

"Yeah," Jetta said. "The village is gone so who cares?"

"Fandrella will care a plenty if Thornton happens to find any surviving Petikins and tell his story. No one was to know she was behind his disappearance, you know that." Charro paced back and forth, gnashing her teeth. "And Fandrella put me in charge of him. Me, me, me. And now he's escaped."

"Aw, don't worry about it," Jetta said.

Charro's pink eyes glowed. "But he was supposed to be dead by now. She wanted him starved and the rope destroyed, so if anyone ever found him, they'd think he'd wandered off and gotten lost in here. And stupid Ruthertold wanted to keep bringing him food and water, and you dimwits wanted to keep him alive for entertainment and I agreed to it, fool that I am."

Tawni giggled and rolled on her back, paws in the air. "Well, what else is there to do around here? Oh it was so fun laughing at him. And biting him until he cried."

"Yeah, Thornton was one big baby," Jetta snickered. "Ugly, too with all that hair on his face. I liked making him say tongue twisters."

"And making him scratch us behind the ears until we told him he could stop. That was the best." Tawni smiled and her eyes looked like gobs of dark jelly.

Charro was not amused. "Well, glad you have your memories, girls, but I won't take my chances of losing my spot as second in command of Fandrellaville. We're going to have to find Thornton and kill him before any of this can get back to Fandrella. In his condition he can't have gone far." Charro started to cross the room, then paused in front of Ruthertold, looking him up and down. "And I suppose you'll go running to try and help the pathetic Petikin," she sneered.

Ruthertold locked eyes with Charro, his face blank.

Charro did not break his stare. "Girls," she said. "We'll have to do one other thing first." Her gaze remained cold, steady, calculating. At last she broke the silence. "Kill Ruthertold."

CHAPTER FOURTEEN

Ellis' heart skipped a beat. Had he heard correctly? Kill Ruthertold? But those dogs were tiny, and Ruthertold was so big.

Tawni and Jetta stood up and cocked their heads, looking at Charro with confusion. Charro's eyes gleamed. Spit flew from her lips as she shouted. "You heard me. Kill him!"

Before Ellis could process what was happening a black and tan blur flew through the air. Ruthertold let out a cry. In less than a second Jetta and Tawni had landed on Ruthertold's back and sunk their teeth into him.

Ruthertold writhed this way and that, like a bucking bronco desperate to throw its rider. But there was no throwing these riders, for they were secured to his flesh like nails in a coffin. Ruthertold's green eyes lit up and then dimmed, over and over, as he barked. But instead of making a cheerful chiming noise his bark sounded like the clash of cymbals.

Charro grinned, drool seeping from her evil smile.

"Between his shoulders. Shred those muscles. I'll get his neck."

Tawni and Jetta released their bite and blood spurted from Ruthertold's wounds. He ran in circles and lifted off the ground, starting to fly. But the two chatzkies were unfazed. They sank their teeth between his shoulder blades and shook their heads back and forth, sawing through fur and flesh to reach the underlying nerves and muscle. Ruthertold's front paws stopped moving. He fell to the ground, collapsing onto his side.

The chatzkies remained stuck to his body.

Ellis couldn't watch anymore. "Stop!" he cried. He ran to Ruthertold and knelt beside the bleeding pup. He leaned down to examine Ruthertold's wounds only to find himself eye to eye with Jetta, her teeth stuck in Ruthertold's flesh like a fork in a slab of ham.

Ellis held her gaze. "Come on," he pleaded softly. "Let him go."

Jetta and Tawni released their grip and Ruthertold moaned as the blood spurting from his gashes turned his white fur crimson. Both chatzkies stared with a look of surprise mixed with curiosity as blood and slobber dripped from their lips.

"Who are you?" Charro's voice demanded from behind him.

Ellis' hands slipped from Ruthertold's fur. He sat all the way down as he turned to face the pink-eyed devil dog. "I'm Ellis. I'm—"

"He's a Kootie!" Jetta leaped off of Ruthertold and joined Charro's side. "Another Kootie has come to Kibblestan to topple Fandrella's rule."

"Actually, I—"

"You're right!" Tawni bounced over to Charro. "I knew the Kooties would be upset. Fandrella's been pulling all kinds of tricks. Bob probably reported back to the Kootie Kingdom about what's been going on."

Charro's eyes narrowed to slits. "Perhaps." Her voice was smooth, icy. She padded back and forth, looking Ellis up and down. "You're here to take over, are you? Are you plotting with Bob?"

Ellis' mouth opened then shut. What should he say?

Tawni smiled and batted her lashes. "Well if he is here to take over, he sure is a much handsomer replacement," she mused. "Look at those gorgeous eyes."

Jetta grinned. "You're so right, sister! He's a mighty big improvement."

Tawni strutted back and forth, then stopped and gave him a sidelong glance. "I like his sun-kissed skin and exotic clothes. And that thick dark hair. Better than any dog fur, that's for sure."

Ellis' mouth dropped open. What the heck. Were they flirting with him? *Flirting?* Ellis started to jump to his feet and scream, "I'm not a Kootie, you psycho dogs!" But the look in Charro's eyes stopped him. These dogs were small but dangerous. Maybe he should just play along.

"Um, sure. I—uh—I'm a Kootie. I'm um, I'm visiting for a while. Why don't you girls go on back home. I'll take care of Ruthertold."

"Home?" Charro said, looking skeptical. "Why would I want to go home when I have such an interesting visitor right here?" Charro's eyes traveled to Ellis' sneakers. "I've never seen a Kootie dressed so strange."

"Huh?" Ellis' heart thumped as he drew his knees up to his chest.

"Why do you cover your talons? That's your main weapon."

"I—uh—uh—Because I'm nice. I—I don't need weapons."

Charro's brows lowered. "Everybody needs weapons. Show me your talons. Let's see how sharp they are."

Ellis curled his toes inside his sneakers. His heart raced. "I don't feel like it. I—I'm a peaceful Kootie so I don't like to show off my talons."

Charro gazed up at Ellis with a knowing look. "Peaceful? Come on. If I didn't know better, I might think you have something to hide. You know all I have to do is give the command and my girls will tear out your throat. Don't tell me you don't need weapons."

Ellis met Charro's flaming gaze and knew she was onto him. He scooted back, pressing into Ruthertold.

The white pup raised his snout and gave Ellis a sorrowful look before his head plopped back down on the ground. Ellis stared at the three chatzkies. Jetta and Tawni's eyes were wide with playful curiosity, but there was nothing playful about Charro's triumphant smile.

"Your talons?" she said silkily. "We're waiting."

Ellis drew himself into a tight ball. It would do no good to run. These chatzkies were way too fast. Sweat crawled through his thick hair.

A voice came from the entrance to the tunnel. "Excuse me, but do you girls know where I can go potty?"

The chatzkies whirled about. Ellis sat up straight, craning his neck to see.

Philecia stood in the entrance, wagging her tail. Her eyes widened as she stretched her lips into a fake, toothy grin. Her neck bulged as she swallowed hard, then she trotted forward, breathing heavily, but never losing the ridiculous smile.

Poor Philecia. This was taking every ounce of courage she had. Ellis leaned forward and tried to make eye contact, but her bugged eyes evaded him. It was so obvious her smile was fake, yet these chatzkies didn't know Philecia. Maybe they wouldn't recognize her fear. Besides, as she stood there shuffling from one paw to another, she really did look like someone about to pee all over.

"Sorry to bug you," she said. "I just really need to go potty, and I wasn't sure where I should go."

Charro looked at Philecia like someone seeing a cockroach who'd started to sing—fascinated and appalled at the very same time. She scrunched up her face. "What are you?"

Philecia smiled wider, tail wagging all too fast. Her nostrils flared in and out and her body started to hunch. Oh no. She was about to pee.

"I made her," Ellis said quickly. "Just like Fandrella made you. She's my creation."

The chatzkies turned and stared. Charro raised an eyebrow. "Continue," she said.

Ellis cleared his throat. "She's called a, uh, a weinerdach. That's it. She's a weinerdach."

Tawni smiled. "Ooooh. A weinerdach. I like the long body."

Jetta sidled up to Philecia, her eyes friendly. Philecia's smile relaxed and she let out a sigh of relief. She instinctively lowered her snout to sniff under Jetta's tail.

Jetta jumped away. "What are you doing?" she demanded.

Philecia's nervous smile returned. "Er—saying hello. You know, making friends." But this must not be the way dogs made friends in Kibblestan. Philecia had tried sticking her tail in Ruthertold's face, and Ruthertold had looked clueless. Kibblestan dogs must not do that sort of thing. At least, not Fandrella's engineered dogs.

Jetta fixed Philecia with an indignant stare and Philecia backed away. The chatzkies moved toward her, ears flattened and fur bristled. A low growl escaped Charro's throat.

Ellis leapt to his feet. "It's the power I gave her," he shouted. The chatzkies stopped their advance and turned toward him. Ellis prayed that he would sound convincing. "You guys have your teeth, Philecia's power is her nose. She can recognize anyone from the way they smell."

The chatzkies' eyes smoldered. They didn't look impressed. Ellis ran a hand through his hair. Think of something else—quick. "Oh—and don't stick your face under her tail," he said. "She can shoot you with air that smells so bad you can't breathe. You could die."

Now the chatzkies' eyes lit up with interest. Slow smiles spread across their blood-stained lips. Were they buying it? Besides, it was kind of true, especially when Philecia ate those dog treats that looked like pepperoni. "Trust me," Ellis continued, "you don't want to get on her bad side. And underground here, with no windows or anything, she could be really dangerous."

The chatzkies looked at each other, then Tawni's face broke into a smile. "A weinerdach with a deadly scent." She pranced over to Philecia. "I like it."

Charro tossed her head. "A deadly scent is nothing compared to our teeth. And we do not intend to let Fandrella be overthrown, do we girls?"

Tawni and Jetta shrugged. Charro glared at them. "If Fandrella's overthrown, I don't get to be second in command. Get it?" Jetta and Tawni looked at each other, then nodded.

Ruthertold made a snorting sound as he heaved a sigh. Ellis bent over the wounded pup. Ruthertold's puncture wounds had clotted, but the rips in his skin looked so painful. Could he even walk? If only these chatzkies would go away for good, Ellis could go back through the tunnel and find help.

But how could he make these chatzkies go away? What would make them believe he wasn't a threat to Fandrella?

Ellis' stomach clenched as he got an idea. It was an awful idea. The very thought of it made him want to throw up. But as he looked at the perfume-soaked chatzkies, Charro wearing a bow, Tawni batting her lashes, Jetta with her crazy blue eyes ... Well, it just might work—though it would take his very best acting skills to pull it off.

"Look," Ellis said, sitting back down and motioning the chatzkies to him. "Can you girls keep a secret? I mean, a really, really good secret?"

Jetta jerked her head, her eyes once again rolling in different directions. Tawni offered a crooked smile and hopped up and down. Charro remained stone-faced. "What?" she said.

"I didn't come to overthrow Fandrella." Ellis paused and drew a deep breath. Here it goes. Make it believable. "I came to marry Fandrella."

All three chatzkies stood open-mouthed, their teeth glistening like silver rows of blood-soaked icicles. Philecia's jaw dropped too.

"And you came all the way from the Kootie Kingdom just to marry her?" Charro said. "Are you after some power grab? You weren't chosen to be a ruler yourself so you figured you'd come down and marry one?"

Ellis' heart pounded. Think. Think. Think. "I'm not from the Kootie Kingdom. I'm from somewhere else. But trust me, Fandrella will want to marry me. I'm the ruler of my land. We can rule two lands together. And we need chatzkies like you to help control all the people."

Charro's eyebrows raised. "People? What's that?"

Ellis flushed. "I mean, uh, Petikins. People is a nickname I have for Petikins."

Tawni stood on her hind legs and clapped her paws "A wedding! How exciting. And this weinerdach will be our sister?"

At last Charro smiled, eyes glowing. "A sister with a lethal smell. We'll be a deadly team."

The chatzkies circled Philecia and rubbed up against her, like cats rubbing against human legs. Philecia plastered on her fake grin and looked over at Ellis like she was about to lose it.

Ellis cleared his throat. "So, girls. Remember, this is all top secret. I want it to be a surprise for Fandrella. Go back home now and don't tell Fandrella a thing."

Tawni giggled and ran in a circle. "Oh, he's so romantic. Tell us, how did you fall in love with her?"

Charro looked up. "Yes," she said, brow furrowing. "How *did* you fall in love with her, if you're from some other land?"

Ellis hoped his smile concealed the fear pulsing through his veins. His thoughts raced. Come up with a story. You can do this. He pictured Fandrella, surrounded by yellow-green flames and black lava rock. He remembered her swamp-washed hair, her gray-green skin stretched tight over her too-big skull. Her tiny square teeth and insane cackle. And he was supposed to be in love with her? Puke burned the back of his throat.

Tawni laid on her stomach and looked up at him through long, batting lashes.

"Tell us the story, Handsome," she said dreamily.

"Well," Ellis began. He thought of a video game he played at home, with portals that let you see into different worlds. "You see there's a portal, from my land into Kibblestan. I can watch Fandrella through the portal and well, I fell in love with her."

"What do you love about her?" Jetta asked.

Ellis felt the barf creeping its way back up his esophagus. "Oh her, uh, I like her hair." That was weak. Think of something else. "And, Fandrella's really cool, the way she flies around and makes stuff like those Snotlins. And she did such a good job making you guys. She'll be great at making stuff in my land."

"What's your land called?" Jetta asked.

"Um, America."

Charro stepped forward, her face very serious. "And if you marry Fandrella and rule by her side, you agree with her plan of fairness for all? Is that what your land—America—stands for?"

Ellis didn't need to think before answering this one. If there was one thing Dad had drilled into his head during his eleven years, it was what America stood for—individual freedom—something that Cuba had denied.

"Freedom," the word spilled from his mouth. "Freedom for all, not fairness."

But Charro didn't like this answer. Her fur bristled and her brows drew together. When she spoke her voice was lower than normal, nearly a growl. "Freedom for all. That sounds like something Bob would say." Charro's eyes became two demonic slits. "Fandrella hates Bob. You're a fake!"

Before Ellis knew what was happening, the flaming-eyed chatzkie sprang to his throat. Charro's jaws clamped down around Ellis' windpipe and the rows of needle teeth tore into his flesh. He let out a strangled cry as his hands flew to his neck. It felt like an evil nurse from his worst nightmare was giving him hundreds of shots on each side of his throat. He grabbed Charro with both hands and pulled, but her jaw only cinched tighter. Her teeth sank deeper. The pain was unreal. The harder he pulled, the stronger she bit, until he couldn't breathe at all.

Ellis fell back against Ruthertold. The injured pup raised his head, his paws moving, trying to get up but it was useless. Ellis heard Philecia barking her dog scream, a sound of all-out hysteria. He turned his head to one side and could see Philecia, eyes bulging with horror even as she snarled and charged toward them.

Charro released Ellis' throat and shouted, "Get her, girls!"

Jetta and Tawni jumped in front of Philecia and each grabbed an ear. Philecia yelped as they played tug of war, her floppy ears stretched out like airplane wings.

Ellis grabbed Charro before she could bite his neck again. He threw her across the room. She ricocheted off the wall and landed in a heap. She made a feeble attempt to rise to her feet, but collapsed and fell forward, landing on her chin. Her pink eyes swelled and darkened, looking like they were filling up with black ink.

Jetta and Tawni dropped Philecia's ears. They ran to Charro and nudged her with their snouts. Charro didn't move.

"You killed her!" Jetta said.

Ellis couldn't believe it. He hadn't meant to kill her. He was acting in self-defense. But that wasn't going to matter to Jetta and Tawni. They started toward him, teeth bared.

CHAPTER FIFTEEN

Jetta and Tawni's ears plastered to the backs of their heads. They snarled and slowly approached, drool oozing from their lips.

Ellis scooted back into Ruthertold, one hand clutching his searing neck. Blood slipped through his fingers as his wounds continued to spill. This was it. One chatzkie attack was bad enough. Two might kill him.

Ellis leaned back and prepared to kick as Jetta and Tawni charged. But when they reached Ellis the chatzkies split, each running on either side of him, before leaping and landing on top of poor Ruthertold.

"Ha! Ha!" Tawni giggled. "Tricked you!"

Jetta hooted with laughter. "You should've seen your face. You were so scared. I love it!"

Ellis let out the breath he'd been holding and slumped over with relief. He felt shaky. But as the chatzkies continued to laugh at his expense, his shakiness subsided and he started to clench his teeth to stop himself from yelling at them to shut up.

There was no understanding these psycho dogs. One minute they acted like they were ready to use him as a chew toy, the next minute they were giggling like a couple of kids with a whoopee cushion. And Charro lay dead on the ground and they didn't even care.

Philecia nudged Ellis' knee with her snout. She crawled into his lap and started licking the blood from his neck.

Tawni grinned. "Come on, weinerdach. Let us show you around. We'll take you to Fandrellaville."

"Yeah, let's get out of here," said Jetta. "I'm bored."

Ellis glanced at the white spotted corpse crumpled on the ground a few feet away. "What about Charro?" He asked.

Jetta shrugged and wrinkled her nose. "Who cares? She was too bossy, thinking she was so cool, second in command, blah blah blah."

"Yeah," Tawni said. "I was sick of doing everything she told us to do. We can leave her here. Maybe Thornton will come back and eat her."

The two chatzkies looked at each other then doubled over with laughter.

"Besides, who needs Charro when we have a weinerdach?" Tawni said. "If anyone gets on our nerves now, we can send the weinerdach to shoot her deadly smell, right sister?"

Jetta nodded and cackled until she choked. She stepped on Ruthertold's head as she bounced off of him and scampered to the round opening in the wall. "Come on, weinerdach."

Philecia's ears drooped. Her body trembled. Ellis hugged her close. "You girls go ahead," he said. "We'll catch up with you later. Uh—the weinerdach is kind of shy. She won't go anywhere without me."

Tawni frowned. "Shy? But we're practically family, with you marrying Fandrella and all."

"Yeah," Jetta said. Then her eyes clouded. "But Tawni, what if Fandrella doesn't want to marry him? She's not going to want to share her throne, especially with someone who talks like Bob."

"You're right," Tawni said. She looked at Ellis. "If you really want Fandrella to marry you, don't mention stuff like freedom, choice, independence—stuff like that. It's too much like the drivel she's had to listen to from Bob all these years. She gets really annoyed with that."

"Fairness," Jetta said. "You can talk about that all you want. Tell her you want everything to be fair and equal in the lands that you rule together, and how everyone should have the same thing. She really gets into that."

Tawni batted her lashes. "And be sure she notices your gorgeous eyes."

Ellis flushed. "Look, I don't know anything about this Bob. I just need to get going."

"Go to Fandrellaville," Jetta said. "If Fandrella's not there, she'll be there eventually. That's where she's bringing the few Petikins she's saved."

Petikins she's saved? Ellis' heart sped up. Jenkins' mom and sister—could they be there? Ellis put Philecia down and stood up. "How do you get there?"

"It's pretty hard to get to," Jetta said. "It's way on the other side of the desert. You're a Kootie. Just fly. We'll bring the weinerdach through the tunnels. We've got a special route that we take that you're too big to fit through."

Tawni tugged at Philecia's ear with her teeth. "Come on," she said.

Philecia whined.

"She doesn't want to go," Ellis said.

"But we want her to," Jetta said, her jaw set.

"I told you, she's shy."

Jetta cocked her head. Ellis didn't like the new gleam in her eye. Or how her stubby tail slowly twitched. He held her gaze as he crouched down to pick up Philecia.

Without warning Jetta pounced, wrapping her paws around his forearm. She bit into his flesh, sinking her teeth down to the gum line.

Ellis screamed. Jetta's teeth felt like two rows of giant stinging wasps. "Let go of me!" he hollered. He pulled at Jetta with his free hand but Jetta dug her teeth in deeper. Pain shot down his forearm, through his hand and out his fingertips. His head felt fuzzy and bright lights flashed at the edge of his vision. He blinked and fell backward, collapsing on the ground.

Philecia barked and snarled. Tawni ran over and snapped at Philecia's tail. Philecia yelped.

"Look, sister," she said. "All we want is for you to come with us. Stop freaking out."

Ruthertold whimpered and shifted his body, trying to get up.

Tawni was upon him at once. She chomped on his neck over and over until blood showered down and the poor pup lay still.

"No!" Ellis cried. He squeezed his eyes shut and tried to block out the pain in his arm as he rose to his feet. His head started swimming and a roaring sound rushed through his ears. The pressure in his head intensified and blackness took over his vision. Everything—the room, the sounds, the sight of Philecia's horrified face—started to fade away. He sat back down and put his head between his knees. He waited for his head to clear as Jetta snarled behind her busy teeth.

Tawni slid off of Ruthertold and ran to Philecia's side. Philecia cringed as Tawni shoved her snout in Philecia's face, her dark eyes glistening like two pieces of raw meat. "You see, chatzkies are used to getting their way. Come with us and we'll leave your Kootie alone. With your help, we'll be the ones calling the shots over the other chatzkies in Fandrellaville. Trust me, you're going to love it."

"Don't listen to her," Ellis said. If he could only catch Tawni and slam her against the wall. If only he didn't feel so shaky and weak. He slowly scooted forward. His arm gushed blood and his head pounded. His vision darkened, then cleared, darkened, then cleared. Don't pass out, he told himself.

Jetta released her grip for a split second then bit again in a fresh spot. Her teeth sank in so deeply Ellis thought his arm might break in two. Tears leaked from his eyes as he hollered in pain. He pounded the chatzkie on the back with his fist but she wouldn't let go. She still wouldn't let go.

"Alright!" Philecia's bark was hysterical. "Stop it! Stop it! I'll go with you."

"No!" Ellis cried. He threw himself toward Philecia, reaching for his beloved dachshund with his good arm. Philecia squirmed away. She ran to the round opening in the wall.

Ellis tried to stand but he started blacking out again. Jetta shook her head back and forth. His arm felt like it was stuck in a meat-grinder. He collapsed on his stomach and looked up through his tears. "Don't go, Philecia," he sobbed. "Please. Don't leave me."

Philecia stared out from the hole in the wall. She should be trembling, whimpering, peeing all over the place.

But she wasn't.

Somehow, somewhere along this crazy journey, Philecia had found courage. Ellis could see it in the way she refused to cower when Tawni jumped up beside her. And in the way her voice didn't shake when she told him, "I trust you, Ellis. You'll find me. We won't be apart for long. Not long."

How was she not freaking out? What was giving her so much courage? Ellis locked eyes with his dog and his heart swelled as he realized the answer. The look in Philecia's eyes was the same look Mom gave when she bent over him after he'd crashed his bicycle, or when she felt his forehead when he was feeling sick, or … Ellis bowed his head and his shoulders heaved with fresh sobs. It was the same look Dad had when he tried to apologize for missing the campout, right before Ellis had yelled those hateful words and ran off.

The look in Philecia's eyes was love.

Jetta released Ellis' arm and spit out a chunk of skin stuck to her teeth. "Oh, don't be such a baby," she said crossly. "You remind me of Thornton." She jumped into the hole with Philecia and Tawni, then grinned triumphantly. "The weinerdach is going to be very happy living with us. And you'll see her again when you come to Fandrellaville."

Ellis raised his arm in a feeble gesture. He tried to scoot toward the hole but his body wouldn't cooperate. "Please," he whispered.

Philecia glanced at the chatzkies on either side of her, then hung her head as she turned and disappeared into the tunnel. Jetta and Tawni followed.

Ellis couldn't believe it. Philecia was gone. His dog had left him. The only link he had to his life back home. The only friend in this miserable land who really cared.

Ellis buried his face on his arm and cried and cried.

What would happen to him now? He was alone. All alone. In a world that didn't care anything about him. Kibblestan didn't care that he was just a kid. It didn't care that he had no parents here to look out for him. And where were Matilda and Jenkins, Thornton and William? Hadn't they noticed he and Philecia were missing? Why hadn't they come back for them? Didn't they care?

Ellis rubbed his eyes with his fist. Even if his parents were here, they probably wouldn't want to have anything to do with him. He'd told Dad he hated him. What kind of a son does that? If only he could go back in time. If only he'd known it'd be the last time he'd see him. He wouldn't have screamed such a thing. No way.

Tears gushed from Ellis' eyes like the blood from his shredded arm. He was a terrible son. And a terrible dog-owner. He couldn't even save Philecia from two crazy Chihuahua wannabes.

Ellis raised up and looked around the room. Everything seemed fuzzy. His teeth rattled. Shivers wracked his body. Man, was he cold. He closed his eyes and leaned against Ruthertold's maroon-stained fur as exhaustion took over. His body relaxed, then went limp as the steady stream of blood continued to flow from his arm. Soon consciousness took a vacation from his body.

When he awoke he had no idea how much time had passed. Jetta's bite marks had finally clotted. Ruthertold remained still.

And heavy breathing sounded outside the doorway.

CHAPTER SIXTEEN

Ellis tried to sit up. His head felt like it was full of heavy stones. He leaned back against Ruthertold and watched the entrance across the room.

The heavy breathing came closer. In and out, in and out. It was labored and wet, rattling through gushy lungs. Ellis propped himself up higher.

Clop clop. Footsteps. Getting closer.

A silver light illuminated the doorway. A haggard-looking animal stepped into the room. It looked like someone's neglected donkey that was put out to pasture for way too long. Its spine and hip bones protruded underneath mottled, gray fur. Its mane and tail were scraggly and colorless. Long strands of sticky drool hung from the corners of its sagging mouth.

The silver light shone from something on the poor donkey's forehead. It twinkled then dimmed, like a flashlight surviving on its battery's last juice. Eventually the light disappeared altogether, revealing a single horn that looked like one of Philecia's old bones—one that she'd gnawed then left in the yard to suffer through wind and rain. It was dirty white, marred with scratches and scrapes, and though the tip was pointed the rest of its surface looked rough and worn.

Ellis squinted. Was he seeing things? It was a unicorn.

The unicorn scuffed its hooves along the rocky ground. Its eyelids drooped over large dark eyes that stared at Ellis in a casual way. It mashed its floppy lips together, then lowered its head and snorted. "Sorry. I'm real sorry."

Ellis' mouth parted. Sorry? What would it be sorry for? He'd never seen it before in his life. Ellis wanted to speak but couldn't think of what to say. His mind felt fuzzy.

The unicorn sauntered forward, its breathing raspy and clicking. It walked right up to Ellis, then nudged Ruthertold's head with its nose.

Nothing.

The unicorn sighed, and drops of spit fell from its mouth. "Oh Ruthertold." It slowly shook its head, then looked at Ellis with a mournful gaze. "Chatzkies?"

"Yes." The word eeked out of Ellis' throat.

"Is he alive?" the unicorn asked.

Ellis turned and lowered his aching head to Ruthertold's body. He buried his hands in the silky fur. Ever so slightly, Ruthertold's stomach rose and fell.

"He's breathing," Ellis said with relief. "What do we do?"

"Part his fur. Show me where he's bit up."

Ellis traced the streaks of blood with his fingertips. He pulled back tufts of fur, exposing rows of deep puncture wounds crowned with dark clots of blood. The unicorn stood over Ruthertold and opened its mouth, letting strands of saliva spill into each bloody gash. As the drool absorbed into Ruthertold's cuts, there was a hissing sound and the clots of blood turned silver.

Whoa. This was freaky. Ellis climbed to his knees, swaying as his brain went for a swim in his throbbing head. He rubbed his temples and squeezed his eyes shut against the dizziness and pain. He forced his eyes open and looked at Ruthertold. "What—what's happening?"

The unicorn turned his droopy eyes upon him. "Unicorn spit. Powerful healer. Works every time."

Ruthertold's paws started to move. Gradually at first, then more and more. A sleepy bark escaped his lips. His eyelids flickered. He looked like he was having one of those dog dreams, chasing something while barking in his sleep. His legs moved faster and faster, until finally gold and silver sparks burst out of his paws.

Ruthertold shot up off the ground. He hung suspended in midair and his green eyes blinked open. His ears perked up as he looked around at his surroundings. When he spotted the unicorn his mouth pulled into a smile. Then he tipped his head back and barked and barked. The noise sounded like church bells.

"Good boy, Ruthertold," the unicorn said. "You're okay. Come down here."

Ruthertold floated to the ground and playfully pounced on the unicorn, knocking it backward.

"Careful, boy, careful." The unicorn smiled. "You know my bones are a little rickety."

Ruthertold stuck his wagging tail in the air and lowered his chest to the ground in a play bow. Then he jumped up and spun in a circle before bowing again. His fur was still matted with dried blood, but his wounds had healed. Now he had more energy than a kid who'd eaten an entire stash of Halloween candy.

He loped around the room, his gangly legs as awkward as ever. He paused long enough to give Ellis a slobbery lick on the cheek before resuming his happy prance.

Ellis wiped his cheek with the back of his hand.

The unicorn gazed at Ellis in a lazy sort of way. "Need some?"

"What?" Ellis said.

"Spit." The unicorn's lower jaw dropped and more drool streamed from the corners of its mouth. Its flappy lips looked like they belonged on a camel.

Ellis' head pounded. He squinted his eyes. He'd never had such a bad headache. He was weak and dizzy. And the chatzkie bites felt like they were filled with fire ants that were eating him alive. But could unicorn spit really help?

The unicorn stepped toward Ellis. "It's the least I can do, since it's my fault you're here."

"Your fault?" Ellis said. "What do you mean?"

The unicorn moved its mouth back and forth like a cow chewing cud. Its eyelids remained half-closed. "Yeah, well, I kind of opened up the forest. Sorry." The unicorn attempted a smile, displaying huge square teeth that belonged on a mule.

"You did this? You brought me here? Why?"

"Well, kinda. It's just … look around you. Kibblestan's a mess. Fandrella's gone nuts and killing everyone with Snotlins, and I got nothing to stop her. Just wisdom. But wisdom's no good when you're trying to tell it to someone who's crazy. And she's so obsessed with power ..." The unicorn shrugged and sighed. "Same old stuff I've seen in your world since the beginning of time. No one ever learns."

Ellis didn't know what to say.

The unicorn paced in a circle. "Was desperate. Saw a chance to break apart the Grand Forest and took it. Rammed my horn between two trees and they split apart. Couldn't believe it. Big light shining through and everything. Knew it was a long shot, but thought maybe someone would come through that could stop all this madness. Didn't know it had worked until I bumped into your friends."

"Friends?"

"Yeah, William and Thornton, and some young Petikin and a very hyper mouse. They were getting ready to come look for you when I found them. I sent them ahead, said I'd take care of you. They needed to warn Rabio and the others before its too late."

"Warn Rabio?" Ellis blinked, trying to clear his vision, trying to process his thoughts.

The unicorn pawed the ground with its hoof. "You don't look so good, kid. Need to get your strength back. From the looks of your neck and arm, you've lost a lot of blood. Probably haven't eaten or drank anything, either. Need to be strong, kid. Come on. Let me give you some spit."

Ellis looked at the strands of drool hanging from the unicorn's lips. He'd love to get rid of his excruciating headache. He'd love to be rid of the pain from the chatzkie bites. He'd love to stop feeling like he was going to black out every time he tried to stand up.

"Okay." Ellis said.

The unicorn smiled and parted its squishy lips. "Give me your arm," it said. Saliva oozed out of its mouth.

Ellis shoved his arm under the stream of drool. The saliva spilled into the angry black bite marks. Ellis flinched. It felt cold. Really cold. Like pouring a slurpee on his arm, yet at the same time magically refreshing.

"Steady now," the unicorn said, opening its mouth wider to increase the flow.

Ellis' arm tingled. There was a hissing sound and his gaping wounds filled with silver. Ellis sucked in his breath. His skin clung to the silver patch, closing his cuts. The silver patch disintegrated, leaving behind a scar of silver glitter where the chatzkie bites had been.

"Whoa," Ellis whispered.

"Now your neck," the unicorn said. Ellis scooted forward and tilted his head, letting the fountain of spit land on the wounds in his neck. The same thing happened—cold, tingling, hissing—then a silver, glittery scar.

"Thank you," Ellis said, feeling his neck where the bite marks used to be.

"It's nothing," the unicorn said. "Now open wide."

Ellis' brow crinkled. Open wide? As in his mouth?

The unicorn took a step forward and put his muzzle over Ellis' head. "Come on. Don't got all day. Tilt your head back and open wide."

Ellis' stomach clenched. It was one thing to put drool on his cuts, but to drink it? Ellis scooted backward. "I'm okay. I'm-I'm feeling much better now."

The unicorn raised a hairy eyebrow. "Look, you can't keep on going with nothing to eat. Least I can do is feed you some spit." The unicorn snorted and shook its head. The strands of its mane was tangled in knots.

Ellis cupped his face in his hands. He squeezed his eyes shut and massaged his temples. The headache was worse than ever, like someone was stabbing his brain with a hot poker. Though his skin had healed, his body had not replaced the blood he had lost. He was dehydrated and weak.

Thoughts rushed through his head. Petikins were drowning. Jenkins' mom and sister were missing. And Philecia was with the chatzkies.

Ellis sighed. He did need his strength. And how bad could a little unicorn spit be, anyway?

Ellis kept his eyes shut. He slowly opened his mouth as he tipped his head back. Pretend it's water. Clear, cool water.

The saliva reached Ellis' mouth. It was cold and slippery—and tasted like cherry. Ellis opened his eyes. The unicorn stared down at him like he hadn't a care in the world. Ellis drank and drank. The stuff wasn't bad. If he could just get his mind off the fact it was spit.

Ellis took one last gulp before the unicorn moved away. He sat up on his knees, wiping his mouth with the back of his hand. His throat felt funny. Tingly. The feeling spread, all the way down his chest to the pit of his stomach. Then down his legs and arms. And finally, his face and head. Ellis wriggled his nose, moved his jaw back and forth. He was tingly all over.

He stood up but he didn't feel faint. His head didn't hurt. He swung his arms back and forth and stomped his feet. He felt strong. Energized. Like he could go do a thousand lay-ups on the basketball court. He smiled at the unicorn as the tingly feeling faded.

The unicorn winked. "Now hurry back and join your friends. Just hope you're not too late."

"Wait. What's going on?" Ellis placed one arm over Ruthertold, who'd come up beside him, wagging his tail. The pup's ears pricked up.

The unicorn frowned. "Fandrella. She somehow found out there are survivors down here. She's sending the Snotlins to flood the Underground."

Snotlins? Flood the Underground? Ellis remembered how helpless he'd felt experiencing a flood of slewedge in a river. But a flood of slewedge in these tunnels? There'd be no way to survive. "Are you sure?"

The unicorn nodded. "Don't know how she found out, but she did and she's furious. She's been in that volcano, stomping around and carrying on. She knows I overheard her plans, but doesn't pay me much mind. I have no power over her, but I do know more about Kibblestan than what she realizes. I knew about Rabio and the habitat. I came to warn him, and that's when I ran into your friends."

"So let's go," Ellis said. "We'll go find Rabio and empty the habitat. Or maybe we can seal it off. Keep the Snotlins from getting in."

"Not we. You," the unicorn said. His jaw moved around like he was chewing gum. "I'm forbidden to be involved in such matters. Can only advise."

Advise? But what about its horn? That could be very useful, especially if some Snotlin got too close. "You can't come help? But—but ..." Ellis stammered.

The unicorn smiled. "You'll have Ruthertold. He's the only weapon you'll need."

Ruthertold? What kind of a weapon could Ruthertold be? His teeth were soft and tiny—the chatzkies called him gummy teeth. But the unicorn didn't seem to care. It started toward the doorway then paused, looking over its shoulder. "By the way, sorry I never introduced myself. Name's Bob."

So this was the famous Bob that Fandrella hated. Ellis looked back at Ruthertold to make sure he was coming. That's when he happened to notice.

Charro was nowhere to be seen.

CHAPTER SEVENTEEN

Ellis ran to the spot where Charro's body had lain. No sign of her. How could this happen? Did she rise from the dead? Did he have to worry about chatzkie zombies too?

Or maybe she was never dead. Maybe she had only been knocked out.

Ellis looked at the white pup. "Ruthertold, where's Charro? What happened to her?"

Ruthertold's only answer was to cock his head and ring out a bark.

Ellis ran into the tunnel. Bob's horn lit the way as he casually strolled down the dark corridor.

"Bob," Ellis called.

Bob stopped and turned. "Hmmm?"

"It's Charro. The chatzkie. The really mean chatzkie. I thought she was dead but she's gone. She's gone!"

Bob shrugged. "So she's gone."

"But you don't understand. She thinks she's going to be second in command. She wants to kill Thornton. She attacked me just because I said something that reminded her of you."

Bob's ears pricked up. "Yeah? What was that?"

177

"I don't know ... we were talking about if I ruled with Fandrella and ... Oh, I remember. I told Charro about my country. How it has freedom for all, not fairness. Then she attacked."

Bob's eyes gleamed. "Interesting." He plodded over to Ellis. "What's your name?"

"Ellis."

"And what country is this, where there's freedom for all?"

"America. I'm from America."

Bob nodded, then turned and continued down the tunnel. Ellis caught up with him while Ruthertold closely trotted at their heels. "So what are we going to do?"

"Sure you'll think of something," Bob said. "Humans are smart. Fascinating, too. Never seen any creature with such capacity to love, yet so capable of incredible cruelty."

"How do you know so much about humans?"

"We unicorns have been watching humans since the beginning of time. We're the only ones who can freely cross from your world to this world, which is why we were made to be Kootie advisers. We've seen your history. The Kootie Council says we bring perspective."

Ellis thought for a moment. Unicorns were supposed to be a myth. So they really did exist? In his world? "You mean unicorns have really been to my world? How come no one's ever seen them?"

Bob smiled. "People see us all the time. Just don't recognize us for what we are. That's because our horns can only be seen by little girls up to the age of six or seven. Then somehow their eyesight changes and they see us like everyone else. Beautiful horses." Bob hung his head. "Or in my case, a lop-eared donkey."

They reached the end of the tunnel and stepped out into the open space by the water-filled crater. Across the way Ellis recognized the tunnel leading to William Wantonburger's old home. He headed toward it. Bob didn't follow.

"Aren't you coming?" Ellis said.

"Nope. This is my stop." He sauntered off along the edge of the crater, then climbed into the middle tunnel on the far wall. "Remember," he called. "You've got Ruthertold." He turned and meandered off into the blackness.

Ellis felt something cold and wet at the back of his neck. Ruthertold was nudging him with his snout. Ellis scratched the pup under his chin. "At least you won't leave me, right?"

Ruthertold's green eyes twinkled.

They walked to the tunnel leading to William's old quarters and paused before going inside. What if Charro was hiding in there? Or a Snotlin? What would he do? All he had was Ruthertold, and though Bob said Ruthertold would be his weapon, the dog's small, rubbery teeth couldn't be much protection. Besides, he had witnessed firsthand what chatzkies could do to the poor pup.

Still, it was better than going it alone. "Come on, boy," Ellis said. He poked his head inside the dark tunnel, half-expecting to lock eyes with Charro's flaming pink ones.

"Ruthertold. Turn on your light."

Ruthertold's eyes lit up. Ellis held his breath, searching for a pair of Snotlin pincers or Charro's silver teeth. He placed his hand on Ruthertold's back as they made their way through and reached William's quarters. Ellis peeked into the room.

Something was wrong. Very wrong.

William's bed was flipped on its side, its tattered blanket in shreds. The mattress lay in the middle of the floor, ripped open and straw spilling out everywhere. The cauldron was knocked over, a crack rippling down one side. The stones that once formed a neat circle were scattered all over the place. And the instrument Rabio had used to de-liquify the starjelo—the long stick with the star-shaped piece of metal on the end—was broken in two.

Ellis slid into the room. Ruthertold landed beside him.

"What happened?" Ellis whispered. His heart thumped faster. Where were his friends? Jenkins and Matilda, Thornton and William. Bob had sent them to warn Rabio. They would have had to come through here on their way to the habitat. Who had met them here? What had they done to them?

Ellis picked up a stone and grabbed the broken stick with the metal star. It wasn't a sword, but at least it was something.

"Ruthertold, hurry!" he called. They sprinted across the room and through the tunnel toward the habitat. They paused at the flimsy door that had once been concealed behind a wall of starjelos, camouflaging this entrance and William's existence.

Now the door stood wide open, ripped halfway off its hinges. Shouts and screams poured from the direction of the habitat. And Leon's burping stench was stronger than ever.

Ellis' hand flew to his nose. The gray amoeba on the ceiling filled his balloon lungs and burped, over and over. In, out, burp. In, out, burp. Leon seemed to be in a state of panic and this was all he could do.

The shouts and screams continued, echoing through the tunnel that led to the habitat. Some of them were panicked shrieks, others sounded like blood-curdling battle cries.

Ellis looked everywhere, but there was no sign of his friends. No Rabio. No Raquel. They must be in the habitat.

Ellis ran into the tunnel and his heart felt like it had been smashed by a bowling ball. At the end of the passageway light flashed. Yellow-green light. Like the bursts of lava in the dark Kibblestan sky. Like the light Fandrella used to communicate with her Snotlins and chatzkies.

He was too late. Fandrella was here, and signaling to her Snotlins to come to the habitat. To come and drown everyone inside.

A sudden burst of anger filled Ellis like the lava consuming the ebony sky. This wasn't fair! It wasn't fair that Fandrella was killing her own citizens. Jenkins was in there. Little Jenkins who'd lost almost everything. William, forced into lonely exile. Thornton, who'd barely survived captivity. Rabio and Raquel, risking their own lives to save others.

Ellis thought of all the refugees he'd seen in the habitat. The tiny mother chipmunk, who struggled to feed and comfort her starving babies. The wild dogs, fighting their instincts to attack the small and weak. The mice, the random insects, doing whatever it took to survive. And the Petikins ... Fandrella had convinced them that anyone who wanted to solve the water shortage and not settle for her spit-laced water, was selfish.

Fandrella was the one who had filled them with hate.

And there was nothing fair about it.

Ellis clenched the stone in one hand and grasped the broken stick in the other. He let out a yell from the pit of his stomach as he ran full force toward the end of the tunnel. He leaped into the habitat, stick raised.

But the sight that met his eyes was not what he expected.

Yellow and blue fireflies zoomed through the air, some flying so close that their lights merged, turning yellow-green—the same color as Fandrella's lava. Petikins shouted at them to go faster, raising fists and cheering as a yellow firefly rammed into a blue firefly and smashed it with a crunchy splat.

Mice scampered back and forth, dodging the heavy paws of the wild dogs who were no longer containing their savagery. They snarled and barked, wrestled and snapped at each other.

Ellis heard a loud squeak and saw the mother chipmunk, hunched over her babies in a protective huddle. Ellis' heart stirred. She looked so tiny. And her babies looked so scared.

Blotu strutted by, chest puffed out as he talked with two other Petikins who looked just as smug. Their eyes lit up as a blue firefly attacked a yellow one and slammed it into the ground. Other Petikins screamed in panic, while some simply huddled together and cried.

"Ellis! Master Ellis!"

Ellis turned at the sound of Rabio's voice.

"Oh, Master Ellis, you've come back. Come quickly!" Rabio led Ellis into a dark corner lit by a single starjelo. Jenkins knelt on the ground, cradling his father's head in his lap as he wept. Raquel stood by his side, patting his shoulder as she tried to soothe him. "There, there, Jenkins. He will be alright. Please don't cry."

Thornton Jabbermeyer's face was one big mess. His eyes were swollen shut, ringed by dark purple circles. His bottom lip was split open and puffy. Blood trickled down his chin. He moved his head from side to side, moaning.

Ellis rushed over and knelt by Jenkins. "Jenkins, I'm here, dude. What happened?"

Jenkins looked up. "Ellis!" He leaned forward and wrapped his arms around Ellis' neck in a fervent embrace. "You're back."

Ellis smiled. "Yes, I'm back. I'm back, dude. What's going on?"

Jenkins released Ellis' neck. "Dad got in a fight. Blotu beat him up. And I couldn't stop him. I tried to but I couldn't."

Raquel nodded as she took a damp cloth and dabbed the blood on Thornton's face. Thornton twitched and groaned.

"Oh, that Blotu," Raquel said. "As soon as we announced we had a new space for the refugees, he declared that the R & R—you know, Fandrella's Resource Redistributors—should be the ones to live there. He and his cronies practically ran Rabio and me over when they saw where William's home had been. They threatened to pull out our tails if we let anyone else in."

"And I am ashamed to say that we complied with their wishes," Rabio said, bowing his head. "We had so many other things we were dealing with. War broke out with the fireflies, the dogs became vicious. It has been trying, to say the least."

"Yeah," Jenkins said. "By the time we got back to William's place it was filled with all those Petikins who hate us."

So that explained the over-turned bed, the cracked cauldron, the stones out of place—and the scrapes and bruises on Jenkins' face.

"I'm sorry, Jenkins," Ellis said. "I wish I was there to protect you. Did you tell Rabio about the Snotlins coming to attack?"

Rabio stroked his chin. "Yes, yes. That is what William told me. He and Matilda are out and about trying to get someone to listen. But look at it out there. It is insane. I fear the war between the fireflies is giving everyone permission to release their aggression."

Ellis stepped from the dark corner. Between the warring fireflies, fighting dogs, and screaming Petikins, how would they get everyone's attention? And time was running out. With the fireflies giving off a light that looked like Fandrella's lava, the Snotlins were sure to find them.

Ellis watched the fireflies' flashing lights and an idea came to his head. It was a crazy idea. Probably impossible. But he had to try something. He quickly made his way through the crowd. "William! William!" he called, looking all around.

He found the stocky Petikin, waving his hands in the air while shouting to a wide-eyed girl Petikin half his size. "I be tellin' ye, lassie, 'tis true! The Snotlins are a comin'. They could be here any minute. Tell your parents, lassie. We must quit all the bickerin' and find a way to survive."

Ellis grabbed William's arm. He jumped in surprise. "Why, Ellis! Ye be back! Where've ye been all this time?"

"I'll tell you later," Ellis said. "Look, I think I know of a way to get rid of the Snotlins."

William's eyebrows shot up. "Do ye now? What ye have in mind?"

"Remember when Ruthertold showed us the past? Remember what Fandrella told Charro about the Snotlins? They can't swim. She was going to send them into a lake and drown them once she was done with them."

"Yes, now ye be mentionin' it, I remember."

"That's what we need to do. If she's sent the Snotlins to explore underground, we need to lure them to the crater that we saw, where we first found Ruthertold."

William's forehead puckered. "Lure them, eh? And just how would we be doin' that?"

"The fireflies. Look at them. When they mix their yellow and blue lights together, it looks like the light from the volcano. Like the signals from Fandrella."

"I see," William said. He reached up and massaged the back of his neck, grimacing. "Ye be right about that. But how in the world can we be makin' the fireflies stop their fightin'?"

Ellis gazed around the room.

Smash! Zoom! Splat! The firefly war went on and on.

How could he make them stop? How could he make everyone stop and realize the truth about Fandrella?

Bob's words came to his head. "You'll have Ruthertold. He's the only weapon you'll need."

And suddenly, these words made sense. Ruthertold wasn't a weapon of strength or power. He didn't have sharp teeth or claws to fight his enemies. He was better than that. He was a weapon of truth.

Ellis searched the room. Ruthertold stood up against a wall, surrounded by five big dogs. His ears were down and he barked and barked. His barks sounded like jingle bells.

"Bark again," one dog demanded in a gruff voice. "Sounds like you're trying to play music."

Ruthertold's tail went between his legs but he barked again. The dogs erupted in laughter.

"Come on," the dog said. "Show us your grinders."

Ruthertold hung his head before curling one lip up to display tiny light gray bumps the size of pimples where his teeth should be. The dogs doubled over in more howls of laughter. Ruthertold turned away, toward the wall.

Ellis walked up to the gang. They sure were big. He cleared his throat. "Hey, you dogs. Go away," he said.

The dogs turned to look at him. The biggest one had bushy salt and pepper fur and teeth that looked like they could rip out someone's guts pretty easily.

Ellis' heart pounded, but he drew himself up to his full height and refused to drop his gaze. "Go on," he said. "Scram."

The dogs weren't intimidated. They lowered their heads and growled.

Okay, this wasn't going so good. Ellis' palms started to sweat. He took a step backward. Then another. The dogs closed in on him.

"Hey, guys," Ellis smiled feebly. "I didn't mean anything. You - you guys can stay. I just need to talk to Ruthertold."

Ruthertold's ears pricked up at the mention of his name. He turned from the wall and when he saw Ellis his eyes sparkled. He wagged his tail then leaped over the other dogs and landed at Ellis' side.

The dogs stared in surprise. Ellis placed his arm on Ruthertold's back and surveyed the canine crowd. "You guys can go on. Ruthertold and me just need to talk."

The salt and pepper dog raised an eyebrow then shrugged and turned away. He slunk off and the other dogs did the same.

Ellis smiled as he petted the beautiful white pup. "Ruthertold, I need you to do something. You've got to show everyone here the past. Can you take us all back so everyone can see what Fandrella is doing? That she is sending the Snotlins here?"

Ruthertold pounced in a play bow and wagged his raised tail. His lips drew back in a panting smile as he jumped back and forth, then leaned forward and planted a long, wet dog kiss on Ellis' cheek before bouncing away.

Ellis followed, calling after the pup. "Come on Ruthertold! Take us back. Please!"

Ruthertold pranced ahead on his lanky legs. Then he paused to give Ellis a wink before dashing off at a speed that no dog could match. Away he ran, around and around.

At first, no one seemed to notice the huge white pup running laps around the room. But when he lifted off the ground and sparks shot out of his paws, everyone paid attention.

Ruthertold rose higher and higher. Petikins stopped their screaming and fireflies paused mid-splatter as gold and silver sparks showered down, encompassing the entire room.

Every refugee stood within the sparkling globe—encapsulated within the glittering walls, and Ruthertold's eyes lit up, ready for the story to begin.

The black pupil formed and an invisible hand plucked at Ellis' insides. He felt himself leaving his body and traveling into the pupil's depths, to a place he had never seen before.

CHAPTER EIGHTEEN

Ellis hovered above a beautiful, strange forest. The trees had leaves that were every color of the rainbow—red, yellow, orange, purple. His invisible self sunk down into their midst, and he traveled through their branches like a sparrow in flight.

When he came to a clearing the trees parted to reveal a stretch of lush, green grass dotted with blue and white flowers bathed in golden sunshine. In the middle of this clearing stood Fandrella, arms folded across her chest as she glared at two bedraggled Petikins who were pulling a bucket of water from a well.

"Hurry up," Fandrella snapped. The woman Petikin's dark hair was disheveled, her bony frame barely visible underneath heavy clothes. She pulled at the rope, arm over arm, to bring a full bucket of water to the top of the well.

A little girl Petikin stood by her side, crowned with golden curls—curls that suspiciously resembled those of Jenkins, except much longer. "Good job, Mama," she said, looking warily at Fandrella.

Fandrella made a face. "Good job, Mama," she mimicked in a high, nasty voice.

191

The little Petikin drew back behind her mother's skirts.

"Carry the water up to the house and do not spill a drop," Fandrella commanded. "I will be there shortly to decide who gets how much. And don't even think about sneaking a drink for yourselves."

The Petikins nodded and started up a gravel pathway.

A scuffling sound came through the trees and a very strange-looking animal emerged. It was the size of a small dog, a bit bigger than Philecia, with long silver tangled fur, vulture head and bloodshot eyes that popped out of their sockets. Ellis remembered this animal from his first visit to the habitat. Jenkins had called it a lizamum, and said it was always telling secrets and saying rude stuff.

When it saw Fandrella it jumped with surprise. "Whoa! Fandrella! Your majesty. You're here!" The lizamum wagged its hairy tail.

Fandrella frowned. "What in the world? Where did you come from?"

"I found my way through the tunnels. What is this place? It's wonderful. Much better than my old village."

Fandrella grimaced. "I'm glad you approve. Now, what do you mean you found your way through the tunnels? What tunnels?"

"The underground tunnels. Under the desert. Rabio and Raquel, they've set up a whole habitat down there. Saved a lot of lives from the slewedge. We've all been living down there but it's gotten so crowded. Rabio showed us another room we could live in and, well, I climbed in another tunnel and another, and before I knew it I was here."

Fandrella's eyes bulged. "What do you mean, habitat? This is the only land for survivors. I saved these Petikins myself. Kibblestan is over. This is Fandrellaville. It's the only place to survive."

The lizamum scampered to a nearby fruit tree. "Pardon me, but it's been so long since I've had a decent meal." It shimmied up the trunk and bit into a round piece of hanging fruit. It chomped away, dribbling fruit juice everywhere.

"Listen to me!" Fandrella demanded. "You mean to tell me there are other survivors? Living underground? Without my leadership?"

The lizamum stopped chewing long enough to nod, then resumed its sloppy feast. It was so consumed with eating it didn't notice the change in Fandrella's color. Her face darkened and her eyes sunk into their sockets, making it look more skull-like than ever. She ran through the clearing, her silver-blue gown flowing behind her. "Alive?" she muttered. "Survivors? It can't be."

Fandrella lifted off the ground and flew over the forest toward Latinab. Ellis floated behind her as she descended into the volcano's depths. She landed with a thud and stumbled to the ground.

Bob was there, slowly pacing back and forth. Fandrella picked herself up and stomped past the unicorn, not bothering to give him a glance. She headed toward a cabinet built into the black lava walls.

Bob's droopy eyes followed her. "What's with you?" he grumbled.

Fandrella remained silent as she clawed through the cabinet, throwing its contents onto the floor. "Where is it? Where is it?" she sputtered through tight lips. Finally she produced the goblet made of bone. "Ah ha!" she cackled. She held it up to a crack in the wall leaking the yellow-green lava.

Bob frowned. "You're not drinking that stuff again. I told you it only makes you crazy."

"Oh, shut up!" Fandrella hissed. "The voice that I hear when I take one sip of this lava gives me more knowledge than what that tiny brain of yours has accumulated in a lifetime. I've learned to make Snotlins. I've learned to make chatzkies. I just haven't yet learned how to make everyone be fair. But I will! I will!"

She held up the goblet. "Oh Spirit of Latinab. Show me what to do." Fandrella put the goblet to her lips and drank, long, slow gulps. She let out a breath and wiped her mouth with her sleeve. She closed her eyes and tilted her head back, smiling as she swayed on her feet in a mesmerizing dance. "Goooood, goooood," she whispered. Her skull grew in size, pulsating like a steady heartbeat. The veins in her forehead swelled beneath her skin, alive like a nest of slithering snakes.

Fandrella opened her eyes and stood up straight. She looked up into the black tube that was the neck of the volcano. She thrust her hands above her head and splayed her fingers as fresh bursts of lava flew into the air.

"All Snotlins hear me now!" Her voice was low and gruff, springing from deep within her gut. "Go underground! Squeeze underground. Find any and all living creatures. Dig them out. Sneeze them out. The ungrateful. The unfair. Those wanting to have more than others. Let them all die a slow miserable drowning death."

Bob's eyes widened and his horn started to glow. "What are you doing? Stop it!"

Fandrella's eyes burned in the volcano's light. Within their depths there was no trace of sanity. Her stringy hair framed her skull face like a lion's wild mane. "Die. They all must die."

Bob's nostrils flared. "Fandrella, no! Stop killing them. It's not right."

Fandrella faced Bob and her eyes glowed dark red. "Not right? Not right?" she shrieked. "What do you know what's right? I swore to myself when I became Kibblestan's ruler that I would make it fair. No one would go through what I did growing up in the Kootie Kingdom. There'd be no rich and there'd be no poor. Every citizen would have the same amount of riches. Everyone would share. But they don't cooperate. Someone always wants more. Someone's always trying to ruin my plans!"

"Because they have free will, Fandrella." Bob scuffed his hoof on the ground. "What you want will never happen as long as there's freedom."

"Then I'll take their free will away!" Fandrella screamed. "The old Kibblestan deserves to die. We will start anew in Fandrellaville, and those whom I plucked from the slewedge owe me their lives. They will have to do what I say. And there's only a few of them, so I'll be able to control them. They will not have freedom but they'll all have the same thing. They will all be equal."

"Equally miserable," Bob said under his breath. He lowered his horn. "Fandrella, you're crazy. Same craziness that's happened throughout history in the Other World. People get an idea of how the world should be, then justify doing evil in trying to make their ideas a reality. And it never turns out right. In fact, just the opposite."

"Don't point that horn my way," Fandrella said. "You have no power over me."

Bob straightened up and took a step back. He tilted his head and was silent a moment. "You're right," he said slowly. "I don't. But Kibblestan does. They just have to believe it."

The force grabbing Ellis' torso sucked him quickly from the scene. The pressure pulled him backward, then up and out of the volcano, through the pupil and into the habitat packed with stunned refugees.

The gold and silver sparkles faded in the dismal room, which was filled with silence.

Ellis grabbed his chance to talk. "See? See? Fandrella wants to kill you. She's the one who sent the Snotlins. Now she's sending them underground, to hunt you down. We've got to do something, quick!"

"But-but that can't be right," one Petikin said in disbelief. "Fandrella, she's always cared about us."

"Cared about being in control," another Petikin said. "I never did completely trust her, what with how she dealt with the whole water shortage. I always thought she was wrong about William and Thornton being selfish."

"Yeah," said another Petikin. "I thought so, too. William and Thornton were the ones who made things better." The Petikin paused and hung his head. "It's just, no one had the courage to say it."

Mumblings rippled throughout the room, but one group of Petikins remained silent. Blotu and his buddies with the RR arm bands glowered.

Ellis shouted over the noise. "Look, I know of a way to get rid of the Snotlins. They can't live in water. There's an underground lake through the tunnels. We can lure them there and drown them."

"What kind of a crazy plan is that?" someone hollered from the back of the room. "How do you expect to lure them?"

"The light," Ellis said. "Fandrella communicates with them through the light from the lava. It looks like the same light that the fireflies make when they're close together. All we need is for you fireflies to combine your blue and yellow light. It'll look yellow-green and will make the Snotlins come."

An eruption of laughter waved through the crowd. "You want the fireflies to work together?" someone shouted. "It'll never happen. They hate each other."

Ellis looked at the fireflies. Even in this moment of truce, the Blues had migrated to one side of the room and the Yellows to the other. It was so stupid. They may be different colors, but they were still just fireflies. A firefly was a firefly, wasn't it?

A quiet din buzzed as everyone started talking and grumbling again. Oh no. He couldn't lose their attention now. Ellis looked around for the great white pup.

"Ruthertold! Ruthertold, come here!" Ruthertold bounded over and Ellis climbed onto his back, gripping his fur. "Okay, boy. Can you give me a ride? Can you make me fly over everyone?"

"Ching! Ching!" Ruthertold barked. His eyes lit up. He leaped into the air and swooped around the room. The awesome spectacle drew everyone's attention. "Look," Ellis shouted. "You're all a part of Kibblestan, and for Kibblestan to survive you've got to stop fighting each other. Fandrella and the Snotlins are the real enemies. You fireflies, Kibblestan needs you. I don't know why you hate each other, but if it's because you're different colors, that's really dumb. It's just a color. It's not who you are."

"Now just one minute," a large yellow firefly flew to Ellis' level. "You don't know our history. The Blues have been really mean—"

"Maybe so." A blue firefly joined the yellow. "But you Yellows are the ones who've thought you were so bright!"

The bugs circled each other like two boxers in a ring. Ellis' temper flared. "But you're both fireflies!" He shouted so loud, the bugs stopped circling each other and looked at him. Ruthertold swooped in between them. "I mean, you're all the same," Ellis continued. "You all eat, sleep, poop ..." Wait a minute. Do fireflies poop?

Ellis looked at one firefly and then the other. "Look," he said. "I don't know who was mean first or what happened, but I do know that we're all going to die down here unless we can drown the Snotlins first. You're our only chance. Can't you just get along for a minute and do this? Please? You may be different colors but you both belong to Kibblestan. Come on."

The fireflies looked at each other and finally the blue one nodded. "I suppose so. For Kibblestan."

The yellow firefly nodded and buzzed away.

Ellis punched the air. "Yes!"

Ruthertold landed on the ground and Ellis slid off his back and picked his way over to Jenkins. Jenkins still cradled Thornton's head but there was an expression of complete joy on the little Petikin's face.

"Ellis! Did you see?" he called. "They're alive. I knew they'd be okay."

Ellis knelt down beside Jenkins. "Huh?"

"Mom! Dreya! That was them, at the well. They're alright!"

Thornton mumbled incoherently, his body twitching.

"That was them?" Ellis said. "Then we'll have to go find them in Fandrellaville as soon as I come back. I promise. In the meantime, take care of your dad, okay?"

Jenkins nodded. Ellis waved at Raquel then strode to the tunnel leading out of the habitat. He called to the crowd. "The fireflies are going to help us. Come on, Yellows and Blues. Me and Ruthertold will show you where to go. Everyone else stay here."

Ruthertold ran to his side as Rabio and William made their way through the crowd.

"Well done, well done, Master Ellis," Rabio said. "I never would believe someone could bring such a truce between the Yellows and the Blues."

Ellis shrugged and looked at his shoes. "I don't know," he mumbled. "Let's just hope they don't change their minds."

"Ellis! Ellis!" The high-pitched squeak could only be one mouse. Matilda scampered toward him with another gray mouse running at her heels. "Where've you been, Ellis, hmm? Huh? I didn't get to talk to you, no I didn't."

Matilda sat back on her haunches and gestured to the gray mouse who perched by her side. He was slightly shorter than her and had a very round face, round belly and unusually large ears. "This is Gustav, yes it is. I told him about the Snotlins. He's the only one who would listen to me, yes he would." Both mice nodded their heads in unison.

"I'm glad you found a new friend, Matilda," Ellis said.

Matilda smiled and reached for Gustav's paw. Gustav grinned, his cheeks turning bright red.

Someone tapped Ellis' back. He turned and saw William's twinkling eyes staring up at him. "Good luck, young Ellis."

"Thanks," Ellis said. He stepped toward the tunnel and paused, as the reality of facing the Snotlins again settled into him like a bad-tasting medicine. He looked toward the dark corner where Jenkins sat. Emotion bubbled up inside him like a shaken up can of soda. "William? Look out for Jenkins, will you? Help him find his mom and sister? Thornton doesn't look so good and if I—" Ellis bowed his head, the bubbles of sadness threatening to burst. He pinched his eyes shut and took a deep breath. "Well, in case ... In case I don't come back ..."

William firmly grasped Ellis' arm. "Oh, but of course. Of course Rabio and me be takin' care of the wee one. But ye be comin' back to us, Ellis." He smiled and winked. "Me knows it."

"I whole-heartedly agree," Rabio said, removing his hat. "Godspeed, Master Ellis."

Ellis smiled a smile he couldn't feel then turned toward Ruthertold. "Come on, boy. Let's go."

They entered the tunnel and the fireflies followed, illuminating the entire way in yellow-green. They made it past Leon and into William's old room.

No sign of Snotlins. One tunnel to go.

They entered the tunnel that led to the crater. Almost there.

Ruthertold stopped.

"Come on," Ellis said. He walked ahead and the swarm of fireflies followed. But Ruthertold lagged behind.

Ellis looked back over his shoulder. Ruthertold's tail was tucked between his legs. He took a step backward and whined. What was wrong with him? There was no sign of Snotlins. "Let's go, boy," Ellis called as he continued down the tunnel.

A familiar odor met his nostrils. Grandma? Oh no ...

Two pink eyes stared up at him.

Charro.

CHAPTER NINETEEN

Charro's pink bow was dirty and crooked, but her teeth were the same. She jumped in surprise. "You! You're not Fandrella. You're that annoying Kootie!"

Loud buzzing vibrated through the tunnel as the swarming fireflies approached. Charro strode past Ellis and peered down the passageway. "But that light. It's got to be Fandrella."

The fireflies suddenly flew at high speed. They surrounded Charro, drowning her in flickering light. Charro shrieked. "Get away! Get away from me!"

"But you smell so good!" they buzzed.

Charro shook her head and swatted with her paws. Ellis followed as she raced out of the tunnel and into the room with the crater. She screamed as the smaller fireflies tried to land on her. "Gross! Don't touch me!"

She ran in circles, biting and swiping, but it did no good. The fireflies simply dodged her blows and buzzed louder.

Ruthertold stepped from the tunnel and smiled as Charro ran across the room, past the crater, and toward the far wall with the five tunnel entrances. She stopped underneath the middle entrance, shaking her head and screaming while she tried to splat the fireflies.

Deep, slurred voices bellowed from within the middle tunnel. It sounded like a herd of buffalo talking with broken noses.

"I hear subthin' screabin'. Think we should keep goin'?"

"Thad's whad Maw said. Find livin' things."

"Bud did she mean screabin' things or livin' things?"

"Uh ... I dunno."

"I'b feelin' sneezy."

Ellis' eyes grew wide. The Snotlins were in the middle tunnel, heading their way.

He ran to the edge of the crater. The bugs needed to hide down inside, so the Snotlins couldn't see that the light was only fireflies and not Fandrella. He waved his arms.

"Guys! Over here! Come over here!"

But the bugs wouldn't leave Charro. They loved her perfume too much.

"What does it taste like?" one firefly buzzed. The smaller bugs landed on Charro and licked her with their sticky insect tongues.

"Aack! Get away! Get away!" Charro shook herself from head to tail. Ellis hollered. "Guys! The Snotlins are in the tunnel. Come on. Remember the plan."

Ruthertold ran back and forth and barked.

The Snotlins' voices grew closer.

"I hear yellin' now. Think id somethin' livin'?"

What followed was a sound that no one could ignore. And the fireflies finally paid attention.

Tchooo!

The sound of the Snotlin sneeze was like the shot out of a cannon. The dirty, metallic stench of slewedge drowned out any smell of Charro's perfume and in the next instant a flash flood of bronze, slimy muck came pouring out of the middle tunnel.

The fireflies frantically batted their wings, propelling themselves above the rushing slewedge just in time.

But Charro was not so lucky. The slewedge swept her away as it gushed toward the crater.

"Aaaaaaaaa!" Charro screamed as she was tossed over the edge and into the water several feet below. She attempted a feeble doggie paddle until more slewedge pounded down on her head. She disappeared below the surface and the only thing to float back up was a tattered, hot pink bow.

Tchoo! Tchoo!

The series of sneezes sounded like an explosion. A tsunami of slewedge burst from the tunnel, way more than the flood that had carried Charro away. This was a tidal wave that could swallow the entire room.

Ellis turned and ran.

"Ruthertold! Ruthertold! Come quick!"

The white pup galloped over but before Ellis could reach him the waves pounded him from behind. Ellis lost his footing and found himself caught in the angry torrent. He screamed and kicked, wildly paddling against the warm, slimy current. But it was too strong. He was headed for the crater's edge.

Just like Charro.

No! No! His mind screamed. He bounced along the rocky ground, bumping his knees, scraping his hip. The slewedge thrust him forward with no mercy. He tried to plant his feet and stand, but the force was too great. He tumbled face first and drank a mouthful of slewedge. Ellis raised his head and thought he would vomit right then and there. He took a breath and saw the crater's opening looming close—a huge dark mouth ready to devour him whole.

It was right there.

And so was Ruthertold.

The great white dog swooped into Ellis path. His leg! If he could only grab his leg. Ellis stretched out his arms and groped for Ruthertold's hind leg. His hands gripped the white dog's paw and Ellis was pulled up out of the slewedge just in time.

Chinkity! Chinkity! Ruthertold's barks sounded off—like a broken music box still struggling to play. He flew erratically, a short burst of climbing high, then plunging back down, veering to his left side—the side that Ellis dangled from.

Ellis' hands started to slip. He looked down below. The belly of the crater looked like a washing machine set on its fastest cycle, churning and churning as the flow of slewedge pummeled the rippling water, turning it the color of a freshly dug grave.

Ellis closed his eyes. Please! Please, Ruthertold. Just get me to the other side. Ellis tightened his grip around Ruthertold's leg. I'm so sorry, boy. I know I'm weighing you down. If they could just get to the other side and land he could climb onto Ruthertold's back and his weight would be centered.

The Snotlin voices bellowed from the tunnel. "Led's go back homb. I want my blankie."

"But Maw might ged mad. Need to find livin' things."

Ellis' hands hurt. "Come on Ruthertold! Almost there."

Ruthertold dipped to the left but was able to muster one last burst of flight, propelling them to the far edge of the crater. On this side there was a ledge only a few feet wide, but it was big enough for Ellis to drop to the ground. Ruthertold landed right in front of him.

Ellis hugged the dog around its neck. "Thank you. Thank you, boy. You saved my life."

Ruthertold nuzzled Ellis' hair.

From the tunnel, "Which way now? I wanna go homb."

Ellis clambered up Ruthertold's back. "Hurry boy! We can't let them get away." Ruthertold jumped into the air and soared toward the ceiling, where the fireflies swarmed about.

"Quick," Ellis said. "I need two of you to go into the tunnel. The Snotlins will see your light and try to follow. Lead them here. The rest of you get down by the water and shine your lights as bright as you can."

The fireflies buzzed loudly and the two largest ones took off toward the middle tunnel. They flew into its opening, being careful to fly above the ebbing flow of slewedge. Soon Ellis heard Snotlin voices.

"Look. Id's Maw!"

"Whad she doin' here?"

"Follow her. Follow her. Maybe she'll tell us a bedtime story."

"Maw!"

"Maw!"

"Maw!"

The repeated sounds of Snotlins calling their "Maw" sounded like sickly cows burping and mooing all at once. Ruthertold hovered toward the ceiling. Ellis watched the middle tunnel, gripping his fur tight. The Snotlins were coming. Any second.

Bzzzzz! The two huge fireflies zoomed out of the tunnel. They soared in a figure eight then dove into the crater.

"Maw?"

Ellis sucked in his breath as a Snotlin squeezed out of the middle tunnel. It landed on the ground then stood up straight, its round, dark eyes shiny, searching the room.

Ellis held his breath. He squeezed his legs together against Ruthertold's back. Don't look up here. Please don't look up here.

The Snotlin didn't look up. It moved toward the fireflies' yellow-green light as a second Snotlin pushed into the room.

"Look!" The first Snotlin pointed to the yellow-green glow rising from within the crater. "Maw! Maw!" It stumbled forward, teetering on the edge for one moment before tumbling over and falling into the slewedge-filled water.

"Uuuuuuuuumgh!" The Snotlin let out a most miserable sound.

"Maw?" The second Snotlin followed the first one into the crater. Soon Snotlin after Snotlin squeezed through the tunnel, and like a group of migrating lemmings, they charged over the edge of the crater after their "Maw."

The water exploded, alive with splashing and moaning.

"Maw! Maw!" The Snotlins gurgled, snapping their pincers and swirling their long, purple tongues. Some climbed on top of each other, others tore at the surrounding walls. They scratched and scratched with their pincers, but to no avail. There was nothing to hang onto, nothing to grab so they could pull themselves up and out of their watery grave. Their calls dwindled as one by one they disappeared beneath the surface.

At last, all was still.

Ruthertold circled around and landed on the ground. The fireflies flew to his side.

"You did it! You did it!" Ellis told them, smiling. But his smile faded as the bugs started darting toward each other. Oh no. Were they going to start their war back up so soon?

But they didn't splatter each other. They simply hit the tips of one another's stubbly insect legs as they buzzed by. Ellis grinned. They were giving high-fives.

Ellis jumped from Ruthertold's back. The slewedge had quickly receded, and was only ankle deep. He sloshed to the edge of the crater for one last look.

Ellis peered over the edge.

The water was still.

Not a ripple.

Nothing had survived.

And yet ... Ellis crouched down, leaning forward. At the center of the crater, deep beneath the water, did something flicker?

Ellis squinted.

Yes, something was definitely flickering. A yellow-green flame. But how could fire survive at the bottom of a crater filled with water?

Ruthertold walked over and stood beside him, examining the strange phenomenon.

"What do you think, boy?"

The white pup cocked his head. His eyes didn't dance. A small whine squeezed out of his throat.

The fire or whatever it was spread bigger. Fingers of yellow-green light crept up the walls, illuminating the entire crater.

Ellis rose and stepped away from the edge of the crater. They should leave. He scratched Ruthertold beneath the chin. "Come on, boy. We need to get out of here."

But Ellis found himself lingering. His heart raced. This was stupid. The Snotlins were gone. He'd seen them drown with his own eyes. It was time to go back and tell the others that they were safe.

He glanced once more at the odd fire.

At least for now.

CHAPTER TWENTY

The news of the Snotlins' demise sent cheers throughout the habitat. Ellis waved as he walked through the celebrating crowds. But he couldn't fully share in their joy, for there was no sign of celebration where he headed—the dark corner where Raquel stood watch over Jenkins and Thornton.

"How is he?" Ellis asked.

Raquel looked up with glistening eyes. "Oh, Ellis. Not good."

Jenkins' head remained bowed as he stroked his father's cheek with his small hand. Thornton's face contorted in pain. Beads of sweat laced his forehead. His breathing was rapid and shallow.

Ellis' heart sank. Thornton looked terrible. This wasn't just from getting beat up. Dark bruising shadowed his swollen eyes but that wouldn't make his breathing difficult. Or cause the sweat to pour from his face.

Ellis touched Thornton's forehead. He was burning up.

"He has fever," Raquel said. "I think it's from the infection in his leg. Look at it."

Ellis had almost forgotten about Thornton's leg. Though Matilda had gnawed through the rope, the iron cuff remained. It sat in a pool of pus and blood that stretched across Thorton's ankle. Red streaks shot out from the wound like angry whip marks. When Ellis bent to get a closer look, the sickening smell of rotting flesh pummeled his nostrils.

Ellis had heard stories about the Civil War, when soldiers had such severe injuries to their arms or legs that the doctors would have to amputate before that stuff called gangrene set in. Sometimes they'd even saw the limb off without any medicine to dull the pain. Infection killed. Would this be Thornton's fate?

Ellis looked around the room. The refugees were done congratulating each other, and now they pushed toward the tunnel, anxious to escape the stuffy habitat. Rabio stood at the entrance. "We cannot do this all at once. Please. Let me go and examine above ground, to determine how safe it will be to proceed. Even in the absence of Snotlins, if the slewedge has not receded adequately, there will still be a grave risk of drowning."

Jenkins looked up at Ellis. "Are you leaving? To find Fandrellaville?"

Ellis nodded. "I've got to go. Philecia's there. I can't leave her."

"And Mom and Dreya. You're going to save them too?"

"Of course I am." Ellis swallowed. He'd sure try.

"I want to go with you." Jenkins said.

"You do? But what about your dad?"

"Raquel will watch him. Rabio ... William ... They won't let him die." Jenkins paused and drew a shaky breath. "Mom and Dreya need help. And Dad can't help them. But I can. I know it's what he'd want me to do."

Ellis nodded and stood up. And now to find Fandrellaville. But how? Ellis rubbed his chin. Jetta and Tawni had said Fandrellaville was across the desert. They'd told him to fly there. What a joke. He couldn't fly.

Ruthertold walked by, nudging Ellis' neck with his snout.

Ellis' hand dropped from his chin.

But of course! He couldn't fly, but Ruthertold sure could.

Ellis turned to the pup. "Ruthertold, can you fly us to Fandrellaville?" Ruthertold tipped his head back and chimed out several barks.

"Oh, Ellis, must you go so soon?" Raquel walked toward him, wringing her paws.

The memory of Philecia looking out from the hole in the wall, a chatzkie on each side, her warm brown eyes so full of love, gave him his answer. "Yes." Ellis said. "There's no time to lose."

Jenkins looked at Raquel. "Take care of Dad, okay? When he wakes up, tell him I went to find Mom and Dreya." He wiped his face with the back of his hand and sniffed. "Tell him I knew it was my job."

Raquel cupped Jenkins' face with her paws. "I will take good care of him, little Jenkins. Please be careful."

Jenkins kissed his dad on the forehead then gently shifted Thornton's head from his lap and stood, giving his father one long, last look. "Raquel? Be sure to tell him ... tell him I love him. Okay?"

Ellis' heart churned. The longing for his own father tore at his soul. He loved Dad so much. He was so sorry for what he'd said, yet there was no way to tell him.

Ruthertold and Jenkins followed Ellis to the tunnel. Rabio stood at its entrance, still encouraging the refugees to stay put.

"Master Ellis?" Rabio tilted his head.

"We're going to Fandrellaville to find Philecia and Jenkins' mom and sister," Ellis said. "If I see Fandrella I'll do my best to beat her up or something. But I think the only way to really get rid of her is if you guys all tell her she can't be your ruler anymore. That's what America did. We were sick of being ruled by the King of England, so we started a revolution."

"Revolution?"

"Yeah. You know, when a country decides it's had enough and fights for change. In America's case, a bunch of guys wrote the Declaration of Independence saying America was going to be it's own country."

Rabio slowly nodded. "But did it work, Master Ellis?"

"Sure. I mean, the king didn't like it and he sent his army and there was this big war, but yeah, it worked. America won."

Ellis, Ruthertold and Jenkins left Rabio, who was stroking his whiskers in thought. They climbed into the tunnel and back to where Leon stuck to the ceiling. At least he wasn't burping anymore. They climbed into the exit tube and Leon blew them up and out with a stinky whoosh of his breath. They landed at the foot of the desert.

The stagnant pond that Rabio's raft had crashed in was still there. Beyond the pond was the dark jungle, but in the other direction mounds and mounds of sand stretched to the horizon.

The sun shined with intensity, and its heat quickly raged war with Ellis' sweat glands.

"Across the desert," Ellis said, covering his eyes and squinting. "Fandrellaville's somewhere out there. You ready to take us?"

Ching! The noise rang out like a clink of champagne glasses and Ruthertold wagged his tail. Ellis and Jenkins climbed onto his back and away they flew, faster than ever before. The peach colored sand whirred by underneath them and hot air lashed Ellis' cheeks. His mouth became dry and sticky and his thick hair whipped every which way.

"Hang on, Jenkins!" Ellis called, tightening his grip on Ruthertold's fur.

Soon the end of the desert was in sight and Ruthertold started to slow. A strange forest lay at the edge of the sand. Its trees had leaves that were rainbow-colored—the same forest he'd seen in Ruthertold's sparkling eyeball.

They soared above the treetops until finding an opening in the branches and zooming through the canopy. Now they flew close to the ground, Ruthertold skillfully swerving in and out of every tree trunk. At last the trees opened up into a clearing, where a quaint little cottage stood.

Ruthertold landed gently on the ground. Ching! Ching! He barked.

"Okay, okay, boy." Ellis hopped off the pup's back. "This is Fandrellaville?"

Ruthertold jerked his head and smiled.

Ellis examined the cottage before him. It stood three stories high with a roof made of copper and walls made of wood. A path lined with stones winded up to the front door. Who lived here? Was this where Philecia was being held? What about Jenkins' mom and sister?

"Come on, Jenkins." Ellis helped Jenkins off of Ruthertold's back. They started toward the cottage but Ruthertold didn't follow.

"You coming, boy?" Ellis said.

Ruthertold's tongue stuck out as he smiled even wider but remained planted at the edge of the trees. Why wouldn't he follow?

Ellis looked down at Jenkins. He hoped his smile looked reassuring, even though right now Ellis wasn't sure of anything. "Come on, dude. I guess it's just us."

They walked up the path to the front door. It was painted a faded blue and looked to be made of wood. Cut into the bottom of the door was a small square opening covered by bright pink cloth. It looked like a doggy door.

Or a door for chatzkies.

Ellis' heart started to patter. He put his ear to the faded wood panels and listened.

Nothing.

"Think we should knock?" Jenkins whispered.

Ellis glanced back at Ruthertold. He sat at the edge of the trees, watching. Ellis gripped the doorknob. He cracked the door open.

He couldn't believe what he saw.

To the right of the entryway was a great room, complete with two over-stuffed chairs and a couch. Chatzkies filled the room, playfully chasing each other or lounging on the chairs.

But the couch was a different matter. Lying comfortably on her back, an orange bow tied around each floppy ear, was Philecia. A little girl Petikin sat beside her and stroked her belly. When the Petikin's pointy fingers hit a ticklish spot, causing Philecia's hind leg to move rapidly back and forth, the Petikin tilted her head back and laughed. The golden curls fell away from her face and Ellis knew immediately—it was Dreya.

Tawni sat beside Dreya, barking out instructions. "Come on, Dreya. Fix the weinerdach's bows. They're crooked. She can't have poor style."

Jetta sat at Philecia's feet, her icy blue eyes surveying the room. Jenkins' mom entered, carrying a silver tray filled with delicious-looking fruit. She paused in front of Jetta and curtsied. "Where would you like this?"

Jetta nodded toward the ground.

Jenkins' mom placed it on the floor and the chatzkies ran to it.

"Wait!" Jetta commanded. "The weinerdach gets to eat first. Who wants to feed her this time?"

Many paws shot up as chatzkies stood on their hind legs and begged to be chosen.

"Me! Pick me!"

"Let me do it! I haven't had a turn!"

Jetta raised her voice. "Control yourselves. You know that it is a privilege I grant only to those who best behave." Jetta pointed to a chocolate brown chatzkie.

"You. I declare that it is your turn to feed the weinerdach."

Grumbles rippled through the room as the chocolate brown chatzkie bounced to the couch and clapped her paws.

"What can I serve you, oh Great Long One?"

Philecia leaned over the couch and licked her chops. "Oooo. The Oingo Fruit is so tasty, but I haven't tried those red berries yet. Umm ... Oh, how about a little of everything?"

"As you wish!" the brown chatzkie piped. It filled its mouth with the red berries then jumped on the couch. Philecia stretched out on her back and the chatzkie dropped the berries into her mouth one by one.

Jenkins tapped Ellis from behind. "What's in there, Ellis?"

Ellis turned and smiled. "Your mom and sister. And—"

"They are?" Jenkins pushed past Ellis and shoved the door open.

"Wait—the chatkies—"

But it was too late. Jenkins stood in full view.

For an instant, time stood still. The chatzkies stared in surprise. Jetta leaped to her feet. But no one in the room was more astonished than Jenkins' mother.

Ravina Jabbermeyer gripped the side of the couch as her knees started to buckle. One fist flew to her mouth and her smoky eyes misted. "Jenkins!" The word was a squeak. She raced to the entryway and scooped her son up in her arms, showering him with kisses—on his hair, his forehead, his cheeks.

"Jenkins!" A young voice giggled. Dreya sprang from the couch. She ran to her brother and flung herself on him. All three Jabbermeyers squeezed in a tight huddle, laughing and crying.

Philecia sat up. "Jenkins?" The bows on her head wiggled as she tried to perk up her ears.

The chatzkies looked at each other in confusion. "What's so big about Jenkins?" Jetta said crossly.

Ellis stepped through the doorway.

"Ellis!" Philecia jumped from the couch. She bolted across the room and in the next instant was in Ellis' arms.

"Philecia! Good girl. How's my girl?" Ellis squeezed his dog tight. Philecia's tail wagged so fast it was barely visible. Ellis cuddled her close to his cheek. "Are you okay? Did they hurt you?"

"Ellis I knew you'd come for me. I knew you would. Everything's okay. The chatzkies love me."

Ellis raised his eyebrows. "They do?"

"They like my long body. It's so perfect for going through tunnels. And the smell I can deliver ... well, let's just say the food here in Kibblestan has ten times the effect on me as those pepperoni treats at home."

Ellis grinned.

"Nobody cares about Charro anymore," Philecia continued. "Jetta and Tawni were right. The chatzkies are happy to have me around."

"What about Fandrella?" Ellis asked. "Did she see you?"

"I haven't seen her. Word has it she got all mad and flew off to Latinab."

"She did," Ravina Jabbermeyer said. Her grip on Jenkins and Dreya did not loosen as she eyed Ellis suspiciously. "Who is that, Jenkins?"

Before Jenkins could answer Tawni danced into the room, clapping her paws while hopping on her hind legs. "Oh goodie, goodie, goodie! The handsome Kootie has arrived. Now we can plan the wedding!"

"Wedding?" Jenkins looked up at Ellis.

"It's not, I mean, I'll tell you later," Ellis stammered. His eyes darted from the gleeful Tawni to the sullen Jetta. She remained on the couch, watching him. The skin on his forearm prickled at the memory of her last attack.

The other chatzkies wandered closer, staring with great curiosity.

"It's okay, guys," Philecia told them. "Ellis is my human. He won't hurt you."

Tawni stopped her dancing. "Human? What's that? I thought he was a Kootie."

Jetta leaped from the couch. "Yeah. That's what he told us. He's a Kootie who wants to marry Fandrella."

Philecia's ears fell and she glanced up at Ellis. "Er—he is. He—"

"Marry Fandrella?" Ravina Jabbermeyer raised her chin as she stepped protectively in front of her children. She fixed Ellis with the same steely gaze he'd seen on Jenkins a dozen times. "If you are marrying Fandrella, then we want nothing to do with you."

Dreya peeked out from behind her mother's skirt, making a face. "Fandrella? Really? Gross."

Ellis took a step back. How could he explain with all these chatzkies around? Would they rip out his throat if he came clean? Every eyeball in the room was upon him.

Waiting.

CHAPTER TWENTY-ONE

Ellis felt the blood run to his face. The chatzkies wanted an explanation. As did Ravina Jabbermeyer. Should he just tell the truth?

"Okay," he said, cradling Philecia close. "I'm not really a Kootie. And I don't want to marry Fandrella."

"What?" Tawni wailed like she'd lost her favorite chew toy. "You mean there won't be a wedding?"

Ellis shook his head. "I don't want to marry anyone. Where I come from I'm just a kid. Philecia and I came from the Other World and all we want to do is get back home."

Jetta's mouth turned down. "Fandrella will be plenty angry when she gets back. She doesn't want anyone in Fandrellaville except for creatures she's made, and Petikins she's saved."

"Yeah," Tawni said. "She only wants things she can control."

Ellis' insides clenched at the thought of facing Fandrella's wrath. When was she coming back? Could he face her alone? If only everyone else would turn against her, too.

225

"You guys need to get rid of Fandrella," he said. "I mean, all she does is boss you around. She practically killed everyone in Kibblestan. What makes you think she won't do the same thing to you someday?" The chatzkies looked at each other but no one said anything. Ellis continued. "I mean, did anybody vote to put her in charge?"

"Fandrella was appointed by the Kootie Council up in the Kootie Kingdom," Jetta said. "There's no voting. Besides, she created us."

"Well, where I come from, there's voting. No one becomes ruler unless the citizens vote on it. Besides, what kind of a life does Fandrella have planned here?"

"Boring," Dreya piped up. "All we do is work but we don't get anything good out of it."

Ravina smoothed her daughter's hair with her hand. "What she means is Fandrella has the few Petikins who live here gather food and water. She has plans for us to build other shelters in this forest, too, but it will all belong to her. Fandrellaville. We do all the work, but she says who gets what."

"Yeah," Dreya said. "And it's not fair. When Mom and I got here we were starving and we worked for hours gathering a bunch of food. But Fandrella took it from us and only gave us one piece of fruit to split. Then she gave the rest to everybody else, and some of those Petikins hadn't even gathered anything that day."

Ravina bowed her head. "It's true. This is not a happy place. Why work hard if you get no reward? If Fandrella thinks Fandrellaville is going to prosper, she's sorely mistaken."

"Where are the other Petikins?" Ellis asked.

"They're scattered throughout the forest," Ravina said. "Fandrella will call to us when she gets back. It's called Gathering Time. Everyone's supposed to turn in what they've gathered that day, though I've heard rumors that some are hiding things they don't want to be forced to share."

"That's where we come in," said Tawni. "We're supposed to spy and use our teeth to make sure everyone's playing by Fandrella's rules. But you know what? It's been a lot more fun hanging out with the weinerdach." Several chatzkies nodded their heads.

"Screeee-e-ech!" An ear-splitting squawk sounded outside. Ellis stepped to the door and looked out.

Ruthertold was gone. And several Petikins were coming through the trees.

"Screee-e-e-ch!" Louder this time. Closer.

Ellis searched the sky, remembering when he'd heard this sound before. Matilda had squeaked, "It's an owl! An owl that is hungry for mouse casserole!"

But it was no owl.

"Gathering Time." Ravina whispered. She rushed out of the house. "They're hearing the call. Gathering Time!"

More Petikins approached, clustering around the grassy clearing. Two pulled heavy wooden wagons, most carried buckets, and one didn't carry anything at all.

Screeeeeeech! The sound vibrated through the air. Ellis winced. Like a broomless witch, Fandrella soared above the treetops. Her arms stretched out to each side while her silvery blue gown flapped in the wind. Her legs were straight, talons curled. She dove toward the ground like a hawk after a field mouse. When she was a few feet from the grass her body shifted. She stretched her legs in front of her, talons first, and gracefully landed at the edge of the trees.

Ravina looked back to the house. "Jenkins," she said, "stay here. Dreya, come on." Dreya ran past Ellis and joined her mother. They trotted down the path to the group of Petikins. Fandrella strutted toward the crowd, a cruel smirk on her thin lips. "You didn't think I'd miss Gathering Time, would you?"

The Petikins looked at each other but did not say a word. They spread out in a circle, surrounding Fandrella.

"Very good," she said, slowly turning as she surveyed each Petikin with a sharp eye. She pointed at one and snapped her fingers. "You. Bring me your goods of the day."

A young teenage boy Petikin with brown hair and a face caked with dirt stepped forward, pulling a wagon. It was so heavy he had to lean with all his weight to move it. "I got a wagonload today," he panted. "Was up before anyone else. I even climbed a tree and got every piece of fruit in it." The Petikin shifted from one foot to the other as Fandrella examined the wagon's contents.

"Good job, Peter," she said. "I think that's the most I've seen anyone bring. You should be proud of yourself."

Peter broke into a smile. "Glad you think so, 'cause I'm awful hungry. I didn't even stop for lunch today." He started to reach into the wagon but Fandrella grabbed his wrist.

"What do you think you're doing?" she hissed.

Peter's eyes grew wide. "I-I was just going to take a piece of fruit. Please. I worked all day, and I'm so hungry."

"But we don't know how much fruit we have," Fandrella said. "We must divide it up equally." She yanked down on Peter's wrist.

"Ow!" He stumbled forward.

"Go on." Fandrella said, releasing his wrist. Peter hung his head and walked back to his place in the circle as the next Petikin approached.

This one looked older than Peter, not a boy but a young man. His hair was dark and shaggy and his eyes were barely visible underneath thick, crooked bangs. He swaggered forward with fists shoved in his pockets and a smirk across his face. He stood in front of Fandrella and blew his bangs out of his eyes while fixing her with a steady gaze. He dug in his pocket and extracted one small round orange fruit. His smile never wavered as he tossed it to the ground.

"Here's my contribution," he said. The Petikin sauntered back to his place in the circle.

Fandrella's eyes narrowed. "Brattley! That is all you gathered today? How is that possible?"

Brattley shrugged and rocked back on his heels. "Just didn't get around to it."

Fandrella's lip curled, but she said nothing. "Next!" Her voice was rough.

One by one the other Petikins tossed what they had gathered into the pile. Some had a full bucket of food, others only a couple of pieces. When it came time for Ravina and Dreya to contribute, Ravina explained. "Dreya and I have been busy tending to the chatzkies. We didn't have time to gather anything today."

Fandrella's mouth twisted down and her cheeks became hollow. She paced back and forth inside the circle. "It seems to me, that not everyone is cooperating." She clenched her teeth. "Some of you are working harder than others." She paused in front of Brattley. Her eyes flickered burgundy. "It is quite disturbing."

Brattley crossed his arms and met her piercing gaze. "Maybe if you let us keep what we work for, we'd be more motivated. Why should I bust my tail when I know you'll just take it away from me to give to someone else?"

Fandrella raised her arms and the shadows beneath her eyes darkened. "You selfish little—" She lifted off the ground and swiped her talons at Brattley's cheek. Brattley jumped back, barely dodging her blow. But while her claws missed his skin, they'd managed to wipe all the smugness from his face.

Fandrella smiled as she slowly clasped and unclasped her talons before his eyes. "Must I remind you it was I who pulled you from the slewedge? You owe me your life. All of you. You will obey my rules, or I will tear out your insides. And if you are hiding food away, if you are trying to cheat, don't think I won't find out. The chatzkies are watching. Always. I will summon them now, must you be reminded of what their teeth can do."

Fandrella shot up several feet into the air and glided toward the house. Ellis quickly stepped back inside the doorway.

"Charro!" Fandrella called. "Charro get your girls and come out here. These Petikins need to be taught a lesson."

Ellis looked at the chatzkies. Tawni and Jetta exchanged nervous glances.

"Who's going to tell Fandrella Charro is dead?" Tawni asked.

Panicked chatzkies chattered through the room.

"I'm not telling her, no way!"

"I hate it when she gets in a bad mood."

"Yeah, and that's all the time."

"She scares me!"

Ellis shifted Philecia in his arms and peered out the door. Fandrella floated toward the house, a look of murder across her tight-skinned face.

"Charro, come out here now!" she shouted.

Oh man. This was it. Time to face her. Fight her. But with what? As she stormed closer Ellis couldn't take his eyes off her talons—black, leathery, lethal. They didn't look like something found on a bird, more like the powerful claws of a velociraptor. And he had no weapons. Nothing to fight her with.

"Him!" Jetta shouted above the chatzkie babble, glowering at Ellis. "He's the one who killed Charro. He should take the blame."

All the chatzkies looked at Ellis. Ellis swallowed. "I know, but I didn't mean to. It was self-defense. It—it—"

Fandrella was right outside. No time to explain. No time for anything.

Time was up.

CHAPTER TWENTY-TWO

Fandrella waited a few feet outside the door, for a Charro who would never come. Any second her patience would run out and she'd tear inside and find out the truth. Then what?

Ellis seized an idea.

He raised Philecia high into the air and shouted to the chatzkies. "The weinerdach is your leader now! Not Fandrella. Let the weinerdach be in charge. She won't make you spy all the time. She won't make you be a police force that nobody likes. She'll let you do what you want. She'll let you be free. Free!"

Ellis put Philecia on the ground. He searched the mob of tiny dog faces. They adored Philecia. But was it enough to make them reject Fandrella?

At last, Jetta shouted. "Hail to the weinerdach!"

Silver-toothed grins rippled through the crowd. "Hail to the weinerdach!" the chatzkies shouted.

Ellis peeked back outside. The Petikins were traipsing up the path. Fandrella hovered a couple of feet above the ground, her face smoldering with rage. She tilted her head back and bellowed. "Charro-o-o!"

Her voice was that of an unleashed demon.

233

Jenkins squeezed Ellis' wrist. "What are you going to do?"

Ellis tightened his lips. "It'll be okay, dude." He called to the room. "Remember, she's only one." Ellis gripped the doorknob, his stomach in knots. He looked at Philecia. "Back me up, okay? Make sure they back me up."

Philecia's bulging eyes darted from Ellis to the chatzkies. But there was no time to wait for her to agree. Ellis flung the door open and charged out of the house. "Charro's not here," he yelled. The approaching Petikins stopped in their tracks, pointing and whispering.

Fandrella, however, did not make a sound. She froze, jaw open, hands clenched to the sides of her gown. The burgundy flame went out of her eyes, and her talons were still. She landed on the ground and squeezed her mouth into a blood-red slit as her eyes traveled from Ellis' hair to his lips—where they lingered a moment—before continuing their journey to his shoes.

Ellis stood on legs that quivered, his heart about to break free of his chest. Every muscle fiber tensed like the strings on a well-tuned guitar.

Fandrella raised her gaze. Her eyes bore into Ellis' with an intensity he'd never experienced. Ellis caught his breath. It wasn't anger in those eyes. It was ... It was ... what?

Fandrella stepped forward. Her nostrils flared and her eyes widened. Ellis stepped back but he couldn't break the stare. Why couldn't he look away? Why was she looking at him like this? Why?

At last she spoke. "Who are you?" Her voice was almost pleasant, that of a normal teenage girl, not a crazed demon. She tilted her head and smiled, but the intensity did not leave her gaze.

Ellis' lips parted but nothing came out. That look she gave him. Was it of a vulture who'd landed beside the juiciest roadkill? Or was it ... was it the look of a girl who'd just found her dream date to the prom?

Ellis swallowed back the bile rising in his throat.

Philecia whined. He could sense the chatzkies watching from the doorway. The group of Petikins closed in behind Fandrella, their curiosity obliterating any urge to run away. Everyone was watching. Better make this good.

"I'm Ellis. I'm from the Other World. And I know what you've been up to."

Fandrella drew back. Her brows lowered. "Other World? No one can come from the Other World but the unicorns. Do not lie to me. You look like a Kootie." Fandrella gave a hint of a smile. "Did the Kootie Council send you to learn about the fairest, most just ruler in history?" Fandrella's eyes traveled to Ellis' lips again and she smiled. "I don't mind." She reached out and stroked his hair. "I don't mind at all."

Ellis recoiled at her touch. He ducked away and circled around. "I'm not lying. You're the worst ruler in history. You made all those Snotlins so they'd kill everyone in Kibblestan."

Several Petikins gasped. Fandrella bit her lip and glanced their way.

"Well, it didn't work," Ellis continued. "The Snotlins are dead. I killed them. And there's a bunch of refugees who survived."

"You lie!" Fandrella let out a bloodcurdling screech and sprang into the air, talons headed for Ellis' face. Ellis dodged away. Fandrella flew past and landed hard on the ground. She turned and started toward him, eyes wild.

Ellis balled his fist.

Fandrella screeched again. Her forehead pulsated, as if maggots crawled just beneath her skin. Ellis charged at full speed. Before she could raise her talons he punched, popping Fandrella right between the eyes.

Fandrella screamed and clutched her face. She bent over and Ellis leaped onto her back. He wrapped his arm around her neck in a headlock and hung on with all his strength. Fandrella choked and cawed, tearing at his arms with her jagged fingernails.

"Charro!" she shrieked. "Charro help!"

"Charro's dead!" Ellis shouted. "The chatzkies aren't yours anymore."

Fandrella screeched again, and Ellis thought his eardrums might burst. She tried to lift off the ground but couldn't under Ellis' weight. Fandrella twisted and Ellis started to lose his grip. He dug his knees into Fandrella's lower back.

A horrible smell wafted through the air and Fandrella started to cough. Her fingernails cut into Ellis' arms, digging bloody trenches as she struggled to take a breath.

"What ... is ..." she tried to talk but her words were strangled.

From the corner of his eye Ellis saw a flash of brown as Philecia ran past. He knew the smell only too well. It was the smell that came whenever Philecia ate too many pepperoni treats, or in this case it was the Kibblestan food. His eyes watered as he tried not to inhale.

"Chatzkies!" Philecia hollered. "I call for a revolution. Attack! Attack Fandrella now! Show her she's not your boss. Show her you're free!"

Ellis pushed off Fandrella and slid to the ground as a tornado of chatzkies whirred their way. The tiny dogs landed all over Fandrella, sinking their deadly teeth into her arms, her neck, her legs, her cheeks. Fandrella screamed a guttural cry that shook the trees. She fell to her knees, grabbing the vicious beasts and attempting to pull them off without success. The chatzkies who couldn't find a spot to bite rallied around, cheering.

Ellis scooted back, breathing heavy as he watched the scene. Fandrella rose to her feet and twisted about, hitting and screaming. She took off into the air in an awkward, sputtering flight. She'd float up, then fall toward the ground, then fly up a little higher. This pattern continued until she was hovering as high as the roof of the house.

"Tell them to release me or I swear I'll go higher!" she cried, her face contorting with pain. "They can't hold on forever. You want them to fall to their deaths?"

Drops of blood sprinkled the grass. The chatzkies cast nervous glances at each other and whined.

"They can't die!" Tawni cried. "Jetta's up there!"

Ellis squinted and recognized the black chatzkie stuck to Fandrella's wrist. Her blue eyes bulged as she watched the ground slip further away. Fandrella's voice was raspy. "I ... will ... kill ... them." She called between strangled breaths. "If ... I die ... they die."

And Ellis realized Fandrella meant it. She would stay up in that sky until either the chatzkies let go or she died of her wounds. Either way, the chatzkies would fall to their deaths.

Philecia nudged Ellis' arm with her snout. "What do I do?" she asked. "They think I'm in charge."

Jenkins stepped through the doorway and joined them. "I don't want them to die," he said.

"Neither do I," said Ellis, surprised that the little critters had grown on him so much.

The mumbling from the group of Petikins on the pathway grew louder. Ellis looked their way. Some were still watching Fandrella, but others were looking toward the trees and pointing.

Jenkins ran to his mother. Ellis craned his neck to see what all the excitement was about. A strange animal scurried toward them. Its silver fur was caked with dirt and twigs and its eyeballs looked like they were ready to explode from their sockets. It was the lizamum.

"Here's the house!" he called over his shoulder. "I told you I could find it again. See? See? Believe me now?"

Trailing the lizamum came an unusual crowd. Buzzing fireflies, barking dogs, chittering mice and a mother chipmunk and her babies, all scampered through the grass. Ellis' heart soared as William marched toward him, leading a group of familiar-looking Petikins. It was the refugees from the habitat—they'd made it!

The lizamum stuck his nose in the air. "I did it! I showed them the way. I'm totally awesome." He pranced in a circle while Ravina, Jenkins and the other Petikins greeted the refugees with whoops and hollers.

However their jubilation was short-lived. Blood showered the ground, and all eyes were drawn to the spectacle in the sky.

Questions buzzed through the crowd of newcomers.

"What's happening to her?"

"What are those things hanging off Fandrella?"

Fandrella flailed her arms but only rose a few inches before her chatzkie-laden limbs fell to her sides. Mud-colored sweat dripped from her filthy clumps of hair. "No, no, no," she rasped. "It's not supposed to be this way. This wasn't the plan."

More blood sprinkled down, and Fandrella's face turned ashen.

Tawni ran up to Philecia, her eyes gaping. "Come on, Long One. Do something! Save them!"

The crowd gasped as a dark brown chatzkie lost its grip. Its shriek sounded like a referee's shrill whistle as it zoomed toward the ground and landed with a sick thud.

Ellis, Philecia and Tawni ran to the chatzkie. It lay on its stomach, legs bent in an awkward position. Its glassy eyes pooled with blood.

"No!" Tawni wailed.

Ellis reached out and stroked the broken chatzkie's head, searching for any sign of life. He found none.

"Ha!" Fandrella cackled. "They can't hold on forever!" Ellis looked to the sky. Fandrella's voice had lost all traces of sanity. She punched her arms in the air and rose higher.

Another chatzkie lost its grip. Without thinking, Ellis stretched out his hands and dove forward. He caught the chatzkie mid-air and rolled to the ground. Ellis lay on his back, panting. The chatzkie perched on his chest and stared into his eyes. It cocked its head and smiled, then hopped off of Ellis and rejoined the others.

Fandrella squawked and another chatzkie fell to its death before Ellis had time to react. He looked at Fandrella and realized with horror that these chatzkies weren't just falling. Some of them were within reach of Fandrella's talons. She was swiping these chatzkies from her body and plunking them to the ground.

Another chatzkie fell and Ellis sprang into action. He ran back and forth, catching as many chatzkies as he could. The crowds closed in, cheering. Two chatzkies fell at the same time. He dove for one while the other fell to its death.

A glossy black fur ball headed to the ground.

"Jetta!" Tawni cried. "No!"

Ellis scrambled to his feet but he was too far away, and Jetta was falling too fast.

"I'll get her!" Philecia hollered. The little brown dachshund ran toward the incoming chatzkie. She threw herself in Jetta's path right before she hit the ground.

The sound of the two dogs colliding was dwarfed by Tawni's frantic screams.

"Philecia!" Ellis rushed to the crumpled pile of fur. Jetta shook her head and slowly opened her eyes.

Beneath her, Philecia lay motionless.

CHAPTER TWENTY-THREE

No-no-no! The word screamed over and over in Ellis' brain. Jetta cast her eyes downward as she crawled off of Philecia's broken body and limped toward Tawni.

Ellis gently stroked the top of Philecia's head.

No response.

He lowered his face to Philecia's snout. Ever so slightly Philecia's breath warmed his cheek. Ellis felt like a brontosaurus had been lifted off his chest. She was breathing, but barely.

A hand squeezed Ellis' shoulder. He looked up. It was Jenkins. The little Petikin's lips trembled as tears welled in his eyes. He didn't say a word, but his firm grip on Ellis' shoulder said enough.

Ellis looked back to his little brown dog. "Philecia," he whispered. "Don't die. You're gonna be okay girl. You hear me? You're gonna be okay."

Ellis stifled a sob as he caressed Philecia's body, running his fingers over the protruding fur where shattered bones were shoved out of place. And what about her insides? Had they gotten crushed? Was she bleeding inside and he didn't even know it?

243

Ellis was numb to the gasps and shouts around him as another chatzkie fell to its death. Time stood still. For a brief moment, nothing else mattered.

"We be needin' a blanket or somethin'. Fast!" The familiar voice pulled Ellis from his fog. He looked around and saw William huffing toward him, flanked by three other Petikins.

"Ellis, me boy," he said. "I's so sorry 'bout your Philecia. She bein' okay?"

Ellis swallowed hard and shook his head. William looked down at the dachshund and whistled under his breath. "Aw, tis shame, it is." He clucked his teeth. "She bein' a hero, rightly so." He tousled Ellis' hair.

Tawni came out of the house, dragging a puffy, lavender blanket grasped firmly in her teeth. She dropped it at William's feet. "Here. From Fandrella's bed."

William grabbed the blanket and turned to the other three Petikins. "Let's go, maties. We be stretchin' this blanket here tight."

William and the other three Petikins positioned themselves underneath Fandrella and stretched out the corners of the blanket until it was taut.

"Hey, ye critters!" William shouted. "Stop yer chompin' and drop down here. We be catchin' ye little boogers. Promise."

The remaining chatzkies attached to Fandrella stared down with wide eyes. More blood rained down and

Fandrella hung her head. She looked close to passing out. They needed to hurry, or bye-bye chatzkies.

"Come on!" Ellis yelled. "You can trust those guys. They'll catch you."

The chatzkies hung like limp rag dolls. A few seconds passed and then one let go. It tumbled toward the ground and bounced off the blanket.

William grinned. "Told ye! Who's next?"

One by one the chatzkies detached their teeth from Fandrella's flesh and fell through the air. Each time the blanket broke their fall. At last, all the remaining chatzkies were safely back on the ground.

Fandrella drifted lower, eyes shut. "Good ... good ..." she breathed.

Ellis turned back to Philecia. She remained still. As he stared at his broken dachshund, rage swept through Ellis like he'd never felt before. He glared at Fandrella as she descended toward the ground. She looked like a pathetic teenage girl from a horror movie, with the blood-stained gown and empty face. She didn't look so threatening now.

Ellis clenched his fists and cried out, "You're no one's ruler anymore! Not Kibblestan's, not anybody's. You don't deserve it. You don't!" Ellis struggled for more words that could shout his loathing, that could describe the gut-wrenching hatred he felt right now.

But the words didn't come. Instead, he fell to his knees and grabbed one of the stones lining the pathway and hurled it with all his might. It smacked Fandrella in the forehead.

"Ow!" she cried. Her hand flew to her face. The hate filling her eyes was enough to kill an army, but Ellis didn't care. He scrambled for more rocks and pelted Fandrella over and over as she came his way. Blood pounded in his ears. His breath came in heaves. Any second he'd be ripped open by her velociraptor claws. He didn't care. He launched rock after rock in a blind fury.

Fandrella's screech tore through his ears. Ellis stopped his mad attack and looked around. Rocks and sticks and clods of dirt flew through the air. The crowd of Petikins were copying Ellis, grabbing anything they could find and lobbing it at Fandrella. Fandrella screeched again and covered her face.

"The lad is right." William shouted. "Kibblestan don't belong to any Kootie. Especially not a psycho like this one."

Fandrella floated into the air, batting at the objects flying her way.

"Get out!" the crowd yelled. "Kibblestan is ours!"

Fandrella's talons expanded, then curled. Her lips stretched in a tight grimace and her eyes looked glassy. "You ... selfish ... idiots," she gurgled from deep within her throat. "You are nothing without me. If I'm not here to control you, who will?"

A high-pitched squeak cried out. "We will, you big meanie! We will control ourselves, yes we will! Yes we will!" The crowd opened up and there was Matilda, jumping up and down and swinging her tiny fists. Her new friend Gustav stood close by, watching her fury with a look of admiration.

Fandrella's eyes narrowed as she lifted a talon. But Matilda didn't waver. Gustav crossed his arms and fixed Fandrella with a defiant scowl. The Petikins moved in and formed a protective barrier.

"Get out! Out! Kibblestan is ours!" They shouted.

"But you need me!" Fandrella bellowed. "I know what's best for you!"

"Hmmm. Nope, not really," a drowsy voice drawled. Coming up the pathway, leaving a trail of slobber, plodded the rickety, gray unicorn. "Fandrella, you're done," Bob said. "Kibblestan's spoken."

Fandrella floated higher, her face a mix of blood and tears. "But I am in charge! A Kootie has to be in charge. It's been that way since the beginning of time."

Bob shrugged. "So." He casually bent down and nibbled the grass.

Fandrella's eyes gleamed with murderous rage. "So? I'll tell you what's so. You are ignorant little fools if you think you can survive on your own. Without my guidance. Without me here to keep things fair. Just wait until one of you gets sick. Wait until someone cheats you. Wait until you injure yourself and you can't gather your own food or water. What then? Who will take care of you?"

"We will!" The crowd's shouts were louder than Fandrella's screeching. "We will take care of each other. Get out!"

Bob looked up, blades of grass stuck to his chin. "You heard 'em. They don't need you. Don't trust you. Always told you, gotta earn their trust, but you wouldn't listen. Just wanted to control 'em more and more, 'til you ended up killing 'em. Don't have trust, can't rule in peace."

Fandrella gnashed her square teeth. She squeezed her eyes shut and clutched the sides of her head. "But-but ..."

"It's over," Bob continued. "I'm telling the Kootie Kingdom. There's been a revolution. Kibblestan's no longer under Kootie rule. Period." Bob lowered his head and chomped the grass.

Fandrella bit her lip. She clawed at her face. "You— you can't do this!"

Bob didn't bother looking up. "'Fraid I can. If the citizens don't want their Kootie, the Kootie is banned from their land." Bob stopped chewing and looked up. "Don't be actin' like you didn't know. You learned all that in your Kootie Academy. Just never happened before." The unicorn buried his muzzle back in the grass.

Fandrella's forehead swelled as the veins beneath it threatened to pop. She let out a demon scream and shot through the air. The last thing anyone heard was her throaty screech. "You'll regret this!" Then she disappeared beyond the trees.

Everyone was quiet for a moment. Was she gone? Gone for good?

William broke the silence with a loud "Waa-hoo-hoo-hoo!" His shout was followed by cheers and hollers. Petikins jumped up and down, chatzkies giggled their crazy laughs, fireflies buzzed at full speed. Jenkins ran to Ravina and Dreya, and hugged them tight.

Everyone was celebrating but Ellis, who knelt by Philecia's side. Her breath was faint. Her eyes remained shut. She needed help. He looked at all the happy faces surrounding him. Didn't anybody care?

Matilda scampered his way, followed by Gustav. "Ellis, Ellis, how's Philecia? She'll be okay, yes she will?" The brown mouse stopped a few inches from the dachshund. Her paws flew to her cheeks as she surveyed Philecia up close—the lifeless body, the protruding bones, the trickle of blood that stained her lips. Matilda shrieked, "No!" She shook her head vigorously. "Oh no-no-no-no!"

"Matilda," Ellis said gruffly. "Listen to me."

The little brown mouse raised her head. Her beady eyes were wet.

"She's going to be okay," Ellis said. "We just need to get her some help. Stay with her, will you? Don't leave her alone."

Matilda nodded. Her lips quivered. Gustav came up behind her and squeezed her shoulders. Their tails intertwined as they stood vigil by the injured dachshund.

Ellis stood up, searching the jubilant crowd. Who could help? Who would know what to do?

In the distance, a small figure lurched from the trees. It limped through the clearing with slow, jerky movements. Jenkins ran down the pathway, Dreya and Ravina close behind. The figure picked up speed and as it drew closer Ellis recognized it—grizzled beard, bald head, bony frame beneath shabby clothes. Thornton Jabbermeyer hobbled toward his family, and trotting closely behind were Rabio and Raquel.

Ellis ran toward them. Thornton collapsed to his knees, embracing his wife, while Dreya and Jenkins clung to his back like a couple of monkeys.

Jenkins shouted. "Dad! You made it! You're alive!"

"Yes I am," Thornton said through happy tears. "That mouse Matilda and her friend Gustav found a tiny bone left behind by the dogs. Gustav stuck it in the lock and pop! It sprung open and that awful iron cuff came off."

Raquel's sapphire eyes sparkled beneath her orange bonnet. "Then Bob came, after everyone had left the habitat."

Thornton nodded, still hugging his family. "That's right. He drooled on my leg and look! It's nearly good as new."

Thornon pulled up his pant leg. Sure enough, the angry red stripes and puddle of pus had been replaced by a silver, glittery scar.

Ellis smacked his forehead. Of course! Bob! Who could help Philecia better than the unicorn with healing spit?

But where was Bob? Ellis looked around, and spied the unicorn at the side of the house, munching grass. Ellis ran to him.

"Bob!" Ellis said. "You've got to fix Philecia. She's hurt real bad."

Bob sauntered over to the dachshund. Matilda and Gustav moved aside as Bob lowered his muzzle over Philecia's face. A long strand of drool plopped onto her snout. Her nose twitched, but her eyes remained closed, her body unmoving.

"Hmmmm," Bob's lips squished together. His heavy-lidded eyes raked Philecia's body. "Don't know how much I can do. Lots of bones broke. Probably crushed."

Tears stung Ellis' eyes. Philecia not fixable? Never. "Just fix her!" he shouted.

Bob raised his wiry eyebrows. "Okay, okay. Do what I can. Just not makin' any promises." He lowered his head. "Open her mouth."

Ellis knelt down and gently turned Philecia's head. He stuck his fingers in the folds of her lips and eased her jaw open. Bob aimed his long strand of drool. He lowered his jaw and more saliva bubbled over his chin and dropped into Philecia's mouth. Ellis closed her jaw and tilted her head back, stroking her throat.

"Swallow, girl. Swallow." Ellis whispered into Philecia's ear. At last the skin under Philecia's neck contracted. She'd swallowed! Ellis scratched her belly, her ears, every favorite scratching spot he knew. "Come on, girl! Wake up."

Slowly, Philecia's eyes blinked open. They seemed glassy, doll-like at first. But eventually the light of life ignited inside them. She lifted her head and looked around.

"What happened?" Her voice was groggy. "Why do I feel so weird? So tingly?"

Ellis smiled through his tears, his hands not leaving her frail body. "Careful! Careful, girl. Take it easy."

Philecia laid her head back down. Matilda clapped her paws and twirled around. "I knew she'd be okay, yes I did."

"You got pummeled by a flying chatzkie," Ellis said. "Do you remember?"

Philecia's tongue slowly wriggled in a slurping motion. She moved her paws to stand and yelped.

Ellis sat up straight. "What's wrong? Philecia?"

Philecia grimaced as she struggled to get up. "It hurts," she grunted.

Ellis looked at Bob. "What's going on?"

"Told you. It's tricky. Spit's good to strengthen, nourish. Heals cuts real good. But broken bones, insides tore up. Helps some, but can't make perfect." Bob looked at the ground. "Sorry."

Ellis couldn't believe it. He didn't want to believe it. He gripped Philecia's body. "Come on girl, stand up. I'll help you."

The little dachshund pushed down on her short legs and whimpered. "Ouch!" Philecia's nostril's flared as she took deep breaths. Her brow lowered in extreme concentration. "Okay. Okay. Let me go."

Ellis let go of Philecia and smiled as she stood on her own four paws. "All right!" he cheered. "Now can you take a step?"

Philecia's teeth clenched as she shuffled one paw forward, then another. Her movements were shaky, but she was moving.

"She just needs to practice, yes she does." Matilda said. "She'll get better in no time, yes she will. She will!"

Ellis looked up at Bob. "Is that right? Will she get better?"

Bob chewed on his lip. "Sure," he mumbled. But he didn't meet Ellis' eyes.

Tawni ran over. "The weinerdach! Great Long One! She's walking!" Tawni bowed in front of Philecia, wagging her stumpy tail.

"Y-yes," Philecia stammered, still wincing in pain. "I can walk."

"I'll go and tell Jetta," Tawni said. "She'll be so relieved you're all better. You've proven your love and loyalty to us chatzkies. We will follow you for life!"

Tawni loped off, singing "Weinerdach rules! Weinerdach rules!"

Ellis smiled down at Philecia. "You see girl? You're a hero. Bet you didn't think you'd ever be someone's hero, huh?"

As Ellis gazed at his beloved dachshund a thought occurred to him. An incredible thought. An overwhelming thought. Something almost too good to contemplate, as he realized what Kibblestan's freedom truly meant.

Ellis whirled around. "Bob!" He shouted, though the unicorn stood only a couple of feet away. Ellis' words gushed forth. "Bob, Kibblestan's free. You don't need me anymore. You can send me back. Me and Philecia—and Matilda if she doesn't want to stay here with Gustav." Ellis picked up Philecia and snuggled her against his shoulder. "We're going back, girl, and I'll take you to a real vet. He'll fix you up nice."

Ellis' heart felt like it had been high-jacked by a hot air balloon. He closed his eyes, imagining that moment of entering his house, his parents sleepless with worry. They probably had all of the neighbors and even the police out looking for him. Was his picture posted everywhere? Had he been on the news?

A smile played on his lips as he imagined his mom showering him with kisses. The Vulture Voyagers giving him high-fives. Maybe even Duane Ratsman would give him a friendly elbow.

But the best part would be seeing Dad. He'd give him the biggest hug of his life and tell him how sorry he was for what he had said.

Ellis opened his eyes. "I just need to say good-bye to my friends real quick, then we can go."

Bob dropped his gaze. He scuffed the ground with his hoof, mumbling.

"What'd you say?" Ellis stepped closer to the unicorn. Bob kept his eyes downcast, still mumbling.

Ellis sighed. "Bob, I can't hear you. Let me go say good-bye to my friends and you can tell me on the way back to my world." Ellis turned and headed toward the Jabbermeyers.

Bob spoke, this time loud and clear. And his words drove a sword into the balloon carrying Ellis' heart.

"You can't go back."

CHAPTER TWENTY-FOUR

Ellis turned on the unicorn. "What do you mean, I can't go back?" he shouted. He felt like punching Bob in his slobbery mouth. How could he magically bring them here, and not send them home? "I'm not staying here. No way!"

Bob stepped back. "Okay, okay. It's just ... the trees are sealed back up."

"Yeah," Ellis said. "They closed up as soon as we got through."

Bob's mouth turned down. "Was afraid of that."

Ellis' brow lowered. "So. You'll just have to open them up again."

Bob's chunky teeth gnawed his spongy lips. Spit streamed everywhere. "Ellis, think we should talk." Bob stepped toward him and cocked his head. His sleepy eyes became clear. "Come. Walk with me."

Ellis clenched his jaw and tightened his arms around Philecia. He followed the unicorn past the crowds, past the house, all the way to the edge of the trees.

Bob stared at Ellis, seeming to choose his words carefully. "Ellis, I don't think it's by chance that you're here. Think there's more for you to do."

Ellis felt like someone had pummeled his back and knocked the wind out of him. How could Bob say this? How could there be anything more to do? Fandrella was gone.

"Look, there's nothing else for me to do. Just send me back. Come on." Ellis shifted Philecia in his arms.

Bob hung his head. "I know you miss your home. Prob'ly have a family—"

"Yes!" Ellis said. "I've got a mom and dad who are worried sick about me. I've got friends and school and Vulture Voyager campouts. I've got a life back there. I can't stay in Kibblestan."

Bob nodded. "I know, I know. But here's the deal. When I go tell the Kootie Council what's happened, they'll ask about sending another Kootie from their Academy to take Fandrella's place, and I'm not going to recommend it. Kibblestan won't be able to trust a Kootie again. Not after it's happened twice."

Ellis' brow puckered. "Twice? What do you mean twice?"

Bob lowered his voice. "Not supposed to talk about it. No one is. Kootie Council just wants it to be forgotten. But I know it's in the back of everyone's mind." Bob's nostrils flared as he snorted. "See, long time ago, Latinab wasn't just some explodin' volcano. Was a real country. And just like all the other countries this side of the Grand Forest, it was ruled by a Kootie." Bob paused and looked around before continuing. "Well, that Kootie lost his way. Became evil. Did some terrible, terrible things. Finally, the whole mountain blew up."

Ellis frowned. "Did the people—or whatever—did they blow up too?"

Slowly, Bob nodded. "Yep. No one knows the full story. No Petikin lived to tell. But plenty of rumors. Rumors that floated from one land to the next. Finally everyone started gettin' all paranoid about their Kootie. What if their Kootie turned evil? Why did they need a Kootie ruler in the first place? When word got back to the Kootie Kingdom that citizens were havin' their doubts, the Kootie Council called on us unicorns."

Bob lifted his head. "We became the advisors. Thought with our guidance, no Kootie would get too powerful, or turn evil, and the citizens' trust would be restored." Bob looked to the ground. His ears drooped. "But, that didn't quite happen. 'Least not in Kibblestan."

Ellis' mouth turned down. "Yeah, but now it's over. You don't need me. There's been a revolution. Kibblestan's free."

Bob looked up, an odd gleam in his eyes. "But will it stay free?"

Ellis buried his face in Philecia's fur. "Come on. Can't you do something to make sure Fandrella doesn't come back?"

"I can tell the Kootie Council. They'll take away her authority. But that doesn't mean she can't come back on her own."

Ellis shifted Philecia to his shoulder. "But—but if she comes back, everyone will hate her. They won't do what she says."

Bob raised an eyebrow. "Wouldn't be so sure. Seen it enough in your world, Ellis. People havin' short memories. Get caught up in their own lives and don't pay attention to what's goin' on around 'em. Dangerous way to live. Evil rises up, and no one notices 'til it's too late."

Ellis shuddered.

Bob continued. "If the citizens really want to keep Fandrella from weaselin' back into Kibblestan, they've got to work at it. Value freedom. Treat each other as equals. And never forget history. Some of the worst evils come about when people start throwin' out labels, putting each other in some kind of group or class, instead of seein' people for what they really are. Just people." Bob smiled, displaying grimy donkey teeth.

Ellis rubbed the back of his neck. What Bob said made a lot of sense. But couldn't Kibblestan figure all this out without his help?

Bob continued. "Ellis, they need a framework. Somethin' that will keep another leader from goin' down the same road as Fandrella."

Ellis sighed. "Okay, okay. Well, you seem pretty smart. Why don't you tell them? Tell them what you've seen in my world—what works and what doesn't."

Bob's eyes fell. "Won't listen to me. Everyone knows me as the pathetic unicorn that Fandrella never listened to. And now, after what's happened, I'm prob'ly considered the biggest failure this side of the Grand Forest." Bob's voice hitched. Was he stifling a sob? Ellis tried to meet Bob's gaze but his eyes remained downcast. He reached out and stroked Bob's neck. "You did the best you could."

Bob slowly nodded. "No matter. Just need to move forward. But I don't think Kibblestan is ready to let you go."

Ellis stopped petting. Let him go? Bob talked like he was a prisoner. "What do you mean?" Ellis' voice squeaked.

"Remember when I told you it was my fault you're here? Well, it's true that I opened up the trees. But never could have done it without that hole."

"What hole?"

"Was walking by the Grand Forest and saw this flicker of light. Real strange. Was a tiny opening between the two largest tree trunks, 'bout the size of a quarter. Never happened before. I mean never. Thought woundn't it be something if the forest could be broken. Rammed my horn into the hole and the trees split apart.

Couldn't believe it. They split apart and must have stayed apart 'til you came here."

"Yeah. So."

"When those trees split, I thought it was a sign. Hoped help was on its way." Bob's eyes danced. "Think I was right about that. But I can't figure out how that tiny hole got there in the first place. Or what made the forest seal back up once you came through."

Ellis opened his mouth but nothing came out. He had no answers, either.

Bob continued. "So that's what's making me think. Maybe there's something else going on. Some kind of bigger plan. Kind of like your world, Ellis. Things happen, and some people like to think of it all as chance. But maybe it's part of something bigger. Something too big for any of us to understand. But just because you can't explain it, doesn't mean it doesn't exist."

Ellis' chest tightened as he looked around. A silver light flickered deep within Bob's granite eyes. "Kibblestan needs to stand on its own. Teach Kibblestan what you know. America fought for its own freedom. It's fought for the freedom of others. Teach them how your country did it."

Ellis groaned. Teach Kibblestan about America? If only Dad were here. He'd told him so much about freedom and democracy. Maybe it wasn't such a waste of time after all. "I guess I can try. So if I teach Kibblestan what I know—try and get their government in place—you think I'll be able to go back?"

Bob smiled. "I think so."

Ellis looked across the clearing. How could he do this quick? In America it'd taken years, what with the Articles of Confederation, and then the Constitutional Convention.

Philecia licked his cheek and Ellis grinned. The Constitution. That's it. Kibblestan needed a constitution.

"I know," Ellis said. "I'll write a constitution for Kibblestan. If I write one, then can I go home?"

Bob winked. "Now you're talkin'." He started to walk off into the trees.

"Wait!" Ellis said. "Where can I find you once its written?"

"Don't worry 'bout findin' me. I'll be findin' you ... when the time is right."

"Wait!" Ellis yelled again but this time Bob didn't stop and turn. He continued through the trees until he disappeared altogether.

Ellis trudged back toward the house. Constitution. Constitution. What had he learned about the Constitution?

The chatzkies still frolicked by the pathway but most of the other animals had wandered off. The Petikins remained clustered around Thornton, who was telling the tale of his capture and imprisonment. When he described the role that the chatzkies had played, some Petikins glared at the little animals.

"Now that we're ruling our own country, maybe we shouldn't allow chatzkies in Kibblestan at all," one Petikin said.

"Yeah," said another. "If we can drive Fandrella away, we can drive them away."

But Jetta overheard the conversation, and the fur on her back stood on end. She snarled and started to creep up on one of the unsuspecting Petikins.

"Jetta! Stop!" Ellis yelled.

The Petikin turned in surprise. Jetta froze, but her eyes flickered.

Ellis caught his breath. What if she'd attacked? What would have happened? Would the Petikins ever be able to trust the chatzkies? Would they be able to live together in peace? Ellis remembered what Bob had said. Treat each other as equals. Maybe it wouldn't be so easy, especially after everyone heard Thornton's tale.

Ellis addressed the crowd. "Listen to me. I know in Thornton's story, the chatzkies were bad, but that's because they were under Fandrella's rule. They won't attack any Petikins now." Ellis paused, looking to the chatzkies. "Right?" The chatzkies cocked their heads, staring back. Ellis started to sweat. Come on guys. Tell me I'm right.

Tawni spoke. "Of course. We were just doing what we were told."

Ellis smiled. "See? The chatzkies aren't under Fandrella's rule anymore." He lifted Philecia high above his head. "The weinerdach is their ruler now. She won't tell them to hurt you."

A few mumbles floated up from the crowd. Thornton pressed his lips together. He still looked wary.

Ellis put Philecia on the ground and the chatzkies swarmed her as they chattered with excitement.

"Hail to the Great Long One!"

"Come in the house with us!"

"Where are your manners? Let the weinerdach go first!"

"The weinerdach gets Fandrella's bed!"

The chatzkies crowded Philecia so much that Ellis could barely see her head as she looked back to him and smiled. She sure looked happy, even though her movements were painfully slow. Would she ever be able to run again?

William and Rabio walked by. "So, me little rat friend," William said. "What ye be doin' now? Should we all be settlin' in these parts?"

Rabio scratched his chin. "I suppose the first order of business will be to proclaim the news to all of Kibblestan. Some of the refugees did not choose to travel here. They did not heed my advice and traveled on to the old parts of Kibblestan instead, to see what is left of their homes."

William looked around. "Ah," he scoffed. "Most Petikins are here. Just looks like some of 'em like Blotu and crew didn't make it."

Rabio nodded.

William shrugged. "Who cares? No hurry in tellin' those ruffians. They don't deserve to enjoy the new freedom anyway. They didn't fight for it."

Rabio shook his head. "William, we cannot think like that. If we are to rule ourselves, we must treat each other as equals."

Wow. Hadn't Ellis just heard that?

"Rabio," Ellis said. "We need to write a Constitution for Kibblestan. It's what America has. It's kind of like a bunch of rules Americans follow and believe in. Kibblestan needs that, but it's got to be agreed upon by the people—or the Petikins."

Ellis thought hard, back to everything he'd learned in school about American History, and about what Dad had taught him. America had had a Constitutional Convention. Time for Kibblestan to have one, too.

Ellis watched the Petikins crowding around Thornton. Many of them stared after the chatzkies, a look of suspicion in their eyes. A shiver ran down his spine. He could write a constitution. But, would they follow it?

CHAPTER TWENTY-FIVE

Ellis sat in the dim candlelight, his pen suspended over the crinkled yellow piece of parchment. "You want what?"

Matilda's beady eyes resembled two shiny black pearls. "Cheese. All mice should get as much cheese as they want, yes they should."

Ellis let his pen drop and sighed. "Come on, Matilda. I can't write that. This is a constitution, not some wish list."

A low grunt came from the dark corner of the cave. "You start writing stuff like that and I'm out of here. But first I'll be pummeling me some mouse brains."

Matilda's whiskers quivered.

"Nobody's pummeling any mouse brains, Blotu," Ellis said. "Besides, I'm not writing anything down that everyone doesn't agree on." He squeezed his eyes shut, rubbing his forehead. "Now can we just get done with this? It's taking forever."

And it really was taking forever. Writing a constitution was not as easy as Ellis had hoped it would be. After he'd returned from his conversation with Bob and explained to the group of Kibblestan survivors that he'd be writing their country's new constitution, everyone went nuts.

Petikins and animals and chatzkies alike had shouted their ideas, screaming louder and louder so they could be heard. Some had trampled over each other, desperate to get to Ellis and cry out their demands. The swirling chaos took Ellis by surprise as the crowds pressed in all around him.

Out of nowhere, Matilda screamed at the top of her lungs. The high-pitched sound was like a nail gun shooting into the ears. The little mouse smiled proudly as it got everyone's attention.

However it was Rabio's calm, cool demeanor that settled the masses. He explained that it would be impossible for everyone to be included in the writing of the Constitution, but that they could have a vote right then and there to choose who would represent them at Kibblestan's own Constitutional Convention. A vote was taken, sending Thornton to represent the Petikins and Rabio to represent the animals. The chatzkies, however, insisted on sending their own representative—Philecia, their beloved weinerdach.

Ellis had invited Matilda along to serve as a witness, but it was at Rabio's insistence that Blotu ended up being a part of the Constitutional Convention.

Rabio thought they should track down the Petikins who had gone to other parts of Kibblestan to inform them of what was going on. He was afraid if they didn't, then those Petikins wouldn't recognize the Constitution and might refuse to live under it at all.

Unfortunately, those Petikins included Blotu and many members of Fandrella's old R & R.

Days passed, until finally Rabio returned with Blotu in tow. The small group took some candles and matches from the house, as well as a pile of parchment and pen found underneath Fandrella's bed, and were off. They holed themselves up in a dank cave that smelled like wet leaves and rotting wood. It was located deep in the woods, where no one would bother them.

Ellis sat with the stack of parchment piled in front of him. The candlelight cast flickering shadows on its yellowed, waxy surface. Everyone sat in an intimate circle except Blotu, who remained in the corner.

"I guess the first thing you guys should decide on is who's in charge." Ellis said.

"We are," Thornton said. "I mean, we the citizens of Kibblestan. Right?"

"Well, yes," Ellis said. "But you've got to have a leader. Not a king or queen, or a dictator that bosses everyone around. But you need someone to take the lead or it'll be chaos."

"That's easy," Blotu said. "Put me in charge. Write that in."

Rabio looked at Blotu steadily. "We are not going to have just one individual in charge. That lends itself to the same risk that we had before—of that leader getting corrupted by power, just like Fandrella."

Blotu snorted. "Then why did you drag me here, if you're not going to take my ideas? I told you me and my group aren't going to follow your rules no matter what you say, unless we like them." Blotu slunk out of the corner. The candlelight lit up his scowling face, his pink forehead a ladder of lines. "This is a waste of time," he grumbled, and headed for the exit.

"Hold on!" Rabio leapt to his feet. "Don't go. Master Ellis, please. Surely, you have some ideas?"

Ellis took a deep breath, his mind reaching for all the constitutional jumbly junk Dad had taught him that he never thought he'd ever use. "Okay," he said. "In America, we have a president. But our Constitution makes it so he's not like all powerful. You see, there's three parts, or branches, of government and the president is only one part, the executive branch. He enforces the laws but he doesn't make the laws. That's up to Congress."

"Who's Congress?" Blotu demanded, folding his arms across his chest. "Is he the president's boss?"

Ellis stifled a giggle. "No. The Congress is a bunch of people. Representatives from each state."

Ellis paused and looked around. The only response was a collection of blank stares. His mind spun. "Okay, you guys had a village, right?"

"More than one, Master Ellis." Rabio said. "Kibblestan had many villages. And we had our own leaders. The Kooties were there to watch over all of Kibblestan, but to my knowledge they did not participate in the village affairs very much—that is, until Fandrella came along."

"Okay," Ellis said. "Now we're getting somewhere. In America, we have states, which are big pieces of land where people live and have their own government. But what makes us one country instead of just a bunch of states is our federal government. Everyone votes on the president and then everyone in each state gets to vote on people to go represent them in Congress."

Rabio fingered his whiskers. "And tell us, Master Ellis. What does this Congress do?"

"They don't give mice cheese, that's for sure," Matilda squeaked. "But Kibblestan's Congress could be different, yes it could."

Ellis ignored Matilda's comment. "It's called the legislative branch," he said. "It makes the laws. So say someone has an idea for a new law, they call it a bill. Everyone in Congress talks about it and votes on it and if it wins the majority of votes, then it goes to the president. Then he can sign it and it becomes a law."

"But what if it's a stupid law?" asked Blotu.

"Well," Ellis said. "If the president doesn't like the law then he doesn't have to sign it. That's called a veto."

"But what if the law wasn't stupid, hmmm? Hmmm?" Matilda asked.

"Like giving all mice cheese? Give me a break!" Blotu scoffed.

"The president doesn't have the final say," Ellis said. "The Congress can vote again, and if two-thirds of their votes are for the bill, it becomes law even though the president vetoed it."

Blotu stood up. "That sounds like a bunch of work just to get a law. It'd be much easier to have the president do everything."

"No, but don't you see?" Rabio's eyes shined. "Why, it is ingenious, really. We'd have a president in charge, with powers that are limited by the representatives of the animals."

"And the Petikins," Blotu said.

"And don't forget chatzkies," Philecia said.

"And mice," Matilda jumped up. "There has to be lots of representatives of mice, yes there does. In the Other World, mice don't get to do anything, no they don't."

"So if you do it that way," Ellis said, "you don't have one person telling everyone what to do. Because what if the president became evil, you know?"

Everyone nodded thoughtfully.

"Oh," Ellis added. "And there's also another branch of government, called the Judicial branch. It interprets the laws. So if people disagree about what a law really means or whether it follows the Constitution, judges can settle it."

Matilda hopped up and down. "I want to be that, yes I do. A judge. It takes much wisdom, yes it does. And I have that, yes I do, I do."

"So a president cannot make a law on his own," Thornton said. "He can only veto a law or sign a law."

Blotu shook his head. "Sounds lame. I'd rather be Congress so I could make the laws."

"Well then, you can be," Rabio said.

Thornton flashed Rabio a look of contempt. "I'm not sure Blotu can be in Congress," he said firmly, avoiding Blotu's hot gaze. "Or that he should be."

Blotu growled as he clenched his fists. He stood up and walked over to where Thornton was sitting. "Watch what you say, Jabbermeyer. You want another beating? This time I might finish you off for good."

But Thornton didn't back down. He stared at Blotu with defiance. "Those refugees out there know the truth. They know Fandrella was trying to kill them. And they know that you were on her side. Maybe not the killing part, but you enjoyed getting rich under her rule."

Blotu's jaw tightened. He leaned over Thornton, staring him down.

Thornton's gaze didn't waver. "You liked being a Resource Redistributor, with the power to choose who did and didn't get water. In fact you profited off of it, while telling everyone else that it was William and I who were selfish. All we were doing was trying to find a way for our village to have our own water, and not be so dependent on Fandrella."

Blotu sneered. "But you would have wanted to get paid for that. You would have made it so that Petikins would have to pay you for the water you made."

Thornton jumped to his feet. His face contorted and the fire in his eyes was not from the candlelight. "And why shouldn't they?" he hollered. "It was an underground starjelo colony. If I was the one with the idea, if I worked hard to build it, and it was something the villagers wanted and needed, why should I not get paid? It's a lot more honest than your system of Fandrella spitting her 'free water' that's slimy and slobbery and never enough. And you got paid in secret not for what you produce, but for your connections to power!"

Blotu's lip remained puffed out, his eyebrows drawn. His nose wrinkled as his eyes appraised the angry, grizzled Petikin. He drew back his fist.

Ellis leapt to his feet. "Stop!" he shouted. His voice cracked the tension in the air, and Thornton and Blotu looked his way. Ellis cleared his throat. "Uh ... let's get back to the Constitution, okay?"

Blotu's fist fell to his side and he took a step back, his eyes locked with Thornton's. Philecia whined. Matilda's ears and tail drooped.

"Come on," Ellis said. "The Constitution. Should I write that Kibblestan will have a Congress? And Blotu, if you get elected you can be in it, okay? Once you get to rebuilding all your villages, each village can vote on a representative to send to Congress. And that person—I mean Petikin," Ellis paused and looked at Rabio. "Or animal—just whoever is elected gets to be part of Kibblestan's Congress. They will make the laws, and Kibblestan's President—"

"How about its Count?" Matilda interrupted. "'Kibblestan's Count sounds better than Kibbestan's president, yes it does."

Ellis rolled his eyes. "Okay, whatever. We can have a Count of Kibblestan that will be like a president, then a Congress, and then once the Count is elected he or she can choose someone to be a judge. How's that for a start?"

Ellis looked around the darkened space. Rabio paced back and forth in deep thought. Thornton and Blotu's glares cooled. Philecia wagged her tail, her brown eyes warm. And Matilda made a clicking sound as she absently preened her fur.

Finally, Rabio stopped his pacing and spoke. "So be it."

Ellis smiled and bent over the parchment, writing furiously. This was it. Kibblestan's Constitution was agreed upon. As soon as he wrote this thing his job would be done. It'd been over a week. Bob was probably waiting for him back at the house, ready to escort him home.

There's no way he'd be stuck in Kibblestan much longer. There wasn't anything more for him to do. Was there?

CHAPTER TWENTY-SIX

Ellis lay on Fandrella's bed, staring at the flaking ceiling. Chunks of it looked like they could fall right on top of him. He didn't care.

The sound of chatzkies playing downstairs held a happiness he couldn't feel. "Oh look! Philecia's coming! Quick! Get her a bone!"

"Dad! Dad! Guess what I found in the woods today?" Dreya's voice stormed the house. "A worm that was stuck in the well. I rescued it, Dad! I did!"

"I'm proud of you, Dreya ..." Thornton's voice faded as Ellis closed his eyes, his thoughts carrying him to another place, another time.

"I'm proud of you, Ellis," Javier Garcia smiled down, his dark eyes crinkling. "You worked hard today, just like a man. Have an ice cream cone."

It was his favorite memory. Just he and Dad, eating ice cream cones one night, long after the shop closed. Ellis was only eight, small enough that his legs dangled from the stool on which he sat. But that hadn't stopped him from helping Dad work the shop that day. He could remember looking at Dad over his double decker ice cream cone, staring into his eyes, and the warm feeling he got when he recognized what was in them. Approval. Love.

This was the memory that Ellis clung to every time that other memory—the hateful words, the pain in those very same eyes—tried to surface. The thought of that stupid fight was plain torture, especially when Ellis lay awake at night, wondering if he'd ever get to see Dad again.

Weeks had passed. Each day Ellis awoke from another restless night, trying to convince himself that this would be the day—the last day stuck in Kibblestan.

"When the time is right," Bob had said. But when would the time be right? Why wasn't it now? The Constitution was written and Kibblestan was doing fine. Great, even.

Thornton had been elected Count, and he'd appointed Rabio as judge, with the election of more judges to follow. Matilda had been disappointed, but her spirits rallied when she was appointed Recording Secretary for all the Congressional meetings. Philecia was the Congressdog of the chatzkies, and Congress was gaining new representatives each day as more and more villages organized and formed.

The volcano had stilled with Fandrella's departure, and the sky was now the clear blue that reminded Ellis of home. It was remarkable how quickly Kibblestan recovered, when its citizens were left to be free.

Ellis rolled over on his stomach and sighed. What more was he supposed to do? He'd offered his advice—quite often at first—but as time went on, Kibblestan seemed to be getting the hang of standing on its own. So Ellis spent more and more time in the house, waiting for a unicorn that never came.

The house wasn't entirely uncomfortable. It had furniture and a well for water and plenty of food, though it was all fruits and nuts and nothing like the cheeseburger and fries Ellis so desperately craved. Since it had always been occupied by Kibblestan's Kootie leader, the Jabbermeyers wanted to move in and live as First Family.

However the chatzkies didn't like this idea. They'd snarled and growled at the Jabbermeyers until Philecia convinced them there was plenty of room for all. They reluctantly agreed, provided their Great Long One still got to sleep in Fandrella's old room, and Philecia insisted on sharing the room with Ellis.

Ellis reached into the nightstand drawer. He extracted a wrinkled, worn brochure stained with dried slewedge. It was the Vulture Voyagers brochure that had traveled with him to Kibblestan in his back pocket. Tears stung his eyes as he stared at the smiling boy on the cover.

Are you a boy who loves adventure? Are you ready to make lifelong friends? Come and join the Vulture Voyagers!

He remembered Mr. Rooper giving him the brochure when he dropped him off from the campout. He remembered the fight with Dad. And he remembered standing in front of the trees, the hot, angry tears burning his throat, as he made that fateful decision that would send him into Kibblestan.

Ellis laid the brochure back in the drawer.

Why didn't Bob come? He'd done everything he could, hadn't he? He played Bob's words over and over in his mind. "If the citizens really want to keep Fandrella from weaselin' back into Kibblestan, they've got to work at it. Value freedom. Treat each other as equals. And never forget history."

Ellis sat up. History. Maybe that was it. Kibblestan needed a record of what had happened in their land, so no one would forget. He could write everything down.

Ellis rolled off the bed and landed on the splintered wooden floor. He reached for the stack of yellowed parchment stashed amongst the dustballs and chatzkie droppings under Fandrella's bed. The parchment was soft and smooth, with a fleshy consistency. Some of the pieces contained Fandrella's old writings—mostly gibberish that made no sense.

Ellis shuffled through the stack until he found some pieces that weren't written on. He dusted them off and grabbed the pen. A dark rust color stained the waxy surface as he formed letter after letter, word after word, telling the story of Fandrella and Kibblestan.

Ellis wrote for what seemed like hours, recording every detail of his journey. He told of Fandrella's trickery, the Snotlins, the destruction of Kibblestan. He told William's story and how he'd been treated, the village's quest for water, and how Thornton was captured and imprisoned. He told of Rabio and Raquel's bravery, and how their determination to save every life, no matter the cost, made it possible for many to survive and make Kibblestan live on. He wrote about how the blue and yellow fireflies learned to set aside their differences to work together to destroy the Snotlins, and how the citizens of Kibblestan finally rose up and drove Fandrella away once and for all, a chapter he titled The Kibblestan Revolution.

Ellis wrote until the sun crept lower, throwing long shadows through the window and darkening the parchment. He released the pen and shook his hand, pain cramping through his thumb and forefinger.

When he was done writing he tapped his teeth with his pen. The nagging feeling that something else needed to be done lingered.

Ellis paced the floor. Kibblestan had a constitution. It had recorded history.

But Ellis stopped short when he remembered one of Dad's many bedtime stories.

Dad never told him the typical stories boys liked to hear, about dragons or knights, or baseball players or monsters. Never any of that. Ellis was always stuck hearing true stories. About history.

After the Constitution was written, many people were still afraid the federal government could get too powerful. Not every state was willing to agree to it without adding a Bill of Rights, which would spell out the freedoms of the individual. So James Madison wrote the new amendments, and the Constitution was ratified.

Kibblestan needed a Bill of Rights.

Ellis grabbed the last two pieces of parchment, their surfaces blank and smooth. He hunched over the paper, running his hand through his hair. What were they?

Ellis carefully scrawled "Kibblestan's Bill of Rights" across the top of the parchment. Number one. "Everyone in Kibblestan can't be told what religion to belong to. And they can't be stopped from worshiping, either." Ellis remembered Grandpa talking about life in Cuba, when communism took over. If you attended church, you couldn't belong to the Communist Party—and that meant it was nearly impossible to find work or get an education. Some of the religious leaders were even sent to labor camps, which was worse than jail. It wasn't fair.

Number two. "Everyone in Kibblestan can say whatever they want and not get in trouble." Ellis swallowed. Grandpa said in Cuba you couldn't just say whatever you wanted. If you said something bad about Fidel Castro's Cuban Revolution, you'd get thrown in jail. Or sometimes, people would get thrown in jail just because they were suspected of not liking the government. The government even had people in Grandpa's neighborhood who snooped around, trying to overhear conversations. It was hard to trust anybody.

Ellis gnawed on the pen. Number three. "Anyone can work in the news and report what they want. But they can't lie." In Grandpa's Cuba, they didn't have a bunch of different newspapers or news channels, with citizens saying what they wanted. All of the news was controlled by the government. The citizens were only allowed to learn what the government wanted them to know.

Number four. "Citizens are allowed to hang out in a big group and protest stuff if they want."

Ellis eyed his list so far. Freedom of religion. Freedom of speech. Freedom of the press. Freedom to assemble. Yep. Everything listed was what America's First Amendment covered. Now to the Second Amendment.

"Everyone in Kibblestan can have a weapon to defend themselves."

Ellis raised his eyes to the ceiling. What else? What else was there? Something about property. The government can't just come in and take your property. Dad had talked a zillion times about that—how he loved that

America gave him the opportunity to have his own ice cream shop. During Cuba's communist revolution, the government took away people's property, businesses and farms. People weren't free to run their own businesses or have their own land.

Ellis clenched his tongue between his teeth, writing fervently. "Everyone in Kibblestan can own property and the government can't take it away."

Think. Think. There were ten of these amendments, but Ellis could only remember a few.

"You can't be thrown in jail without going to trial."

Ellis put down the pen. He closed his eyes and rubbed the sides of his head. His eyes hurt from trying to write in such dim light, now that the sun was almost down. He stacked his writings in a neat pile and placed the last blank piece of parchment on top. Ellis paused, then picked the pen back up. These writings needed a title.

THE CHRONICLES OF KIBBLESTAN

He wrote the words in big, bold letters across the page. There. Now he was done.

He flopped back on the bed and waited. Philecia should be in here any minute. She always came around this time of day, to check on him and try to cheer him up.

But she didn't come.

And something crashed into the window.

CHAPTER TWENTY-SEVEN

Ellis jumped off the bed and ran to the window. A small crack marred the center of the pane. He looked through the glass and automatically ducked as a silver blur zoomed toward him.

Crash! It hit the window with a loud thud, and the small crack shot out in many directions, like the spidery veins on an old lady's leg. Ellis crouched on the floor, his heart pounding. Moments passed, the only sound his own breathing. He waited a few more seconds before slowly rising up. He peeked out the window.

A few feet away a butterfly hovered in mid-air. It was shiny and silver and looked to be made of some type of metal. Ellis stepped back from the window, as the butterfly was huge—the size of a raven. A chill went down his spine as he thought of the bird associated with bad omens and death.

Clink-clink-clink-clink! Its wings beat back and forth. As if on cue, when Ellis ventured closer it swooped toward him again, and this time the window didn't just crack. It shattered.

Ellis jumped away, dodging the flying glass. He stumbled backward and fell onto the bed. Before he could get back up the strange butterfly landed on his chest.

Ellis turned his head to one side, making a face. Ick! He'd never been face to face with a butterfly before, and up close they looked really freaky. The butterfly stared with thousands of teeny tiny eyes blanketing two bulging black spheres. Two shiny antennae sprouted up in between the gruesome eyes, and its sticky insect tongue was bluish-black and coated with stubble.

"Wh-what do you want?" Ellis managed. The butterfly slowly beat its wings. Click- clack.

Ellis rose up on his elbows. "Get out of here!" He waved at the insect, trying to scare it away.

It didn't budge.

Ellis' chest rose and fell. Could he smash it? The wings and body were metal, but the creepy eyes looked squishy, and he really didn't want whatever was inside those eyes to explode in his hand.

"Ellis, how are you—whoa!" Philecia stood in the doorway, eyes wide. "What-what is that?"

"Butterfly ... I think."

Philecia walked toward Ellis, her movements stiff and awkward.

Ellis tried to sit up. Maybe the butterfly would get the hint it needed to move. But when he started to rise pain poked his chest. The butterfly's legs had pierced his shirt and now its hard insect feet were digging into his skin.

"Yap! Yapyapyapyap!" Philecia barked as loud as she could. The butterfly turned from Ellis' face and looked at Philecia. Then it flew away and landed on the nightstand.

"Whew, thanks," Ellis said, sitting up and rubbing his chest. He lifted Philecia onto the bed. "I don't know, girl," he said, watching the butterfly. "It crashed through the window. Weird."

The butterfly was still. Philecia lowered her wriggling black nose within inches of the insect. The butterfly shot into the air. Philecia yelped and almost fell off the bed. Ellis reached out and steadied her. The butterfly flittered erratically around the room.

Click-clack-click-clack.

Philecia shrugged. "I guess it's just another weird bug in Kibblestan. Remember how big some of the lightning bugs were?"

Ellis nodded as the butterfly fluttered out the window and into the dusk.

Philecia jumped from the bed and yelped as her back legs gave way. "Ow!" She cried. "I've got to remember, I'm not the dog I used to be." She hobbled toward the doorway.

No she wasn't. The old Philecia could have scampered off the bed with ease, but would have stained the floor yellow at the sight of the butterfly.

"Come on," Philecia said. "Time for dinner. I've got to get down there. The chatzkies refuse to eat until their weinerdach eats first." She grinned.

Ellis' stomach knotted. "You can go. I'm not hungry."

Philecia walked over and nudged his leg with her wet nose. Her soft brown eyes were sad. "I miss home, too," she said. "But it's not so bad here. I kind of like it. Give it a chance."

Ellis' lips tightened. Easy for her to say. Unlike him, she was accepted here, and loved by the chatzkies. She didn't have everyone looking at her with suspicious eyes, keeping their distance because she looked like a Kootie. And she didn't have parents or friends to get back to. In reality, he was the only friend she had back home.

Ellis collapsed onto the bed and drifted off to sleep. When he awoke it was morning, and two silver butterflies were sitting on the window ledge.

Ellis sat up and Philecia stirred under the covers. He swung his legs over the edge of the bed and tiptoed across the room. He held his breath. *Click-clack.* The butterflies' wings slowly batted together.

"What do you want?" Ellis whispered.

The butterflies took off, crossing each other as they flew in a graceful figure eight, before circling Ellis' head, again and again.

Ellis waved his arms. "Hey! Cut that out. Not so close." The butterflies flew out the window, then turned and zoomed back, circling his head again.

Ellis moved to the bed, shaking his head and flailing his arms. "Get away!" he yelled.

The small lump under the covers stirred and then moved toward the head of the bed. Philecia peeked out. "What's going on?" she said drowsily, one floppy ear inside out.

"The butterflies!" Ellis said as he swatted. "There's two today. They won't leave me alone."

Philecia stood up and barked her best yap. The butterflies flew out the window but remained close.

"What's their deal?" Ellis said with frustration. He sighed and turned from the window. As soon as he did, the silver butterflies returned, this time with three friends.

Now there were five butterflies swooping about the bedroom, diving at and circling Ellis' head. "Aaaaaaaah!" he hollered at the top of his lungs. Philecia yapped and yapped. But this time the butterflies were relentless.

Ellis ran out of the room.

The butterflies followed.

He tore down the stairs.

The butterflies pursued.

He ran outside and spun in circles, fists flying.

It made no difference. The clattering wings clanked on and on as the butterflies continued their torment.

Jenkins joined him outside. "What's going on? Ooo—what are those?"

"Butterflies!" Ellis grunted as he slapped. "Won't leave me alone." The clanking noise grew louder and Ellis realized two more butterflies had appeared out of nowhere.

Philecia came outside, followed by a group of chatzkies. "Okay," she instructed. "When I say go, everyone bark at the same time. One-two-three-go!"

The group of chatzkies exploded in feverish yipping. The butterflies swarmed higher in the air, giving Ellis one moment's rest, before they dodged back down and continued their assault.

"Aaaargh!" he screamed. "Help me kill these things!"

Jenkins came closer and punched toward the butterflies, but he was too short to reach them.

"Where is everyone?" Ellis said through squinty eyes and clenched teeth.

"They're gone," Jenkins said. "Had some kind of meeting or something. I know, why don't I throw something?" Jenkins picked up a stone and threw it, missing the butterflies and striking Ellis' shoulder.

"Ow!" Ellis cried.

"Sorry." Jenkins didn't try again.

"I know," Philecia said. "I know just what to do. Hang in there, Ellis."

Ellis couldn't see what was happening. Three more butterflies had joined in and now all he could concentrate on was the clanking silver blur that surrounded him. His flailing arms ached, the butterflies too fast. It was useless. He plopped on the ground.

"It's okay. Everything'll be okay." Jenkins' voice soothed him as Ellis buried his face in his hands, praying for the swirling madness to stop.

After what seemed like forever a painfully shrill, all encompassing shriek cut the air. The clattering diminished.

Ellis slid his hands from his face. He no longer saw a silver blur. Instead, he saw Matilda's infectious smile.

"I scared them away, yes I did, yes I did." She danced back and forth on her tiny mouse toes.

Philecia walked over. "I figured if the chatzkies' yipping couldn't do it, Matilda sure could and I was right!"

Ellis heaved a sigh of relief. "That was the weirdest thing ever." He stood up, his legs shaky. "Thanks, Matilda. Maybe you should stick around and be my bodyguard."

But then he heard a far off clanking ... getting louder ... and louder. He looked up into the sky. A huge swarm of dozens of butterflies zoomed straight for him. Ellis didn't think, he just ran. He ran as fast as his legs would carry him. He blindly ran, not knowing where he was going and not caring, either, as long as he could get away from the clattering madness that was slowly driving him insane.

Clack-clack-clack-clack. The din behind him sounded like hungry prisoners pounding steel cups against the iron bars of their cells as mealtime draws near. Ellis ran and ran, through the clearing and into the trees. He raced ahead, leaping over twisting roots and shuffling through brambles. Blood pounded in his ears, his lungs burned.

He dared to glance over his shoulder only to find the butterflies closer than ever. Ugh! He cut to the side, zigzagging through the trees. Soon he was struggling for breath, his energy spent. Maybe he could hide. He dove behind a boulder, and landed in front of two white paws. He looked up. Ruthertold stood before him with a panting smile.

"Ruthertold!" Ellis managed between gasps. "So here's where you've been. Good to see you, boy."

The clanking noise was getting louder. Ellis stood up. "Quick," he whispered. "Give me a ride."

Ruthertold wagged his tail as Ellis climbed onto his back. "Get me away from the butterflies." Ruthertold took off at a trot.

"Buddy, you've got to go faster," Ellis said, watching over his shoulder. "There's these like psycho butterflies after me. I think they're trying to drive me crazy."

But Ruthertold didn't go faster. He picked his way through the forest as if they had all the time in the world.

"Dude, you're not hearing me. You think you don't like the chatzkies, you're not going to want any part of these butterflies. They're—"

Clank-clank-clank. Here they came. Now Ruthertold could see for himself.

But the butterflies didn't give chase. As soon as they saw Ruthertold, they backed off and dispersed through the trees.

"Whew!" Ellis said. "They're gone. You have no idea how bad they were. They were attacking me like crazy."

Ruthertold padded on through the forest. Ellis looked around and realized he had no idea where they were. "Um, Ruthertold? You know where you're going?"

Ching! Ruthertold rang out his melodious bark.

Ellis relaxed and raked his fingers through Ruthertold's fur. He'd missed his big white buddy. "You know, the chatzkies aren't that bad now, boy. I know they were mean to you and all, but really, you should give them another chance."

Ruthertold shook his head and sneezed.

"Okay, okay," Ellis said. "I guess you don't have to take me all the way back to the house if you're still scared of the chatzkies. If you get me to the clearing, I can find my way back. Just don't know what I'll do if those butterflies are there."

Up ahead bright sunlight shined through the trees.

"Thanks so much for the ride—" Ellis started to say, but his lips fell silent when they stepped into the sunshine. Mounds and mounds of amber sand stretched as far as the eye could see. Ellis swallowed. "Dude. This isn't the way to the house. It's the desert."

Without warning Ruthertold leaped into the air.

Ching! Ching! He barked his crazy bark as they took off through the sky. Ellis gripped his fingers tightly around Ruthertold's fur as the ground fell away. He squinted and leaned forward, like a jockey racing a horse. The sun scorched his skin and the wind slapped his face, turning it pink and splotchy.

"Woo-hoo!" He couldn't help but shout, the ride was so exhilarating. Soon there was no longer sand underneath them, but the lush green treetops of the jungle's rainforest. It was the first time Ellis had seen this part of Kibblestan without the shadows of rolling black clouds and floods of slewedge. The sun shone down on a beautiful landscape, and after they passed the jungle, a wide swath of grassland stretched out before them. Ellis could just make out small buildings and tiny dots moving around, that had to be Petikins going about their day, rebuilding village upon village.

On they flew, over a rippling field the color of pale golden straw. And at the end of this field stood an ugly gray forest, with thick solid trees.

Ellis' heart crept into his throat as he recognized this forest. The Grand Forest, the barrier between Kibblestan and home.

Ruthertold circled, lower and lower, until his paws gently met the ground. Ellis sat still for a moment, his eyes and mouth sticky and dry, his windblown hair standing on end. Finally he slipped off of Ruthertold's back.

"Okay, boy," he said quietly. "Why'd you bring me here?"

Ellis gasped as he realized the answer.

CHAPTER TWENTY-EIGHT

Clomp! Clomp! Bob's splitting hooves made a clunky sound as he stumbled along. His bony hips bobbed up and down with each labored step.

Ellis ran to the unicorn. "Bob! Bob, it's me, Ellis!"

"Hey." Bob grunted. He silently chomped a thick wad of spit as he lazily looked around. A cluster of swollen lumps that were crusted with dried blood dotted the poor unicorn's forehead. Ellis' smile faded. They looked really sore.

"Am I going home now?" Ellis blurted.

The silence that followed made him uneasy. He glanced at Ruthertold, who turned in three circles before plopping down in a comfortable spot, curling up and sniffing the air.

Bob gazed at Ellis through stubbly lashes. "If you really, really want to, you can go."

"Yes!" Ellis shouted, punching the air. "Finally! I'm going home!" He swung his arms around the unicorn's neck in an impulsive hug. "You don't know how much I've been ready for this. My parents have got to be going nuts!"

Ellis released his neck.

"Where do we go?" He looked at the trees. "Through here? Like before?"

Bob shook his head. "Won't work," he said. "Been tryin' and tryin'. My horn goes through the trunks but nothin' else. Won't crack apart like before."

So that explained the lumps on Bob's forehead. Ouch. He'd bashed his head against those tree trunks how many times?

"So, how will I get home? What's the other way?" Ellis said.

Bob scuffed his hoof, avoiding Ellis' eyes. "Only one other way that I know of. Never been done before. Don't know if it'll work."

Ellis' heart beat faster. Why did his palms suddenly feel clammy? "Um, what? What way?"

"I take you back myself."

Ellis let out a sigh. Go back with Bob? Even better. No traipsing through a scary forest all by himself, with creepy trees that move on their own.

"Okay, that's cool," Ellis said. "Do we leave from here? I need to go back and get Philecia and see if Matilda wants to come, too."

Bob cleared his throat. "Don't think so."

"Don't think what?"

"Don't think they'll go."

"What do you mean? Of course they'll go. Well, maybe not Matilda. She's pretty happy here. But Philecia's going. She's my dog."

Bob finally met his eyes. "Ellis, the journey's dangerous. No guarantee. We go up so high, cross the Other World barrier. It's a thin membrane that unicorns go through, but the non-magic ..." Bob dropped his eyes. He slowly paced, looking miserable. "I - uh - I don't know that you can survive the trip. Unicorns are magic. Humans aren't. Neither are dogs."

The knot filling Ellis' stomach exploded, traveling up his chest and squeezing his lungs, making breathing difficult. What was Bob saying?

"But ... but I came through it before. What's the big deal going back?"

"You came through the forest, on foot. I think you got here because something wanted you here. And not just you, but that dog of yours and even the mouse."

"What are you saying? You think Philecia, Matilda and me were chosen to come here? That's crazy. I mean, Matilda's just a little mouse, and I'm just a kid, and Philecia—Philecia's not some huge vicious dog. She's the biggest scaredy cat I know." Ellis paused, brow furrowing. Well, she used to be.

Bob sighed. "Might be what you see. What I see is a dog with enough love to find her courage, a mouse with enough optimism to never see defeat and a boy with the knowledge of what it means to be free. All three very useful to a land trying to survive against evil. Was it by chance that you came here? Perhaps. But who knows? Seen it in your world plenty of times. Heroism comes from those you might least expect."

Bob circled Ellis, his ears twitching. "No matter. Don't have all the answers, prob'ly not supposed to. What you've got to decide now is how badly do you want to go back. Is it worth risking your life?"

His life? Ellis' brain was in a tailspin. Thoughts dove at him from different directions, but it was hard to grasp any of them. The very idea of staying in Kibblestan made him physically ill. He couldn't stay here, the only human. No way.

Dad's face floated before him. Smiling. Warm.

"I hate you!" The memory of his shouted words shattered the image, and Dad's loving look turned to shock, then pain. Ellis remembered the cold feeling of satisfaction as he stood in front of the humongous gray trees. "I'll show him," Ellis had thought. "I'll go in the woods, and he can't stop me. And if I don't come back, he'll know it's his fault. His fault for being such a mean dad. He'll know he made me run away and he'll wish he'd spent more time with me instead of the stupid shop. He'll be sorry for the rest of his life."

Ellis' stomach lurched and he almost threw up. How could he have been so selfish? How could he ever wish that kind of lifelong torture on his own father? He couldn't do that to him. He couldn't stay in Kibblestan, knowing Mom and Dad were looking for him, mourning him. And those angry words could not be the last words Dad ever heard from him.

"I'll go." Ellis said. "I don't care. It's worth the risk."

Bob nodded. Then cocked his head. "Philecia?"

Tears sprang to Ellis' eyes. He couldn't leave Philecia. After everything they'd been through? She was more than just a dog. She was his family. He couldn't have gotten through this adventure without her, the only piece of home that he had.

"I - I can't leave her. She's coming with. No matter what."

Bob held his gaze for a long time. Now it was Ellis' turn to look away.

"We need to go back and get her," Ellis said. "But I warn you, there's these psycho butterflies—"

"Won't bother you."

"Hopefully not, but they were—"

"Chasing you to Ruthertold."

"No, they—huh?" Ellis wrinkled his brow.

"I sent them. Couldn't convince Ruthertold to go back to the house to get you." Bob shook his head and sighed. "He's afraid of those chatzkies."

Ruthertold whined and laid his head on his paws.

"So - so you sent the butterflies?"

Bob nodded. "To chase you to Ruthertold. He travels much faster than my rickety old bones."

Ellis crouched down and pet the pup.

"If you really want Philecia to come," Bob said, "better go get her now. It's just ..." Bob raised one eyebrow. "Make sure your decision is for her, and not you."

Ellis' face grew hot. For her? Of course Ellis was thinking about her. He wasn't leaving his dog in this strange land all by herself. Stupid unicorn. What did he know about the love between dogs and humans? She'd be lost without him.

Ellis stood up. "Come on, Ruthertold. Fly me to the house real quick. I'll grab Philecia and be back in a flash."

Ruthertold stood up and shook himself. Ellis climbed on his back and gave Bob one last look. He didn't like what he saw. Bob's expression was piercing, as if he could see something that Ellis couldn't—or refused to—see.

Back at the house all the coaxing in the world could not convince Ruthertold that the chatzkies would leave him alone. So Ellis settled on being dropped off at the end of the walkway to the house. As soon as Ellis slipped off his back Ruthertold sprang into the air, hovering high above the rooftop, safe from any roaming chatzkies.

Ellis ran to the house and burst through the doorway. "Philecia! Philecia! Guess what?" He paused, catching his breath.

Philecia sat up on the couch, a chatzkie on either side of her. Rabio stood in the middle of the floor. One chatzkie rubbed Philecia's back with her paws, another held a tray with bright fruit, should their Great Long One get hungry.

Philecia waved a paw. "Just a minute, Ellis." Philecia looked back at Rabio. "What were you saying?"

Rabio nodded at Ellis, then turned to Philecia. "As I was saying, the Congress is seeking your vote for a new currency for all of Kibblestan. It must be something the chatzkies will value as well, so we need your astute opinion."

"Oh, of course, of course," Philecia said, opening her mouth while a chatzkie popped in a berry. "When is everyone meeting?"

Ellis stepped back from the doorway, a tide of unwelcome thoughts flooding his brain. He gripped the doorframe to steady himself, as his stomach clenched like it had been punched.

Philecia was happy.

He tried to bury the thought but there was no denying it. She was more than happy. She was radiant. And her happiness had nothing to do with him. Kibblestan loved Philecia. She was treated like royalty here, and adored by the chatzkies.

"Make sure your decision is for her, and not you." Bob's words hit him like a sledgehammer as he realized a truth he didn't want to accept.

Philecia was better off in Kibblestan. She didn't need him anymore. How could he ask her to go back home, to a life where she spent hours each day alone in a crate, while he was at school and his parents were at work? How could he ask her to return to a house where she wasn't allowed on the furniture, except for his bed? And where meals were the same, day after day—dry dogfood that probably tasted like cardboard.

Fresh tears stung his eyes. If he took Philecia home, it would be for his own happiness, not hers. And the worst of it was he'd be putting her life at risk to do it. What if she didn't make it?

Ellis wiped his runny nose on his sleeve. He turned and hurried down the pathway.

"Ellis!" Philecia's voice behind him. He started to sprint. "Ellis! Come back. You know I can't run."

Ellis bent over at the waist, gasping as he choked on his tears. Philecia hobbled down the walk, her face contorting with the effort to go faster than her damaged bones would allow.

"Philecia, stop!" He called. "I'll come to you." He traipsed up the walk, his eyes never leaving his loyal dachshund. Her brown eyes shone with a love that was complete. If he hadn't stopped running, she would have followed, no matter how much her bones hurt.

His stomach twisted. What if she didn't agree to stay in Kibblestan? What if she insisted on following him no matter what the cost? No. He couldn't let that happen.

"Ellis, I'm so sorry. I didn't mean to ignore you in there. Did I hurt your feelings?"

Ellis dropped to his knees and scooped up the dachshund. "Of course not, girl. I know you love me."

Philecia wagged her tail and licked his cheek. "Are the butterflies gone?"

"Yeah, they are."

"So what did you want to tell me?"

Ellis hugged Philecia to his chest. He could feel the patter of her heartbeat against his. He squeezed his eyes shut as his fingers raked her soft fur. *Oh, Philecia. I'm going to miss you so much!*

"Let's go over here and talk." His voice was a squeak. He carried her to the side of the house and sat down on a patch of cool green grass. Philecia settled onto his lap. Her tail twitched back and forth as she looked up expectantly.

For a few moments they sat in silence as he petted her behind the ears, massaged her back and scratched that ticklish spot at the base of her tail. Philecia leaned into his fingers and closed her eyes. When he stopped she slowly opened them. She cocked her head when she saw the long tear trickling down Ellis' cheek.

"Ellis, what's wrong?"

Ellis tried to speak but his throat closed up. He drew a shuddery breath and tried again. "Philecia. It's time. It's time for me to go home."

"Go? Now? How do you know?"

"The butterflies. They didn't come here by accident. They were sent by Bob. To come get me so I can go home."

Philecia wagged her tail and nuzzled his ear. "You get to see your mom and dad again. That's great." Her forehead puckered. "When do we go? Will I have time to go to that meeting? Kibblestan really needs my opinion and—"

"We won't be going," Ellis said quickly.

"Huh? But you just said—"

"I said me, not we. It's time for me to go home."

Philecia crumpled. "Wait. What? What do you mean?"

"I mean I'm going home." Ellis took a deep breath. "And you're staying here."

Philecia climbed off his lap and backed away. "You're leaving me? Here? By myself?" Her eyes welled with tears. "You can't leave me. I-I'm your dog. You're my human. We-we're family, Ellis."

Ellis picked her up and hugged her tight. His tears spilled on her golden brown fur, giving it a dappled appearance. "You don't understand," he sobbed. "I can't take you with me. You could die."

Philecia pushed her hind feet into his stomach, her nails digging into his skin. He held her out in front of him and stared into her face. She looked mad.

"Put me down," she said. She wriggled and squirmed until he released her. "I don't care. I'm going with you."

Ellis stood up. He knew she'd still want to come despite the risks. And what would prevent her from convincing Bob some day to take her back just to find him? Her life was worth more than that. He had to give her more reason stay. "Look. Kibblestan needs you. Bob didn't want to send me back until I'd helped Kibblestan get a government in place and wrote a constitution. And now there's no need for me to stay anymore. But you - you're a leader here. Part of Congress, and the chatzkies love you. In fact, if it weren't for you, Kibblestan may not have peace because the chatzkies wouldn't have anyone telling them to be nice."

Philecia slowly nodded.

"And, Fandrella could come back. You and Rabio and Thornton need to make sure Kibblestan stays united. Kibblestan needs you, girl."

Slowly the anger melted from Philecia's face. She nuzzled into Ellis' arms and cried.

CHAPTER TWENTY-NINE

"**Y**ou want me to do what?" Ellis looked at Bob, his eyes wide.

"Dump it over your head. Won't hurt you. It's just spit." Bob smiled a toothy grin. "Just glad I could get so much drool in one place."

Ellis wrinkled his nose as he stared into the bucket. The gray liquid looked stagnant, slimy, edged with froth.

"Go on, Ellis," Philecia urged. "You don't have to drink it. Just pour it."

Matilda hopped up and down. "Pour it! Pour it! It will feel refreshing, yes it will."

Refreshing? Getting doused with a bucket of warm unicorn spit? Hardly.

But at least it couldn't hurt anything. Bob thought if his skin and clothes were soaked with unicorn drool that maybe a little unicorn magic would coat him and help him slip through the barrier to the Other World.

Ellis picked up the bucket and dumped it over his head. The spit felt warm and slimy, just like it looked. Ellis stared out behind his dripping bangs at all who had gathered in the clearing to see him off.

William grinned and saluted with a thick, stubby hand. The Jabbermeyer family stood arm in arm, Thornton solemn and Jenkins tearful. Raquel waved a blue handkerchief that she used to dab at her equally blue eyes. Gustav and Matilda stood with tails intertwined, exchanging glances and giggling. Ruthertold swooped overhead, a safe distance from the chatzkies below. Jetta and Tawni flanked their weinerdach, with silver smiles and crazy eyes.

And then there was Philecia. It was almost too painful to look at her.

"Master Ellis!" Rabio called from the front door of the house. He ran down the pathway to where Ellis stood. Six mice followed, carrying what looked like a book.

"Master Ellis, we wanted to show you something before you go." The book crawled forward, the mice underneath it barely visible. "We took your writings and bound them together," Rabio said.

Ellis wiped the unicorn spit out of his eyes and examined the book before him. The cover was made of dark brown hide, and on the front, etched in ink, was the title. *The Chronicles of Kibblestan.* He picked it up and thumbed through. Sure enough it was all there. Kibblestan's Constitution. Kibblestan's Bill of Rights. And all of the history—his firsthand account of his adventures in Kibblestan.

"Wow, Rabio, this is really cool," Ellis said.

Rabio bowed in a gallant gesture. "It was the least we could do after all that you've done for Kibblestan. We will miss you, Master Ellis. You may be far away, but you will never be forgotten."

"No you won't!" Jenkins ran forward and hugged Ellis tight. "Thank you," he whispered through his tears.

Ellis returned the little Petikin's hug, then knelt and looked into his face. "I'll miss you, dude. You've been like my little brother. Can you do me a favor?"

Jenkins sniffled.

"Look out for Philecia, will you? Your dad's the Count. Make sure she's always happy, okay?"

Jenkins nodded.

Bob snorted and Ellis knew it was time to go. He crouched by Philecia and patted her head. "Be a good girl. I love you so much. You'll always be my dog and I'll always love you."

Ellis stood up and walked toward Bob. Philecia started to follow but made herself stop. Her eyes dripped big canine tears.

Ellis climbed onto Bob's back.

"Hold on super tight," Bob instructed. "Gets cold up there."

Ellis clenched his legs against Bob's ribs and his fingers firmly grasped his coarse mane. His heart pounded so hard it felt like he'd swallowed a drum. His stomach felt like he was climbing the first hill of an insanely high roller coaster, where gut-wrenching anticipation builds with the sound of each click. However this roller coaster had no straps to keep him from falling out, or emergency brake if it lost control. This was it. He was either going home or going to die.

Bob strolled through the clearing and Ellis closed his eyes and said a prayer. Did God hear prayers in Kibblestan?

"We'll take off at the edge of the forest," Bob said. "See?"

Ellis opened his eyes. The trees were getting close.

"Be ready," Bob said. "On the count of three. One-two-"

Ellis' knuckles turned white. He bit his lip as his stomach cinched tighter.

"Three!"

They shot straight into the air like a rocket ship, leaving Ellis' stomach behind. Ellis gasped for breath as he dug his knees into Bob's sides and gripped his mane with all his strength. Frigid wind whipped his hair and stabbed his cheeks, making his eyes water and his throat dry. A shrill ringing sounded in his ears as they climbed higher and higher, into the clouds and higher still.

"Hold on," Bob shouted. "Take a deep breath while you still can."

While he still can? Ellis opened his mouth and sucked in air. His chest expanded, but it wasn't enough, his lungs didn't fill. He tried again, taking in air, but the oxygen—the air didn't have enough oxygen.

Ellis panicked. He needed oxygen. He had to breathe. He gagged as he opened and closed his mouth, like a fish that's been hauled to shore. His head felt fuzzy.

They left the blue sky below and entered a dark void of nothingness. Bob leveled out so they were no longer climbing. He stretched his legs and glided, letting the freezing air currents jostle them along toward the eternal darkness ahead.

Ellis' heart slowed. His breathing useless. No oxygen. His brain wandered. So this is how he would die. On top of a unicorn between two dimensions. The thought didn't scare him. He felt an odd sort of peace.

Ahead patches of light reflected like the rainbow of a prism. Ellis leaned forward and rested his head on Bob's neck. His fingers slipped from Bob's mane. They were frozen solid, having lost feeling a long time ago, just like his toes and his nose. He was tired. Don't fight it. Just sleep.

Ellis closed his eyes and let the cold blackness suck him away.

Ellis awakened to the colors of the setting sun. He lay on his back and blinked until everything came into focus.

He took a deep breath, and reveled in the fullness of his lungs, gulping the oxygen.

He slowly sat up. It felt like a razor blade was stuck behind each eye. Ellis raised his hands to his face. His fingers could hardly move. They were bright red and stung like they'd been stuck in a wasp's nest. He groaned as he rose to his knees and looked around. Where was he?

He plopped back down when he saw the gray trees. Oh no. The forest. He was still by the creepy forest.

"Ellis!" The shout sounded far away. Ellis climbed to his feet and grunted as pain shot through his spine. He felt like a grandpa with arthritis instead of an eleven-year-old boy. He turned toward the voice calling his name.

Silent tears ran down his cheeks.

Houses. Not Petikin houses or chatzkie houses, but human houses, ones that belonged in his neighborhood. He looked to his right and there it was. Home. Only a football field away. He started toward it but stopped when something caught his eye. Across the field stood a light gray donkey-horse with droopy eyes and long strands of saliva hanging out of the corners of its mouth.

"Good-bye, Bob." Ellis whispered.

"Ellis!" The voice again. Someone calling him. Someone looking for him. Someone who missed him.

Dad.

Ellis took off running, as fast as his sore body would let him. *I'm coming! I'm coming Dad! I'm okay!*

Ellis plowed through the field and found the trail that led to his driveway. Standing on the pathway, his hands cupped around his mouth as he prepared to shout again, was his father. Ellis' legs nearly buckled as he threw himself into his father's arms and cried and cried.

The arms holding him tightened. Ellis pressed his cheek to his father's chest and drank in the familiar scent of sweet ice cream and aftershave. It felt so good to finally be surrounded by the strong arms of someone who loved him. Dad. Oh Dad.

At last Javier Garcia gripped Ellis' arms and forced him back, breaking the embrace. Ellis stared up into his father's face and saw not tears of joy but a look of utter bewilderment.

"Ellis! Ellis!" Javier gave him a gentle shake. "Calm down. You're scaring me. What happened? What is it?"

Ellis' eyes grew wide. What is it? He'd been lost for weeks, and Dad had to ask what is it?

"I - I," Ellis tried to talk but the words wouldn't come.

Javier straightened up and looked past Ellis to the field. "Was somebody messing with you?"

"Messing with me?" Ellis stared through his tears.

"I told you I don't like you playing out here by yourself. What happened? Why are you so upset?"

Ellis shook his head and couldn't believe what he was hearing. How could Dad even ask such a thing? And why wasn't he upset? Didn't he care? Hadn't he been searching for him all this time?

"Dad, I've been gone. I - I missed you."

Javier's mouth twisted down while an eyebrow shot up. "You missed me? That's what this is all about? You went off and sulked for twenty minutes and now you're all upset because you missed me?" Javier folded his arms across his chest. "I find that a little hard to believe."

This wasn't right. How could Dad be acting this way after he'd been gone for so long?

Javier took his arm and gently steered Ellis to the house. "I know we had our fight, but I didn't know you were so upset about it. If I'd known, I'd have followed you out here. I just figured you wanted to be alone. I was giving you space."

Ellis walked to the house like a zombie. Nothing felt real.

They walked across the driveway and through the garage. Javier paused in front of the back door. "Ellis, wait." He dropped Ellis' arm and looked toward the floor. "Look. I'm sorry I didn't make the campout. I guess I've had time to think and I'm sorry about a lot of things. Sit down a minute."

Ellis joined his father on the concrete step. Javier stared into his lap for a moment, rubbing his palms back and forth against his jeans. Then he looked at Ellis. "You know, growing up I never did all these extra things like you do. I never got to play sports, do campouts, none of it. Grandma and Grandpa were too focused on working round the clock to bother with any of my stuff. But it was okay. I understood.

"When we came to America, we were living in tents. Grandma and Grandpa had no choice but to work hard to get us out of there and make a better life for me and Uncle Enrique and Aunt Maria. Grandpa worked two jobs and Grandma worked one. They relied on me to take care of the house and watch over my brother and sister. While other kids got to play baseball after school, I had to walk Enrique and Maria home. I had to make sure they did their homework, feed them dinner, then do homework of my own."

Ellis leaned against his father's shoulder. The story wasn't new, but Ellis' reaction was. For the first time he felt sorry for Dad. Growing up, Dad never got to do anything fun. He never got to be a kid.

Javier continued. "Man, how I wanted to play after school. I wanted to hang with friends, do sports, join a club. But if I ever complained to Grandpa, I got the same answer. Life was hard, but we were free. And some day my station in life would be even better than his. That's how America worked, if people just seized the opportunity."

Javier wrapped an arm around Ellis' shoulder. "And you know what? They were right. All their hard work, their scrimping, their saving, put a roof over my head and food in my belly and an education in my brain. And now look at us. I have a son who gets to do the things that I didn't get to. But I'll tell you one thing."

"What?" Ellis searched his father's eyes, and was surprised to see a tear.

"I'm sick of missing out." Javier squeezed Ellis' shoulder. "Maybe I didn't get to do those things as a kid, but I can still do them as your dad. And I don't want your memories of me to be the same as mine are of Grandpa. Someone who loved me and took care of me but who I hardly got to see. I want to spend more time with you. And I'm going to find a way to do it, okay?"

Ellis didn't say anything. He couldn't. He hugged Dad tight, hoping that would say his words for him.

Later that evening Ellis' mom came home acting as if nothing had happened. And nothing had happened, at least in this world. Ellis figured that Kibblestan must have a different time zone, and if you're unlucky enough to get stuck there, no one in this world notices.

Ellis didn't tell anyone about his adventure. He knew no one would believe him. He went through the motions of looking for Philecia, and posting reward signs for her return. His parents became convinced she'd gotten out and wandered off into the forest.

Well, that was kind of true.

His parents offered to get him a new dog but Ellis refused. Loving a dog could only end in heartache. Besides, no one could replace Philecia.

Ellis thought about Kibblestan every day. What was Philecia doing? Was she okay? Sometimes he stood outside the forest, contemplating whether to go in. Maybe the forest had opened. Perhaps he could slip through for just a quick visit.

But each time Ellis abandoned the idea. He somehow knew that Kibblestan didn't work that way. It didn't open up for just a quick visit. It only opened up if it was in dire need.

As Bob had said, heroism can come from those you'd least expect. A dog with enough love to find her courage, a mouse with enough optimism to never see defeat and a boy who knows what it means to be free.

Who would Kibblestan call on next? Or would it call anyone at all?

EPILOGUE

Ellis stood in his driveway, watching the movers unload furniture into the house next door. So far he'd seen a piano, a couch and a table being carried inside. Still no evidence of whether the new neighbors had kids.

"Ellis, you ready?" Javier called from the garage.

Ellis turned toward his dad. "I think so. I loaded the tent and the sleeping bags into the car. Did you remember to pack marshmallows? It's our turn to bring them for the troop to make s'mores."

Javier Garcia snapped his fingers. "That's right. Your mom said they were somewhere in the pantry." Javier trotted into the house.

Ellis smiled wistfully as he thought of what happened to the marshmallows at the last campout, four months ago. Philecia had peed all over them and the Vulture Voyagers did not get to make s'mores. Ellis swallowed the lump that crept up his throat every time he thought of Philecia. *Don't think about it. She's in a better place with the chatzkies. She's happy.*

Ellis walked up his driveway. *Yap! Yapyapyapyapyap!* Ellis froze. Was he hearing things? *Yapyapyapyapyap!*

317

The barking was high-pitched, nervous … and coming from behind his house, from the field … and the woods.

Ellis' heart swelled until he thought it might burst. *Could it be?*

Ellis raced down the path, his sneakers slapping the gravel and throwing up dust. He cut through his backyard and stopped short at the edge of the field.

His heart shriveled.

Yapyapyapyap! Two tiny dogs with jeweled collars chased each other as they yipped and played. When they saw Ellis they snarled and barked as if he were a wildcat threatening to clobber them. A skinny girl with long dark hair who looked to be about his age traipsed toward him, looking over her shoulder.

"Hurry up, Ria!" she called. "We're supposed to be helping unpack!"

The girl turned back around and locked eyes with Ellis. Her mouth gaped in surprise. Ellis remained speechless, his grief at seeing this girl and her dogs instead of Philecia gumming up any words in his throat. The tiny dogs barked louder, sounding like dueling squeaker toys. The girl scowled at the dogs. "Speckles! Sparkles! No! Be quiet!"

The dogs ignored her.

The girl gave Ellis a sheepish grin. "Er—sorry. They're kind of like that around new people."

Ellis fought the tears trying to surface. If he spoke his voice might crack. He looked away and shrugged.

"Kinzie! Kinzie!" A little girl about the age of five or six ran up to them, followed by a squatty mutt with floppy ears and a head that was too small for its overweight body. "Guess what I saw by the forest, Kinzie! Guess!"

The tiny dogs ran off as the pudgy dog jumped up on the girl called Kinzie. She dropped to her knees and the dog licked her all over the face. Ellis' mouth turned down. It was just like Philecia used to do.

"This is my dog, Mo," Kinzie giggled as the dog started to snort from excitement, spewing snot everywhere. "She's the best dog in the world."

At those words Ellis turned away, hot emotion searing his insides. That girl didn't know anything. The best dog in the world didn't waddle around and spray snot everywhere. The best dog in the world was in Kibblestan.

"You can pet her if you want!" The girl called. Ellis walked away without answering.

Javier called from the front of the house. "I got the marshmallows. Come on, we've got to go!"

Ellis lifted his chin and the stone in his heart started to soften. He might not have Philecia, but he had Dad. And this campout was going to be the best one yet.

Ellis grinned and started to run. He disappeared around the corner of his house, leaving the girls and their dogs to stare after him.

"Kinzie! Kinzie!" The smaller girl pulled at Kinzie's shirt.

"What?" Kinzie answered, her eyes lingering where Ellis had disappeared.

"I saw one! I did! I did!" The little girl bounced up and down with excitement. "Come and see!"

Kinzie looked down at the girl. "What are you talking about, Ria?"

"A unicorn!" Ria's wide eyes sparkled. "I saw a real live unicorn by the forest. You've got to come see!"

Acknowledgements

As anyone who has ever written a novel knows, it's a long process and it doesn't happen alone. I'd like to thank Teri Jones, whose feedback was invaluable in the writing and revisions of this book. I will forever be grateful for how much I learned and grew as a writer from those weekly meetings at Starbucks. I'd also like to thank my cover artist, Tim Jessell, whose incredible talent brought my vision to life in a way that was beyond my wildest dreams. To Rixys Alfonso, an amazing woman who was kind enough to share her inspiring story with me, about what it was like to live in Cuba, then come to America. To Missy Brewer, School Librarian Superstar, who took the time to read not just one but two Kibblestan stories and tell me what she thought. To Aiden, Laney, Hayden, Nick and Matthew, my first beta readers who assured me that yes, kids will keep turning the pages. And to Mr. Hooton and his fourth-grade class. Best Test Market Ever!

In addition, I would be remiss if I didn't thank my family. Mom and Dad, you gave me a childhood that was so happy that part of my brain has stayed there, allowing me to see the worlds I create through the eyes of a child. Thank you for that most precious gift. To Russ, Maren and Colin, I couldn't have done it without your steadfast support and encouragement, which made me believe that maybe, just maybe, I had a story worth telling.

Andrea Rand started writing stories in the first grade and never stopped. After graduating from Oklahoma State University with a degree in business, she built a career in sales before leaving the workforce to raise a family. She currently resides in Texas with her husband, two children, two neurotic dogs and two cats. She would love to add a pet rat or pot-bellied pig to her menagerie, but for now her husband says their Ark is full. *The Chronicles of Kibblestan: Revolution* is her debut novel.

To keep up to date with what's next in Kibblestan, visit her website: andrearand.com.

DISCUSSION QUESTIONS

1. Ellis' father has experienced communism firsthand, and loves America for its freedom. America's economy is based on free market capitalism, where the individual can own a business and run it as he or she sees fit. How has capitalism made America prosperous? What's the difference between communism and capitalism?

2. Bob says to maintain freedom, you must "value freedom, treat each other as equals, and never forget history." Explain why these three things are important for a free society.

3. What are some of the things that Ellis includes in Kibblestan's constitution? Why are they important? If you had to write a constitution, what would you include?

4. Matilda wanted the constitution to say that all mice should get cheese, but her idea was rejected, saying they were writing a constitution, not a wish list. Why can't a constitution be a wish list?

5. What are your thoughts on the story of William Wantonburger? Discuss his treatment by the village. What effects did Fandrella's talk of fairness and her "free water service" have on the village, both in terms of the economy and the Petikins' attitudes?

6. In Chapter 14, Charro asks Ellis what America stands for. What is Ellis' answer? What do you think America stands for?

7. Do you think Kibblestan will remain free?

   Hint: This question will be answered in the next book in the series, tentatively titled *The Chronicles of Kibblestan: Canines.*

For more information please visit andrearand.com.

Made in the USA
Middletown, DE
23 November 2021

53245649R00196